TAKING MEDUSA

A ROMANTASY GREEK MYTH RETELLING
DARK GODS RISING BOOK ONE

S.M. McCOY

Broken Books
Kent, WA 98030
First published in the United States of America by Broken Books LLC, 2023,
First Edition Print All Rights Reserved
Second Edition ISBN: 978-1-7322475-8-1
Copyright © 2023 S.M. McCoy , Sky Robert
Cover Design by Taurus Colosseum/Ravenborn Cover Design
Editing by Amaze Inn Proofreading

There is a monster in all of us,
it is whether we wield it,
or it wields us that makes us...
villains or heroes.

TABLE OF CONTENTS

Chapter 1

Prologue: The Kidnapping of Medusa

It was up to Theo to finish what the fates had put in motion, because she was the only one of her sisters that could undo what was once turned to stone. Taken from her very grasp centuries ago, Theo knew it wasn't the last she'd see of her sister. Medusa was too important, too kind, and the fates had known the gods would seek their vengeance on the sea god through his weakness: his heart.

Finally, she had everything she needed to revive Medusa, and she felt ashamed that it had taken her this long. Times had changed over the years, and the world wasn't what it used to be. The gods had found more discreet pursuits, choosing to rule more carefully amongst the mortals, being more subtle in their games. That gave her the opening she needed to right the wrongs of the past.

Theo didn't know how long it would take before the gods found out what she had done, or why she had done it, but her sister was the only hope she had of having a normal life, one where monsters didn't have to hide from the gods. She believed in Apollo's prophecy, but she knew better than most that a prophecy was only one possible future, and she wasn't leaving things to the fates alone.

The day she poisoned the only man she'd ever loved was the very same she went to find Medusa all those years ago, only to find she had been beheaded in her sleep. Perseus had disappeared, supported by the gods, and Landon turned to stone in the gardens at the end of the worlds waiting for the day Medusa would return and bring him back.

Athena hid her shield amongst mortal relics, and it took Theo some digging to finally get the timing right. Removing her sister's head was almost too easy. Granted she was one of the very few capable of undoing petrification from the flesh, but the gods had become comfortable with the mortals, believing the gorgons were gone. Regaled to the likes of myth and legend. It had taken a long time for the gods to become unguarded for her to collect what she needed.

Medusa's head was exactly as she remembered it, unmarred by time. She'd done it. She'd finally recovered her from Athena. She was sure eventually the goddess would know her aigis was gone, but the shield remained, and unless someone was looking close enough, what reason did Athena have to be taking up arms again. The mortals were perfectly capable of enough wars without her heading the front lines as a rallying cry.

The yellow snakes about her sister's head lumbered limply against her skull as she placed it gently in the bag. Against popular belief the power to turn beings to stone was not automatically triggered by gazing into her green eyes. Theo snarled even thinking about what mortals and the gods had used her mother's children for. Always the monster, never the tool they would insist. Every time her siblings were used by the gods to defend, to betray, to kill they were hunted all for some other's sick will.

Not this time, Theo swore.

She was not their monster anymore. Her fiery red hair billowed in the wind of the ship she boarded to reach her final destination. The sea god had slumbered for so long, he would not stop her from plundering his underwater memorial. It was his fault her sister was caught up in this curse to begin with, and this time when Medusa was reborn, he would not know who she was in this new world.

Under the sea's depths the mountain with Medusa's body stayed hidden from all those that would try to use her to kill their enemies. Theo plunged into the murky waters, as soon as her skin touched the salty surface scales knitted her legs together, and her tresses turned to red serpents. Slithering deeper than any mortal would dare, so close to the golden castle of Atlantis, King Triton could not venture to this sacred place without the trident of Poseidon, and this was after the swell of the seas when the trident was known to leave his hands, waiting for the true ruler of the seas to return. It was now or risk being found by the gods once again.

The waters churned in a torrent around the mountain, reminding her why even Poseidon's son couldn't enter here without the trident. She couldn't give up now, not when she was so close to her goal. Her mother knew this would happen and gave her the last shell to have been blessed by Poseidon. It could only be used once, but it carried the oath of Poseidon to calm the waters of the sea with a single purposeful breath.

Theo couldn't hold her lungs under the water indefinitely without passing out. She couldn't die from this, but she couldn't tell where she'd wash up should it happen. With her final breath she blew into the shell, and a siren's song floated around her, parting the waters, and sending her plummeting on the rocky cliff of the mountain below covered in old coral tearing up her scales as she tumbled down. The impact shocked her body, leaving her questioning if she wasn't better off drifting in the sea's current before the water swallowed the mountain whole again.

Blood streamed through the dark water as she struggled to enter the closest cave opening. Within, a giant squid slept, lulled asleep by the shell's music. Making it past the defenses set up by Poseidon, Theo surfaced in a pool opening up into a cavern glittering with the lost treasure of Atlantis, at the center stood a plain stone statue missing its head.

The heart of Atlantis, the shrine of Medusa, and Poseidon's only true love.

Theo only had one shot at this. There was only one drop left of her cure-all blood, the last drop given to the king of Athens, who had mistakenly used the one drop that was deadly poison, then remembering that his mother had been raped to conceive him, he didn't risk the other drop being anything but another chance to murder him or his family should he try to prolong their life with her 'gift'. The gods were vindictive, her siblings knew this fact intimately, most of them died for their amusement. She had nothing to lose if the king was right about Athena's vengeance, and everything to gain if she was telling the truth about one drop being capable of bringing someone back from the dead.

Unstopping the vial, Theo let the single drop of blood, still fresh even after all these years, further proof that this blood was life, not death, fall on the neck of the statue. Then placing the stoic head of her sister atop it, she released her sister's body from its stone confines. For a moment Medusa's body stayed solid before she had to catch her, easing her to the ground.

All that was left was hope.

Hope that she wasn't wrong about the blood, and hope her sister wasn't as mortal as myths betrayed.

She stroked the serpents atop her sister's head resting on her lap, their venom couldn't harm her so she was not afraid. Her own red snakes uncoiled as she leaned over Medusa's face. They gently nudged the yellowed pallor of their fallen kinship pleading for their revival. Theo cried over the still-cold corpse lamenting her failure.

The neck was red where the blood had knitted the skin back together in a raw jagged line, all too familiar to Zeus's lightning. She had been right about the blood being curative, but she had been wrong about bringing her from death's grasp. It should have been immediate, yet nothing stirred within the cold husk of her sister.

Her body was healed, the soul was gone.

Did she have to pry her sister from Hade's kingdom and force the soul and body together once again? Did she wait too long, too late to save her sister or her love? Was it not enough to steal from two gods that she must steal from another to right their wrongs?

A small red snake coiled up to wipe away some of her tears from her cheek, while a few others nudged Theo to think about where she was. Frozen in place, holding the lifeless corpse she thought about staying here, amongst the lost treasures of the sea. She could turn both of them to stone, and let the quest given to her by the fates end here. In failure. Unable to have her sister or her love, she could give up. The gods could win again.

Another monster defeated in their selfishness.

Her lungs burned, and the scales ripped from her flesh seared from her fall down the coral bringing her back to the present. She didn't heal the same as Medusa, it took excruciatingly long to heal when she was injured. Immortality didn't lessen her pain, and it certainly didn't make waiting for her body to heal at the same speed as a mortal any easier. She had to push through and leave now before the squid woke up, and before the waters were no longer calm, and definitely before she passed out from blood loss. She wouldn't die here, but by the time she recovered she'd wish she were if she got eaten by a mutant squid or was stuck here forever. Or worse, still here when Poseidon woke to find that she had intended to steal Medusa from his shrine without seeking to tell him about it. He wasn't dumb, he'd know she was betraying him. She wasn't strong enough to keep her serpent half around her legs, it wasn't her natural state like her mother to be a lamia. She'd have to swim to the surface without it, or have the currents drag her away. She didn't have to be conscious for the whole journey, eventually her body would come to again, and she'd deal with her predicament then.

What would her mother say about defying the gods, she was one after all. The mother of monsters.

Her mother didn't care about all of her children, most of them were forced upon her, and taken from her. It would hurt too much to let herself feel the loss, so there were very few of them that she acknowledged. When Medusa was around Theo's mother had let herself feel something. Protecting her from the gods by pretending she was mortal, and it was the first time Theo felt love. Many times, Theo had thought she should have been jealous, should have been vengeful. So similar to the lessons she had learned from the gods.

But she didn't, not when her mother finally smiled, finally saw her as something other than a tool for the gods, a monster. And that love had grown inside Medusa, known as the protector and the light of the gorgons. Theo smiled, another tear dripping down her chin to land on her sister's head. Medusa had shown her love, and she couldn't even save her. Clutching the head to her chest, her red snakes lamented with her, stroking the yellow and green snakes still limp beneath her sobs. With everything she had left in her, she swore under her breath.

The gods can't have her.

If it was the last act of rebellion she could do, she would take her sister's body back with her, away from this shrine of trinkets and treasure in her honor. Linking her arms under her she dragged Medusa to the pool of water at the entrance to the cave. Her gifts didn't include extra strength, and she was too spent to transform. Taking a golden chain from the ground she wrapped it around herself, and her sister then dragged them both into the water. With one deep breath she worked her way through the mountain, around the squid, and then watched in horror as the waters stirred, shaking the massive sunken shrine.

She knew then, taking Medusa's body from her underwater grave had woken Poseidon. Theo's only hope was that by the time he realized why he'd woken she'd no longer be in the sea.

Chapter 2

Superstitious

T heo got hurt all the time, but you didn't see mom fussing over every nick, scratch, or bruise on my sister. Even she developed mom's strange neurosis for cleaning up every drop of blood, and burning any clothes that she swears detergent won't solve.

"You have to be more careful," mom chided, like I was still six years old. And according to her I was still her baby, a miracle that she had to wait lifetimes for. It was an exaggeration, I knew, but I was going to college now, and they couldn't keep me bound to this small town in the middle of nowhere forever. I had dreams, and one day I'd get to see the ocean, the sea, and travel to different countries.

"It's just a scratch," I insisted. It really was, I hardly saw a single drop of blood before it clotted these days. Theo shook her head in sympathy. She at least understood that mom was intense, but she shrugged and smiled in a way that begged for me to let our mom have this final moment of caring for me. I knew she meant well, so I'd put up with it a little longer.

Theo promised she'd come with me wherever I wanted to go, and assured our mom that not once has holding someone prisoner ever worked out well in history, and it was time. And good glory, sweet sea water, it was absolutely time.

Time to live!

"I'm not sure it's okay, you know, for you to leave just yet. Maybe we can reschedule this adventure of yours?" Mom pleaded with her doe eyes, and for a moment I could have sworn they vibrated before I blinked the thought away. She could be scary when she was worried, and I could sympathize considering she was told by the doctor when I was born that I would be prone to reinjury.

It was a story I'd been told many times, to remind myself to do my best not to fall, not to get hurt, not to get into trouble. The umbilical cord wrapped around my neck at birth, and without enough oxygen, I'd almost died, and all of my muscles were weak. It was a broken song track sung on repeat that I could fall and snap my neck. I could bleed to death if I wasn't careful. I'd since learned how to look up my "condition" myself, and knew right away that my mom had been traumatized from almost losing me, but also there was no reason I couldn't live a normal life.

She'd have to get over it.

"Mom," I tried to bite back my annoyance, "This *is* happening. I'm not a child anymore, and I'm completely recovered. I won't bleed out on the street. I've pricked myself with a thumbtack and not a single drop of blood. My clotting platelets are fine." I scoffed. "More than fine. I'm pretty sure I'm like superhuman with how fine I am. Even this scratch, look," I swatted her fingers and cleaning swab away before she could give me a bandage, "Not even a mark." My mom always did that, insisted I keep a bandage on for weeks even when I'd peeked to see I'd already healed.

I had a harsh pink scar under my neck, but that was the only sign I'd ever had an issue. My childhood was a blur, I had trouble remembering much at all, a symptom of brain damage, but I could remember everything from the last few years just fine.

Mom nodded her head, acquiescing, but not without turning to Theo for some kind of backup. My sister clutched mom's shoulder warmly, giving it a knowing squeeze. This was hard for her, letting go.

"I'll be with her." Theo tossed the gauze into the fireplace for mom's benefit. She hated the sight of even a speck of blood. The fire roared to life, sparking, reminding me of my sister's bright red hair. I was grateful that she'd be coming with me, but if she tried to smother me like our mother, I'd ditch her the first chance I got.

Not for long—I did love them both—but long enough to feel normal. To feel free.

I smiled tightly at my mom, trying to keep myself from saying something that would change her mind about me walking out that door. Her only stipulation was to stay away from the sea and all of the sharks that could eat me alive. I begrudgingly agreed, with my fingers crossed in my pocket.

My mom narrowed her brows at Theo, putting all of her expectations on my sister to keep me safe before grabbing both of my hands and making me look her dead in the eyes. They were round and full of conflicted emotions. She'd let me go, but she didn't like it.

"I know you will change the world," she saw the eagerness, and the promise of great things to come, my mom was nothing but my biggest cheerleader, "but," she paused and I hoped she wasn't reconsidering, "there are always monsters in the world that will do anything to keep things the way they are. Fearful of change."

"I know mom." I shook my head. Monsters weren't the only ones fearful of change. I smirked at her incessant worrying. Nothing but a nobody, I thought; any changes I made to the world would go mostly unnoticed. But that was my mom. Overprotective as usual.

I was going to college, not a war zone.

As home disappeared behind us in our yellow, beat-up pickup, the large plot of wheat fields rolling along the hills, I thought to myself, I could finally go to the University of Apollo to become a doctor. I could help families just like mine, make sure parents never have to lose a child if they don't have to. Theo and mom tried to keep it a secret, but I knew in my bones there was something special about me, about my blood.

I could save lives.

I *would* save lives.

"Does mom know where we're going?" I asked nervously, tugging on the seat belt so it'd mimic the tension I felt about going against what I knew my mom would be okay with. She could hardly stand the sight of blood, and as a doctor, I'd be around a lot of it.

"She'll understand. She just doesn't want you to get hurt."

"I won't be the one hurt," I defended.

Theo sighed and nodded.

"What?" She had something to say. She always did that when she was holding herself back. "Just say it."

"Not all pain is physical, Aless. One day you'll understand that, and you'll find that when you seek to pull souls from the brink of death, there will always be others who pull them back." She paused to let that sink in, and a chill ran down my spine on an otherwise warm, sunny day. "There is a reason why mom doesn't wish for you to speak of the gods–"

"She's superstitious," I joked, but the tone in Theo's voice was anything but jovial.

"It's because she's lost too much to their games. Gaining their attention is a curse, and she doesn't want history to repeat itself. They are real, they are just more subtle in their games now. You think this college is called Apollo's University because someone was like, that sounds like a good name. He was a mythical god of healing and diseases?" Theo gripped the steering wheel so tightly her knuckles changed color from pink to white to red.

I held my breath, holding myself back from asking what neither my mom nor my sister have answered before. She flexed her joints and sighed like an inexplicably heavy weight was lifting from her shoulders.

"You died, Aless. It was never an illness. You don't remember your childhood because you died. You caught the eye of a powerful god, and they played with your life for fun. We are nothing but amusement to them. Remember that."

I sucked on my lower lip, nibbling on it, uncomfortable at the conversation, but not wanting to piss off the one person who was helping me. She was my sister, and I loved her, but this was beyond my family's normal superstitions. I was alive. If I had died, then the doctors revived me, and it had nothing to do with gods.

My sister could always read my expressions, and today was no different. She shook her head, resigned.

"You don't have to believe me. It's better that you don't. Faith is a very powerful thing, that they tend to be attracted to. But," she turned off the road, with the hazards blinking, and she turned to make me promise, "swear to me you'll never use your blood to save someone. This medical school may not be Apollo's main source of entertainment, but sure as shit, they will catch salt of your ability and I'll regret not locking you away like mom wants to do."

I gasped, slapping my hands over my mouth to cover my shock. She knew. Of course she knew.

Then why was she helping me?

"I'm not blinded by hope like our mother. I know you've been experimenting with your blood. A little bit in the dirt to see if the wheat grew thicker. The bird that fell from the tree too soon. Or purposefully hurting yourself to see how fast you'd heal."

"You knew..." But the wheat didn't grow any taller, and the bird never recovered.

She shrugged. "I was curious myself. It was exhausting staying up all night to make sure the wheat was the same height as the rest of the crop, and giving the bird a sedative to make sure I could free it in the woods without mom deciding to kill it, so you don't gain the attention of the gods."

"Mom would kill it?" I shuddered at the thought of someone as sweet as my mom harming a spider let alone a bird.

"She'd do it for you," Theo's words were weighty as she cupped the sides of my face. Fingering my blonde hair, she let the strands fall in waves. "It's our turn to decide our own fates, sis. The gods have decided who gets to be heroes and who they turn into monsters for too long. Learn to be a doctor, save lives, but promise me never use your blood. Stay under the radar."

It was hard to say no to Theo when she believed so strongly that I could be a hero without the extra help. I owed it to her, and my mother, to use every other means first, if only to ease their worries. I may not have believed in the gods, but that didn't mean there weren't people out there that could try to use me to save lives. I knew what desperation could do to a person, and I'd be very careful not to be noticed by gods or otherwise.

This was my life, not theirs.

"I'll be careful," I promised, and she reluctantly eased her hands from my cheeks, driving in silence with the weight of knowing I hadn't agreed to not use my blood. She didn't press the issue, knowing as well as I did that I'd risk the ire of the gods if someone needed my help. How could anyone expect me to let someone die if I had the power to stop it?

Chapter 3

Drowning

Washed up on the shores of Jacksonville, another person was found seemingly uninjured aside from the amnesia of how they got there, and signs of water in their lungs. It might have been considered one of the hundreds of drowning accidents in Florida that didn't end all that badly... if it weren't for the one thing all of them repeated in their accounts. They all swore they saw someone drowning, and when they tried to help they got caught in the current themselves.

All of them cited to be excellent swimmers, surfers, and even certified scuba divers with no sign of the drowning victim, unless you counted the people themselves.

Beach accidents weren't all that uncommon, but my sister's voice kept on nagging me to stay away from the water until things calmed down. She knew I liked to sneak off at night when the beach was empty. There was something about the ocean that called to me, but I kept my promise to my mom from years ago, at least partially in spirit.

Staying away from the sea was because of the danger of sharks, so I always stayed close to the shore, never farther than I could stand. Most of the sharks that would come in this close are not aggressive, and well, I'd be more in danger of a stray jellyfish sting.

I dug my toes into the damp sand. Even on days I went without my wet suit, the cool water felt warm to me, but I knew what my mother would say. She'd remind me that cold water can cause muscles to cramp and sometimes all it takes is for the water to shock your own body temperature, even if the water is warmer than freezing. It took concentration not to take the insulation suit off, but I wore it. I wasn't going to let my dull senses trick me into a false sense of safety. Most of the odd near-drownings were down the shore where surfers liked to catch the break, and there was no reason to think someone else was out here. So I let the water rise, lapping at my shins. The dull shine of the moon reflected off the water's surface as I waded in.

I wouldn't go out too far, I promised myself, but the call of the sea was always so difficult to resist. Being away from it for so long as I grew up only made me want it more.

Then I heard her screams.

All thoughts about how others had remarked on saving a drowning man had left me, and all I could do was act. Where were the noises coming from? Where were the sounds of disturbed waters loudest? Whipping around trying to find the screams, I turned frantically in a panic.

"Where are you?" I called out desperately.

"Are you–" her voice muffled and choked on another lungful of water. Was she another victim like the others? I was barely trained for this. Everything I'd learned so far was basic first aid, and normal primary college curriculum. None of it so specific to how to save someone from the water without drowning myself, sure I'd learned

CPR, but that didn't really help me drag a drowning person out of the water.

It wasn't like I was a lifeguard.

Should I go to her? Should I run for my phone on the shore? Or can I hope someone else comes by to hear both of our screams? She wouldn't last long if I called for help; I knew that. It was me or no one, and I didn't finally get accepted into the medical program to let someone die on my watch.

But what kind of help would I be?

Did it matter?

My help was better than no help. I swam out to where her noises were louder than the crashing of the waves on the shore.

"I'm coming!"

"–coming," she gurgled, and I hoped I'd get to her in time.

The waves were swelling larger here, and even I was having trouble keeping my head above them. Black waters pushed me, and I had to dive through the current to reach her. I bobbed to the surface again straining to hear her, but the only sound was the waves on the rocks.

My heart rate picked up, thinking the unthinkable. I was too late. I didn't make it. It was much too dark to find her under the water by feel alone. I was just as likely to grab hold of a shark as I was to grab a human body, or scrape myself on the rocks, or reef. The reef... how far out did I swim? Where was the shore line?

Unless she came above water again for me to find her.

She was gone.

Scolding myself mentally, I should have went to shore and grabbed my phone. Should have called for the police to set up a patrol. Get the coast guard to search the waters with lights and boats. And trained professionals.

Maybe she wouldn't be lost then, if I had done things differently.

Another wave crashed over me, catching me off guard and pulling me under. I tried to remember which direction the shore was, which direction I should have been pedaling to prevent myself from being swept out to sea, but I had been so focused on finding the girl. I got turned around.

Swim across, not against the current, I reminded myself. But which way was which? It was all so dark now.

My screams echoed in the water. Salty water burned in my throat in place of air. The tides taking me farther away from the shore. Pushing my arms and legs as hard as I could, I tried to make it back to shore, but the distance kept slowly gaining on me.

Was this what it was like for those other swimmers found on the shore half dead? The terror of realizing your fate was in the hands of the consuming sea whether you made it back as a statistic or alive?

It would have been worth it, I thought, if I had saved the girl. Seemed so final, and so unacceptable to trade my life for nothing.

My arms were aching, and my legs cramped up, seizing to a stop. So this was what drowning felt like? I guess Theo was right after all—the sea was a dangerous place.

It wasn't the sharks that got me this time mom, I thought about how she always mentioned the sharks as the excuse to stay away from the sea. How I had used the sharks as the excuse to say I still kept my promise to her by staying safe by only dipping in a little.

My lungs burned, and by all accounts, I should have been unconscious. I didn't remember the last time the waves allowed me the chance to breath. Even if I touched the surface, my lungs had no room left for air.

Yet, I stared ahead in the darkness as my body floated with the current, until the seaweed wrapped itself around, holding me in place.

Tangled up, the seaweed rolled me to the surface. Swaths of my hair were gently pushed off my face.

If I had breath to give, I would have given the goddess before me all of it. The moon lit her up in an ethereal glow, and her eyes were large and bright, like a tropical mango. She was the most perfect dream, that I wondered if I had made it to the beach at all, or if I had decided to stay at home with my sister and I was tucked into bed.

This could only be a dream, and a sense of relief came over me.

Bizarrely enough, the goddess brought my hair up to her face, marveling at the blonde strands. Twining it with her own dark waves, I would have gladly given her my hair if she asked it of me. Then her orange eyes met my own, and she startled at realizing I was observing her.

My mouth opened, water spilling from the sides, wanting to speak with her, but only the sound of gurgles escaped. Whatever remaining bubbles in my lungs were now gone, and the tightness in my chest grew until I was seeing spots.

Razor-sharp teeth gleamed in her mouth, as she glared. A vicious-ness taking over the playful beauty she once wore. Her sticky hands grabbed the thick of my scalp, and pulled me under to twist with the surrounding kelp.

Under the water I heard her voice, "What are you doing away from the sea little nymph?"

My eyes grew wide as the dark spots closed in around me. Her dark hair glinted green, floating around us both, blurring my vision. I tried to speak again, but no words came.

All I could taste was the salt, before I heard the word 'no' echo in my ears. This didn't feel like a dream, but a painful nightmare I couldn't escape from.

"You know the rules," she sounded torn, though I couldn't decide whether that had more to do with talking through the water than any conflict to do with not eating me alive with those sharp razor fangs. "I'll tell you what; I'll delay telling the Lord of the Sea about your land dwelling if you give me your legs."

And before I could answer her, or even be shocked by the obvious insanity of her offer, a last ditch effort to breathe had me clawing for the surface. Then darkness consumed my vision. The last thing on my mind were those gleaming chompers as she gnashed in annoyance.

***

Waking to achy muscles, I felt like I'd ran a marathon, or in this case swam one. Despite the soreness, I was oddly comfortable. Blinking several times, my eyes had to adjust to the brightness before seeing myself in a cushion of colored tentacles. If my body listened to me, I would have jumped up in a panic.

"I had the anemone sting you so that you wouldn't harm them when you woke. It'll wear off soon, but I don't recommend moving unless you want them to excrete more toxins. They are harmless to most sea nymphs, you just have to give them a few fish to eat or some algae and they're happy enough," the girl from my nightmares explained. In the light of the day, her hair was the same color as the kelp, a rich green, and her eyes were a warm mango yellow. She was inhuman, but she didn't seem as scary now as she did in the moon's glow, but she also wasn't flashing me those flesh-tearing grinders.

My head was propped up on the rocks with a few anemones for a pillow, and the salty water calmly sloshed against my ears. We were in some sort of enclosed pool, blocking the harshness of the sea's waves, and my host's head was peeking out from the water in front of me, her mouth thankfully below the surface so I could pretend she wasn't going to eat me.

"I can't decide what kind of sea nymph you are," she pondered, though her mouth was still hidden, and I only now realized I was hearing her through the water still clogging my ears, "I've never seen one quite like you, at least not in my lifetime. Most of your kind don't look so much like a mortal, not since King Triton ruled that any offspring with mortals be stripped of their gifts at birth if they don't live in the sea."

She spoke as if I should know about what she was talking about, and all I could do was stare. My throat was raw, and my mouth felt like cotton, but I could breathe.

I thought I would croak my response, but oddly enough, I sounded normal. "I'm not a nymph."

Waving me off, she continued, "I don't care that you're a rogue, betrayer of the gods. Fuck them," she said flippantly. And as she leaned back to float on her back, a large fin burst from the water, splashing me with salt water. "Times have changed. They don't want mortals to ruin their entertainment by being too aware of them. They get enough of a power boost from the myths and bullshit media worship. They don't want the responsibility of managing a bunch of temples and prayers again."

My mouth opened and closed like a guppy, and she stretched, her fin on full display, sparkling in the sunshine like a rainbow. She was a freaking merperson.

"Plenty of people lose their phones in the water. I'm not completely cut off from the land dwellers... Plus, we like to take a few mortals for fun every so often," she admitted sheepishly, but all I heard was the word 'we'.

There were more, somewhere around here.

Wherever here was.

She leaned in, gathering her green hair to one side over her shoulder. "Have you always had legs?"

I sputtered on some water that crashed over my mouth remembering her previous question about bargaining for my legs. Was that why I was here? My wet suit was gone, and my legs were exposed, still numb from whatever toxin the anemone gave me.

"I won't tell King Triton. I'm under oath to tell him, eventually, that you exist, but," she shrugged, "we can negotiate when that will be, and between just us fishes he's not particularly fond of mortals, and let's us do what we want as long as we stay in the sea, and clean up our mess." She winked, then glided up next to me, lifting herself onto the rocks.

And by mess, the only image in my mind, was merpeople chowing down on human meat.

"Do you eat them?" I couldn't help but ask, now that her smile was on full display, along with her large fin. She seemed pleased by this assessment and laughed. The sound that came from her throat was like sandpaper and metal on metal grating, nothing like the voice I was hearing earlier. Even the anemones that had no sense of sound were startled into sucking all their tentacles back into their bodies by whatever awful vibrations that noise produced.

Rock met with the back of my skull, no longer cushioned by the sea creatures. My body slid down the slope into the pool of water. Still numb from the anemone toxin, I only floated at the top for a moment before my face sunk under with the rest of me.

"The Petite Mermaid was only half right," her voice was melodic once more, "We do have beautiful voices... but only under the water." Now that I thought about it, the only time I heard the cries for help the other night was when I was swimming with my ears in the water. Frantically searching for where the girl was drowning... I'd heard nothing.

I sunk deeper into the depths of the hidden alcove, surrounded by high rocks and beautiful colors of sea life. I had been tricked by merpeople to drown, and I didn't even believe in such things. This was a nightmare designed to make me feel bad for not believing my sister about the myths of gods and monsters.

Leave it to a dying breath to start believing I should have, considering what my own blood could do, but I had convinced myself that there was a scientific explanation. Something in my DNA, a mutation, an evolution of the human condition that lets me heal faster.

This time when I sucked in a breath of water, my lungs knew what to expect, and the shock of the salt burning wasn't as bad. That's what I told myself to cope with how desperately I wanted to claw at my throat. The merlady's green hair covered her exposed breasts and was seemingly plastered in place as she circled around me, her fishy scales refracting like a silver rainbow fish. My eyes stung to watch her, but I'd face my death head on; I wouldn't turn blindly into my final moments—I tried to convince myself.

That was easier said than done, when the anemone took my choice away of trying to run.

She was a deadly dream that might have been lovely to see if it didn't mean it was the last thing I'd know. The vulture of the sea. She circled me, not making a move to save me from my fate.

"You've been away from the sea for too long, nymph. The sea won't drown you, but it won't let you rejoin it without a cost either. I can take you to King Triton, where you can swear your fealty, and most definitely receive punishment for trying to defy him." I shook my head in panic, and this time when she laughed, it was musical, surrounded by the sea's filter for her horrid screeching. "Or you can give me your legs, in exchange for my fins and the sea's acceptance."

Also equally terrifying and unacceptable.

I shook my head once more, only this time it wasn't a laugh I received in response. She clutched her hands around my neck, tightening, bruising my larynx.

A twitch in my toes told me the toxin was running its course. Survival was the only thing important, seeing Theo again spearheading my drive. I had to have the chance to tell her she could have been more convincing about staying away from the sea if she knew monsters like this existed.

What was the point in being vague about merfolk wanting to drown people?

Just the sea is dangerous, that's all she had given. What bullshit! It didn't matter that I might not have believed her. She didn't even try.

My hands suddenly clawed for traction with the fishy bitch. Nothing quite beats adrenaline to speed up the process of filtering out anemone toxins, and it didn't hurt that I'm sure whatever else was in my blood helped out. Was it magic? Was it a scientific anomaly? Did it matter? Thrashing in the water, she had more mobility with her fin than I did with my non-webbed extremities.

With our hands, legs, and tail preoccupied with trying to gain the advantage, I'd forgotten about the one key feature of this green merterror. Sharp rows of razor teeth ready to rip flesh from my bones.

When they tore into my shoulder, I hadn't seen it coming, and the last bubbles of air trapped in my lungs filled with salt water. I was so angry blood pumped from my wound, turning our surroundings red with pain... and vengeance. I stopped trying to pry her hands from my throat and instead wrenched on her hair to pull her from my shoulder.

"You'll never," she choked on her words, "leave the sea." Her grip sagged, and sickly black lines traced around her lips webbing out across her cheeks and racing down her neck towards her heart. If she even had one.

An echo pulsed through the water, pushing me back against the rocks. My vision blurred, but I could see large shadows quickly approaching, and I knew better than to hope they were sharks. At least that would have been normal, and this day was anything but normal.

"Seize her!" They ordered like there was some military guard that would come swarming behind them before reaching my attacker. For the briefest of moments, I thought they were possibly here to save me from her.

"Princess Coraline!" It was clear they were not my reinforcements, or there to save me from her. They were more concerned with her wellbeing than my own.

"She's not responding! How is this possible?" Their panicked voices faded. The rough arms of the other merperson, I had forgotten Coraline had mentioned there were more of them, dragged me across the water, barely conscious.

Just as she had warned, the sea wouldn't let me drown, but it wouldn't end my suffering, either. Tiny bubbles entered my nose and the corners of my mouth, working their way to my lungs, enough to keep me alive, enough to keep me awake, but not enough to feel like my lungs weren't exploding, burning acid and frying me alive.

Who knew the sea cared so much to make me suffer, but not enough to let me die?

Maybe the sea was as vindictive as I was?

I was more than willing to let this merterror die, if it meant I didn't. And it wasn't that long ago that I had thought the opposite. So willing to risk my life to save her when she was drowning.

Not when she was trying to murder me for my legs.

Not very princess like...

King Triton, if he was real too, would not be pleased if princess meant something more than a title. Could I get to her in time to give her my blood? Could that heal whatever happened to her?

I wasn't certain any more.

Not when I was debating if it was my blood that was poisoning her to begin with. The black veins in her face turned gray, chalky, and her skin took on a sickly pallor. Even her claws and the tips of her fins were draining of color.

I was still bleeding from my shoulder, and I had reason to wonder if that was also the sea's doing.

Healing fast was normal for me, but not now, not in the sea. I had to worry if maybe the princess had a toxin like the anemone. One that would prevent me from clotting, chumming the waters so even if she couldn't kill me herself, something else would.

"She's gone," a merperson whispered, "we can't be the ones to bring her back like this." Princess Coraline's nectarine eyes stared off in the distance, vacant, and as the blackish-gray veins reached them they too lost their vibrancy.

"He'll kill us all for letting it happen," he warned his partner.

"If we're lucky, that's all he'll do."

"We need to bring her close enough to the palace without being seen. Someone else will find her."

"What about the nymph?" I wanted to cringe, but I was convinced now that whatever Coraline's bite did, it definitely included a paralytic. Even if I wanted to... which I did, once she let go of me. I was too late.

I couldn't save her now.

My heart clenched.

This wasn't how I'd imagined losing the girl I thought was drowning, but somehow I'd lost her, anyway. Guilt tugged at me for being the reason she was gone. I had felt so angry, that in that moment I had wanted her dead, and now that she was, I wish I could undo it. I was so willing to give my life for hers when I thought she was drowning, and yet when it came down to it I couldn't let her have mine.

Not by force, not that way.

I'd die anyway, but now both of us would be gone.

How was this possible? How did everything go so wrong so fast?

"Something else can eat her. No one can survive this much blood loss from Coraline's bite." She did have a venom, but it didn't just paralyze me... it stopped me from healing.

"She's poisonous," I wanted to scoff as them, so was Coraline, "I don't feel good about letting her body rot so close to Atlantis."

Were they talking about the Atlantis? The lost Atlantis? The sunken city of myth? I'd be excited if it weren't for the circumstances. But they couldn't be serious.

"You won't feel good about what Triton will do to us if we stick around either. Princess Coraline always bends the rules and does what she wants. There's nothing tying us to her. She has her pick of any Atlantian, and there's too many for Triton to kill everyone that might have seen her last."

"She's his last living daughter..." he doubted his comrade's assessment, obviously concerned about what King Triton would do to them, and considering if doing his daughter a kindness of at least bringing her back to Atlantis would ease their punishment in some way.

"Was," his co-conspirator amended.

"Fuck. We're taking a risk even attempting to go back home. He could destroy the entire city just in the hopes that he kills someone that is associated with her death. He won't care who's collateral."

"If they don't go home then Triton will probably assume they had something to do with it and only target them instead of the city," I thought. I mean, "Better them than an entire city, but how messed up is Triton for that to even be an option?"

"How is she still conscious?"

Did I say that out loud?

Under water?

Barely alive?

"The sea won't let her drown..." The kinder of the two seemed to be in awe of me, and as my hair swished over my eyes, I saw him swim towards me.

"But she killed the last daughter of the seven seas. Why would it save her?"

I scoffed. Save me? I was being tortured.

Waterboarding was a real thing, and I was living through it. Worse than anything I could have imagined. Trying to breathe, but opening my mouth didn't change the fact that my lungs were already full of liquid. Full of salt that burned and shriveled up my sensitive tissue, all while still being completely aware of what was happening.

Every pocket in my lungs felt like it was being seared, then healed, then seared again. I could only begin to question if it had something to do with my superpower of being able to heal so fast, but fast enough that I was still alive. And little bubbles of oxygen found their way in only enough to stave off death. It was excruciating.

The sea wasn't saving me; it was getting revenge.

"It doesn't matter. The sea can't stop her from bleeding out, but she's right."

"About what?"

"They'll be looking for someone to blame when they find Princess Coraline."

"This unknown nymph is not enough."

"Exactly," he schemed, "but we aren't the only ones that could be missing from Atlantis. All we have to do is plant some of the princess's poisoned blood on anyone that returns. The city is saved, and then so are we."

"You're both sick. Willing to murder someone else on the chance that your own lives will be saved," I choked out.

How I was able to speak through all the water was still a mystery, but maybe the princess wasn't wrong... maybe I was a sea nymph?

"Not any different from you," he retorted while yanking me through the water. My vision was still blurry, unable to make out his features, other than I was certain he was half fish like his friend dragging the dead princess's body. Her green hair floating in a blur beside me.

"If you had died the princess would still be alive, and we wouldn't be trying to fight for our right to live. So who's the real monster little nymph? Whoever we have to take care of to live is on your soul, not ours."

"It's not ideal," the other tried to explain; at least one of them had a small bit of conscience, "but if we took you back with the princess and explained things it would only make things worse. We would both die, and it's very likely many innocent Atlantians would be punished in Triton's rage. Doing it this way may seem cowardice, but we may well be saving more lives this way," he trailed off and sighed. "Even if we end up dying in the end, our avoidance of punishment and schemes will distract Triton enough that the city may be saved."

"Why are you trying to defend ourselves to her? She's the reason we have to do this."

Was I not any different from them? How is there not another way? Why are they so sure Triton will murder a entire city when I'm right here?

"Wait..." I couldn't believe I was even going to suggest this, "there's another way."

"Fucking sea storms, just let her die already!" The scheming fish traitor groaned in exasperation.

"I wish there was, but we can't even be certain Triton won't break his oath to the other gods and wage war on the mortals over this. The best we can do is cause a distraction that lasts long enough that he will see reason. I highly doubt we'll be alive much longer than you. May Hades take mercy on our souls."

If it weren't for the more reasonable one of the bunch, I wasn't sure I'd force myself to follow through with an alternative. But it wasn't just about them, it was about the people of Atlantis, if the place even existed. Or the victims of the other merperson's schemes.

"She's supposed to be immortal right? The daughter of a god?"

"Where is she going with this? Even gods and titans have been bested, though not usually by a rogue nymph." He was obviously not my fan, and it didn't matter if he was, but his jabs were making it difficult for me to still want to help them before I died as they so delicately informed me of my fate.

I had no extra air to huff out in frustration, and I was barely keeping it all together as it was. "There's a chance I could save her."

It was unlikely— mean dead was dead—and not even I think my blood could bring the dead back to life. Then again, if she's the daughter of a god, and technically immortal... maybe. I mean, worse-case scenario, I'm dead and they drain me of my blood to save as many people from the king's wrath as possible.

"Plus... how do you know she's actually dead?" Even I knew that part was a stretch. She was definitely dead. Dead as stone. She looked frozen.

"I don't think you realize how much time has passed since we left the outpost," the kinder merman pitied my naivety. "It's been hours since her death. Your poison has turned her veins black and her skin gray. There is no way for you to save her, us, or yourself."

It felt like minutes had passed. I must not have been as conscious as I thought. Who knew how much I had actually missed of their conversation during that time?

Still, I pressed on.

"Let me do it."

"Do what?" The one with the kind voice humored me.

"Take her to Atlantis." It would be like a two for one deal. I could see Atlantis before I died, and the princess wouldn't be floating around the vicinity waiting for discovery in the sea. I suppose I could tack on these two would probably survive the king's psycho streak because they wouldn't be involved.

"That's exactly where we are taking you," the merman I might not feel so guilty about endangering snapped.

"If I'm still alive when we get there, let me swim to the guards," they must have guards there, "with the princess."

"What good would that do?"

"Why are we even talking with her? She's not going to live long enough for it to matter if the sentinels find her or if she finds the sentinels. And if she did live long enough, we should probably knock her off now, so she doesn't lump us in with her treason."

That didn't go the way I had planned. I was offering to take the blame and maybe explain with my dying croak that I had no idea how I killed her, but it was me. Maybe the sea was keeping me alive for this reason alone; atonement. So that I could be brought to justice, though I honestly don't know why the sea was capable of keeping me on the edge of life and not an immortal mermaid, and daughter of a god.

,

"Dead enough that Triton will probably have to give her metamorphosis if there is any life left in her. It's quite a beautiful ceremony. His youngest was turned to sea foam so she could still touch the land every time a wave rolls onto the shore."

"She doesn't need to know that." The merman holding me squeezed my arm with a jolt.

"We don't have to make her last moments tragic." Ignoring his partner's sentiments, he continued, "I find stories to be a pleasant distraction when I'm in pain. Coraline's mother was a sea nymph, you know. Against the wishes of Hera, Triton never wanted to marry and settle down with a goddess. So, he picked his mistresses among immortals that she wouldn't force the issue with."

He wasn't wrong; listening to his soothing voice was making the pain more tolerable. And I wasn't opposed to finding out more about the life I'd taken from this world. It was only right that I come to terms with the fact that no matter how justified my self-defense is, to someone else, this monster was a daughter.

"Did Coraline keep you around as bait? How did a guppy like you ever get chosen by her?"

"Maybe for the same reason Triton picked her mother, and any other mistress he's had," he wasn't so much of a push over after all, smoothly he transitioned right back into the story of the sea god's family, "His father favored him the most out of his children, and gave him the highest honor of guarding the trident, ruling Atlantis, and being his messenger. Triton's word was as good as Poseidon's himself, and even if it wasn't, the sea god stood by whatever decision Triton would make. Rumor spread the reason Triton never married was because of how unhappy marriage made his own father. It was used to control him in the game between the gods."

"You're mucking it up. Poseidon pissed off Hera when he double-crossed her during her attempt to overthrow Zeus. Triton knows that if he marries, Hera will fuck it up like she did with his dad making sure he's stuck with a goddess that he doesn't love, and having anyone he ever did grow to care about killed."

"Shit," the revelation threw the storyteller, "what if that is what this is?"

"Nah, Triton's been a right prick, even to his daughters after what happened to his youngest."

"But all of them are dead now."

I was following both of their logic the best I could, and from what I was gathering, Triton was being punished for his father's sins. But how did I fit into all of this?

Chapter 4

Atlantis

S tory time quieted both the mermen the rest of the journey to
Atlantis, or perhaps I was too far gone to be aware of when
they were talking anymore. The revelation of Coraline's death being
anything more than self-defense, wrapped up into a whole age-long
grudge between powerful gods was hard to swallow. Though anything
would be when your lungs were full of salt water, but my two escorts,
which was putting it mildly, were spooked. Even the surly one had
lightened his grip, and the surrounding current seemed to rip past at
a faster speed for him to be rid of me.

Since I wasn't dead yet, I couldn't dismiss the idea of ancient gods
as easily as I would have yesterday. Hell, yesterday merfolk were off
the table. Today, sea magic prevented me from drowning, though not
from the feeling like I was. The pressure in my chest was enough to
make me wish the sea would release me, even if that meant dying.

Cowardly, I knew, but healing fast all my life had made me soft to
pain. I just wanted it to end.

For the briefest of moments, an ethereal light in the distance had me believing this was the end of my story. The thing people talked about what the dead saw when the pain was over—when the reaper took you past the pearly gates into the afterlife.

"Drop them here. The sentinels will find them, eventually. She's been cold all night now, even her eyes are glassy. The sea has released them to Hades. It was a nice thing you did talking to her in her last moments."

"Coraline was pressing her luck with the gods. Messing with the mortals like she was, the nymph didn't deserve to die so young. Not even old enough to have sworn fealty to the sea and gain her gills."

They were talking about me as if I had died, but all I could think about was, would I have sprouted gills? Wouldn't Theo have said something? Why would she keep it a secret? Was my sister a nymph, too?

"You can't dwell on that stuff. The gods may have taken a different approach to things these days, but whatever they have planned, we'd only get in the way."

"She's beautiful, even now," his voice was gentle and I thought it was sweet for him to care so much about Coraline, but then it was my face that his hand caressed, brushing back my blonde strands. I still couldn't see anything but the light fogging in the distance, but I could feel the pressure of his lips on my forehead as his frame blocked the light from view.

"I didn't know you were into nymphs," his friend mocked, trying to lift the mood of heady darkness.

"You know she isn't like the rest of them."

"Wasn't," he corrected, "and I'm not blind." He cleared his throat, uncomfortable with saying anything kind about me, even if it was superficial. "Never seen hair as gold as hers except on the gods themselves."

"Her eyes were as green as the tropical seas before the life left her, and I'd never seen a nymph with wings."

Now, that stumped me. Wings? What were they talking about?

"Not having a tail, I can imagine they are some kind of fins that were meant to help her swim without one. Not even her hands have any webbing."

"Reminds me of a sea robin."

"She does look more bird than fish with double fins like a right proper angel. But she's gone now, and whatever plot she's part of, we need to be in the city before they find her."

Considering Coraline had a mertail, and that meant they had to be speaking of me like I was some fascinating scientific discovery to marvel at.

"What are you doing?"

"Taking insurance."

"We already have the princess's blood. What do we need the nymph's hair for?"

"For the sea witch. Now let's fuck off before we attract attention."

The softer merman gave me a squeeze and whispered into my hair, "May Poseidon bless your passage in the Underworld fair soul. I wish you would have let your legs be stolen, for I would have defied the gods to get them back for you." Then he kissed my temple before releasing me into the sea's embrace to drift alone.

"Poseidon hasn't answered anyone's prayers for a long time. You're wasting your breath." Then the sounds of their voices were gone, and all I had was the small light in the distance that reached beyond the fog of whatever death consumed me. I had hoped the light was my end, that when I reached it, I could rest so I tried to move closer. But my limbs were too numb, and I drifted only by the grace of the water's current.

Until all I saw was light... and then nothing.

I woke with a fit of coughing, clutching at my chest. Gulping in air, luxurious, burning yet joyous air. One heave at a time I was breathing, and it was equal parts excitement to feel alive, and dreadfully painful to actually be alive. Because if this was death, there was no rest in peace.

"I'll inform Triton that you've woken," a deep silky voice relayed from my bedside. I was on a bed, and I wasn't alone. When I opened my eyes, I stared, unable to look away.

His eyes were the clearest blue, and as soon as I could pry myself from their depths, all I could see was his bare chest with chiseled muscles. Not bulky, but toned and sleek with large broad shoulders. He let me drink him in without a word, waiting for my mouth to close before a knowing smile touched his lips. I'd have been mortified, if I wasn't still so elated at discovering the last day of memories was possibly some horrible nightmare that I had concocted in my delirium.

He probably found me washed up ashore, and brought me back to his place instead of the hospital.

So much relief lifted from me as I plastered my attention on this handsome stranger. And just as suddenly his words cleared up in my mind, inform Triton. Triton. For salts sake, I had better be letting my mind run away again. He could not have said the name of the mythical King of Atlantis, a name I clearly would not be hearing if I didn't die drowning in the sea after murdering his daughter. In self-defense, but still not a good first impression. Plus, I was so certainly dead if all of that was true, if not now most assuredly soon, and definitely worse than drowning.

Horror replaced my previous expression. He lifted a dark brow, musing over the flip of my emotions from pure blissful relief to a stark, ghastly realization of where I was. And why was I in such a nice room instead of a dungeon?

"Where am I?" My voice was still gravelly.

"Atlantis." He certainly wasn't one to elaborate, but that one word was enough to confirm my fears. Yesterday happened, and my sister was probably freaking out when I didn't return home. Mom would murder her for confirming all of her fears about leaving town for college, and then I'd meet up with Theo in the afterlife, where she would murder me again for not listening to her about the dangers of the sea.

Mr. Half Naked and Gorgeous watched me curiously as a series of my thoughts played out on my face trying to process my life and groaning at how little of it I actually got to live. I grew up sheltered by an over-protective mom, and only recently graduated college to finally work towards my medical degree. Only to be fated to die in some public showing of the king's choosing for killing his daughter before I even got to make a friend that wasn't my sister.

That's how pathetic I was... my best, and possibly –definitely– only friend was my sister. Not knocking my sister, she is everything I could have asked for in a friend, but I had focused so much on studying that I pretty much didn't put myself out there to get to know anyone else.

And by anyone else, I mean romantically.

So, the blush that was surfacing on my cheeks from the man wearing nothing but a pair of black lounge pants wasn't something I was used to. Now that I was trying to divert my attention to anywhere in the room except for him, I noticed the bed was black silk sheets, and there was a fair amount of masculine taste in the room. This wasn't a dungeon, but this wasn't a room for me, either.

"This is your room?"

I pulled up the covers over the button-up shirt that I was wearing. Suspiciously made of the same matching material as the lounge pants. Soft, and obviously not my size.

"Not usually," he answered while walking to a small kitchen in what appeared to be a studio room. He was being aggravatingly vague, and not at all helpful in offering up any sort of explanation for why I was here, with him, in his room. And not in some dungeon waiting for an execution.

I sucked in another purposeful gulp of air.

"Isn't Atlantis under water?" I kind of expected where the merfolk were taking me was under the sea, given the whole half fish thing.

He continued casually pouring himself a cup of what I assumed was coffee. Waiting until he took a sip before responding, he was in no hurry.

"It is," he confirmed, but left it at that.

I burned to know more. We obviously weren't swimming in water, and he was walking on two legs.

"Are you purposefully being obtuse about this whole thing?" I waved my arms around the room, and in front of myself. There was a stranger in what is 'not usually' but still, obviously, his bed. That stranger being me. We were sharing half of what were fancy men's pajamas, and I was unconscious for the part where we met. If I didn't distinctly remember putting on my wet suit and still feeling the raggedness of my throat from salt water then I might mistake this for a one-night stand after too many drinks. But I've never had any sort of night on the town that would involve having friends that weren't so paranoid about bringing unwanted attention to ourselves, like my sister. We keep our parties inside with wine, movies, and ice cream.

Again, he took forever to answer. How hard was it to plot what he should say to me when everything he has said was two words or less? Well, except for that first time. But that was when he initiated the conversation to tell me he'd inform Triton I was awake, but he hadn't made any move to follow through with his threat to do so.

"You can tell me why you are here, or you can see how Triton decides to greet your arrival. Which do you prefer?" I might have been better off when we were using fewer words. He placed his coffee on the small kitchen island and waited for my response.

I opened my mouth only to close it again unsure of how to proceed. He knew something of the kind of reception I would receive or he wouldn't look so smug, right?

"I was hoping you'd tell me?" I couldn't help the uncertainty in what I was trying to make a statement, but ended up coming out more like a question. Telling him I recently killed the princess didn't really seem like the best move right out the gate. Did he know or didn't he? Did they find Coraline's body?

A slow smile lifted the corner of his mouth. Under different circumstances, the action could have been considered handsomely cheeky, something that would have gotten me excited about what he had planned. Anxious energy filled me, and I shifted on the bed.

He nodded once and then lifted his coffee mug in challenge. Taking a sip, he then moved around the kitchen island to open a closet on the other side of the room. Still carrying his mug, he reached in and grabbed a suit and headed to the bathroom. Returning clothed in his new outfit, I sucked in a breath at the sight of him. The air scratched my throat, and I coughed, bringing his attention to me. He glanced up from adjusting his cuffs, a regular high society prince. His blue eyes twinkled, and he knew exactly how he affected me.

"Not many escape the sea as you have, but it seems as though it valued your life. It didn't value your comfort. Why is that?" I opened my mouth to respond, but he lifted his hand to silence me at the door. Hovering in the door frame, he added with a sigh, "It's not the correct question. The why is predictable, because it is intriguing. Intriguing enough to keep you alive," he tapped the door with his palm, "perhaps," he said, more to himself, then he stared down his nose at me to instruct, "Find some clothes and join me outside."

The door closed behind him, and I was so distracted with his deep blue eyes I missed seeing his hand grab the handle, making the whole action seem as if it were done by a phantom.

Did I have any choice other than that door? Searching the small studio, there were no windows in the bathroom, so it really was stay in this room or join him outside.

Tugging on the hem of his top, I wrung the edges nervously. Was I only going to dress for my execution, or did what he say give me hope that the king would keep me alive because the sea did? The closet only had a few items. He was a man of simple needs, it seemed. I ran my hands over the fabrics of a few suits, similar to the one he was wearing, almost like a uniform, albeit a fancy uniform. And he was probably the only man who would decide to hang up a pair of ripped black jeans, and a plain black cotton shirt. In stark contrast to the worn, easy attire, hung the sparkling dress he was probably referring to when he demanded I get dressed. Considering, it was the only female clothing available, making me wonder if it belonged to his girlfriend. I didn't find any other evidence of him living with another person, but the place was sparse, so a lack of evidence wasn't evidence enough for ruling on a lack of co-habitation.

The dress was beautiful, but a bit too revealing on top for meeting my fate. I grabbed an over-sized white shirt, switching it out for the black lounge button-up, then slipping the champagne-colored sparkles over it. Layers never hurt anyone, and the dress cinched in the extra fabric of the shirt made to cover the large shoulders of the man who most likely waited for me just outside that door. I smoothed out the shirt's wrinkles under the dress, and actually thought the combination looked presentable, toning the evening wear down to a more comfortable casual that I wasn't offended by. Better than having my chest on display with the plunging neckline his girlfriend was okay with showing off.

I slipped on the heels underneath and forced myself to open the door.

My escort took in my choice to borrow his shirt and seemed amused, but didn't say a word until we made it to what I assumed was a throne room. Considering it did indeed have a throne, made of gold no less, and happened to be filled with elegantly dressed people on either side of the large hall.

At the center, sitting on a golden stair that led up to the throne, with his fingers steepled to the crease between his brow, was a white-haired man wearing nothing but golden armored greaves and boots. His elbows on his thighs, he did not appear to be ready for an audience, either in deep thought or distressed by the loss of his daughter. I assumed this man was the king I was to be presented to.

Walking down the aisle with my escort at my side, the king lifted his head, and all eyes were on me as I was announced to the room.

"Conqueror of the Coral Sea, Maiden Alessandra, and her escort Sentinel of the Atlantic, Dion."

So much for them not knowing about killing Coraline. I was pretty sure Triton named his daughters after the seven seas, if my knowledge of myths was accurate, and that kind of introduction was puzzling, to say the least. Conqueror could be seen as a compliment, but the way the king sat there, not in his throne, only served to heighten my nerves. When he lifted his blue eyes to greet me, I was surprised to see features that would have made me think he wasn't older than thirty.

His white hair was cropped short, unlike what any mythical portraits of his likeness have shown, with long hair and a bushy beard. He did have a blue-tinted shadow of a goatee, but not what I would have expected when meeting the king.

My sentinel escort, Dion—his name glided in my mind like a sin, but I pushed the thought out of my mind as he bowed his head to the king. Knowing I should show some kind of respect, I bowed deeper, bending at the hips with a rigid back, too anxious to look up from my feet to see the hatred that I suspected would show on the king's face. It wasn't a curtsy, but it would have to do.

The hall was so silent, the people could have been holding their breath for the king to speak.

"I've grown weary with the games Maiden Alessandra," he said with a velvety voice. It was as if all the merfolk had alluring music in their words, though we weren't underwater, and I was beginning to doubt whether they were, in fact, merpeople like Coraline. Plus, I couldn't stop myself from freaking out about them knowing my name.

Still not able to divert my gaze from my feet, I remained silent for him to continue.

"The sea torments me to bring such a beauty at the cost of reeling me into the net of vengeance." He didn't sound upset, just contemplative, and I risked lifting my head to see any glimmer of hope that might lie there in his eyes. He still sat on the stair of his golden platform, watching Dion instead of me. Dion's gaze was straight ahead, unwavering.

From what I heard of the king from the mermen that brought me here, vengeance wasn't unfamiliar to him. They risked their own lives to let someone else discover Coraline and myself in hopes that his vengeance would stay small instead of destroying the whole city.

The bare chested, golden bottomed king rubbed his face like the decision exhausted him. He didn't wear a crown, but he didn't need to. Despite sitting on a stair instead of a throne, uncrowned, and sporting a white-blue goatee, he still exuded an otherworldly power that was palpable in the room. He sighed, resigned to continue talking since no one else dared to. Were they as scared as I was at what he would do? Were their lives just as at risk as the mermen had feared?

"A lost nymph, unsworn by fealty, saved by the sea, conquered a princess of the Coral Sea. Unprecedented. Tell me, nymph, and answer honestly, for I will know a lie when I hear it. Which god has sent you to force my hand? Whose favor do you seek?"

Both loaded questions, if I were sent by a god. If I were fulfilling some weird oath to the gods to slay his daughter then it would have been a tough answer. Out of all the questions he could have asked, these were the least scary. He could have asked, did you kill Coraline? How did you, a simple nymph, kill my daughter? Those would have had me shaking, but instead I stared at him dumbly and found it easy to speak.

"None."

"You seek no favor?" He clarified.

"No." I shook my head, still stunned by the way he watched me.

"No, you do, or no you do not?"

I cleared my scratchy throat, coughing a bit. "No favor, no gods." I blinked at him, and found this entire conversation laughable, as if this were the most elaborate hallucination before I died of drowning in the sea, because this certainly had to be my mind coping with death. With that sudden certainty, I whispered softly while scanning the room, "I thought we would be underwater."

Dion chuckled before pretending to clear his throat.

"My father did not wish to drown his people when he sunk the city," the king answered. "He lowered the island into the sea to protect it from war. Many of Atlantis's residents are mortal, and those who are not are allowed mortal form within its borders. Even sea nymphs that have abandoned their true forms may live under the blessing of this land beneath the sea." He said sea nymph pointedly referring to me as the one who abandoned my true form, and thus the blessings of breathing under water. I pressed my lips flat, underestimating how great the king's hearing was. If this was all real, then he was the son of a great sea god, and thus a god of the sea himself. I tried not to take a step back at that realization.

I looked out at the people gathered in this room with fresh eyes—some of these people were human and have lived on this island for generations since whenever that war with Athens happened. Were they ever allowed to leave? They probably couldn't survive drowning in the sea to reach the surface. Pity wrenched in my gut. Were they happy in this gilded cage surrounded by merpeople? My eyes softened with sadness, forgetful of my own fate. I knew what it felt like to be trapped, even surrounded by a family that loved me. I ran away, and I didn't regret it, even now.

I regretted living the last four years of my life as if I was still trapped at home with my over-protective mother. I should have gone out more, I should have said yes more, I should have risked getting hurt more. Maybe then I could have faced the king's wrath with less disappointment.

I shoved my fears aside.

"How long have they been here?" But the king was no fool. He knew what I was actually asking. Were they ever allowed to leave? How long were they his prisoners? Even my mother understood that's what I was if she didn't allow me to leave home. It didn't matter that her reasons were understandable. Even if the king's intention was to protect his people, if they couldn't leave, they weren't free.

The young-faced white-haired king stood, and the crowd's murmurs filled the air, a hum of curiosity on how the king would respond to such a question. Who would dare ask the king such a question? Who indeed, I thought, but a woman that was certain she would die either way.

The grin on his face stunned me as he replied smoothly, "All of my subjects are free to leave Atlantis." I was not expecting that, and he seemed pleased that I had miscalculated the situation. "Do not many mortals live their lives never traveling beyond their own borders where you were raised?" He was careful not to say 'from' but 'raised' as it was clear to him that I had rejected the sea that I should have been raised in. He was right, many people never leave the town they're from.

"True," I squared my shoulders, still feeling I was on to something, "but I've never heard of anyone saying they are from Atlantis either, and I find it hard to believe not one person wanted to travel." My voice was more timid than I would have preferred, but there was no taking it back now.

"Spoken like a true conqueror," he said with contemplation. I didn't know if he was complimenting me or dishing a blow. "I assure you, all subjects are here of their own will, maiden. As for you—unsworn as you are—it isn't so simple. I must avenge Coraline's death or favor you for what some would consider a heroic feat."

My eyes grew wide at the suggestion that he would give me favor for killing his daughter. The merman was right to say there were no feelings lost on his daughter if this was one of the options. He didn't even seem that torn about offering it.

"You must think me cold to consider allowing you to live." The king shook his head, baffled by my response to his statement. "Do you not consider me merciful? Such a strange creature you are. It makes more sense as to why the sea would save you as it did. Should I not show the same thoughtfulness as the sea that serves my will? Did it not know instinctively what would serve us both best?" The king paced the platform, then stopped. He motioned for someone to join him, and to my surprise, Dion left my side.

"The gods are not as direct as they used to be. She may not know who she's in bed with," Dion all but told the king I may still be a spy, an unwitting spy, but a spy nonetheless.

"All the more reason to change the tides." And in his case, he really could change the tides—not just metaphorically. "After so many years, I had grown hopeful that the gods had moved on from punishing my father. It was too much to ask for. With Coraline's failure, Atlantis is at risk." He shook his head in disappointment—not at me, but at his own daughter.

"Apollo's prophecy," Dion confirmed his king's thoughts.

"My father will return," Triton agreed, completely ignoring the audience of well, me, and hundreds of Atlantian subjects. The crowd hushed to listen, and even I was curious what they were fussing about that intrigued them enough to stay my judgment. Though I hoped too soon, Triton's blue eyes captured mine before he spoke again, "I pray for your sake Maiden that you are as virtuous, and naive as my sentinel claims you to be." He sounded serious, and though his words hinted at a promise of less than death, I didn't think I was being released to go home either. The audience of lavish voyeurs murmured at the king's suggested mercy. I wasn't sure if the hum around me was relief that their own lives would be spared from a wrathful god's vengeance by proxy, or if they were as twisted as the gods and disappointed by the lack of excitement at living instead of dying.

I pressed my luck to clarify.

"Whatever you think I'm involved in, I am not. I tried to save someone I thought was drowning, only then to be nearly murdered by a merlady that wanted my legs. I'm still considering the possibility that I'm actually dead already, or in a coma from drowning. I honestly didn't intend on 'conquering' anyone. I was simply defending myself." I cringed after I said it, realizing only after that the king probably didn't want to hear from me about how his daughter was a murderer, and I was actually a victim. At least, not when I was the one alive and she was dead.

On reflection, I probably should have left that part out, and replaced it with something I thought might actually help my case, and not increase the likelihood of being executed. Like how all she did was bite me, and then we both passed out, so it was possible that someone else poisoned her? Or it was all an accident, because maybe whatever kind of nymph I was didn't cohabitate well with mercreatures? Like those small octopuses that are found in tide pools and coral reefs considered the most venomous marine animal. Though I doubted I could blame her death on the octopus, considering their poison is a neurotoxin, not really known for causing black veins and gray pallor.

I quickly added, "Are we certain I was the one that conquered the Coral Sea?" I mean, really, all I did was yank on her hair and wish her dead after she bit me. I grew more confident about this analysis, considering all I knew my blood to do was heal, not kill. They couldn't prove anything! I smiled at my sudden realization. Test my blood on, preferably a human, and they will probably heal, not die. But what if it had the opposite effect on merpeople? Was I willing to risk someone else's life to prove my blood heals and doesn't kill, all to save myself? Grimacing once more, I shook my head. I couldn't do it.

"Odd creature indeed," the king observed me. "Plenty of sea nymphs are poisonous, though to be strong enough to kill a daughter of the seven seas is quite unusual. Which is why I am inclined to agree with you. You, alone, did not conquer the Coral Sea." The emphasis on 'alone' was clear, and I couldn't bring myself to beg that he test my blood and risk another life to prove it couldn't have been me. What if it was?

"I'll let the fates decide what to do with you. But be grateful, Alessandra, that I do not like my hand being forced by another. Whatever god you serve–"

"I don't," I insisted. He nodded, a glimmer in his blue eyes, but it was not him that I was staring at, but my sentinel beside him. His black hair was perfectly unkempt in a sexy way, and his deep ocean blue eyes were just as captivating as his king's. Triton didn't miss the interaction, and he peered at my attire once more, re-evaluating why I would be wearing a man's cotton shirt under my silky dress. He lifted a brow between us, and I forced myself to turn my attention away, embarrassed at how taken I was with a man I hardly knew.

The king continued, "Unwitting as you may be, whatever god you serve did not wish for you to live. Anyone willing to use you to begin Apollo's prophecy knew what should happen to you."

I shivered. He seemed satisfied by this, and then he descended the stairs towards me.

"Cities have fallen for less. I've turned my enemies into sea monsters and traitors into chum for my warriors." If his intention was to frighten me, he was doing a marvelous job. "Even those who stood by while others defied me have met with my wrath." I gulped, wincing at the tenderness of my salt ravaged throat. Instinctively, I searched Dion's face for comfort. Why did I feel like he would help me? He worked for the king, he had no reason to defend me, and yet I still silently begged him with my eyes to not let the king threaten me. But Triton was the king, and what would one sentinel do for a stranger, risk his life? No, and I wouldn't want him to. I forced myself to stand tall, so only I would be the one that was punished.

Triton was standing in front of me now, and everything in me wanted to run, to step back, but I didn't.

"I will not be another god's pawn. If they wish you dead, they must do it themselves," his voice commanding and firm. I felt my lower lip tremble at his growing anger at being used.

"What will you do with me?" I finally asked.

He smiled then, and it was anything but assuring. Filled with schemes and a promised fury for those that dared to cross him, even with an unknown nymph like me.

"If they want you dead, you are dangerous to them alive." His eyes lit up, and it was as if he was looking through me, not at me. A swirl of possibilities running through his head, plotting his moves. "The sea has gifted us with an opportunity to end this ridiculous grudge between gods and seek vengeance against those that would harm us." He spoke as if we were a unit, and his plans were beneficial to me as well. That both of us could exact our dues. My heart raced with the thrill and terror of what he was implying.

"Send for the fates, Dion. I must know that they support this decision."

What decision? His mind was moving so fast, I couldn't keep up. One moment he was threatening me with death, and putting the fear of god in me, and then the next he's concocting revenge plans that I'm supposed to assist him with somehow. Against a god or gods that had somehow sent me after his daughter.

Was I really that predicable that some god manipulated me into being the reason Coraline died? How did they know what my blood would do? I had more to worry about than the why, as Dion had said earlier. The why wasn't important anymore.

It's what was I going to do about it now?

Or what could I do?

I may not even be asking the right question, even now, but Dion nodded to the king, and before Triton could cup my cheek in his outstretched hand Dion grabbed the sleeve of his borrowed cotton shirt to pull me away. King Triton narrowed his eyes at the shirt that Dion had somehow brought his attention back to, and I felt a sudden flush to my neck at the implications my mind rushed to.

Was Dion purposefully goading the king with insinuations about why I was wearing his shirt? My heart pounded at the thought, and quickly dismissed it as foolish as Dion's hand touching my arm released me when he was certain I would continue following him out of the hall.

"What was that about?" I narrowed my eyes at Dion, now aware of what kind of trouble he was stirring for me, and my momentary giddiness lapsed into more appropriate agitation. Was he trying to get me killed?

"A bit of jealous lust never hurt to sway the king's decision towards keeping you alive," Dion said playfully, but the distance he kept between us was in direct opposition to his tone. "It was smart of you to steal my shirt, though also very risky," he explained. "None of Triton's consorts live long."

I blanched. "I'm not trying to be his consort!"

Dion stopped, and I nearly slammed into his broad form. He turned and assessed me; the scrutiny made me squirm. "Why did you wear my shirt?" I stumbled at the question, not expecting this turn of direction in conversation. I blushed thinking about the fact that Dion didn't have many clothes, and in one day I had worn two of his shirts. Shirts that had touched his tanned, toned muscles, and smelled like a warm summer day at the beach. The kind of beach that didn't gobble me whole and try to drown me. I thought about earlier when he was much more relaxed in his studio with his shirt off.

Now, I was the one taking forever to respond. His blue eyes stayed pinned on me, taking in every twitch, and change of expression. He was reading me like a book, and I couldn't stand it. Then, as I stretched my shoulder, the strain of my tender flesh where Coraline bit me gave me the perfect excuse, and I wasn't sure why it had taken me so long to think of it. I winced at the dull pain. Obviously, my blood had healed most of it, but the toxins from the princess had somehow slowed my recovery. I moved the fabric over to look at the gash with a grimace.

Realization dawned on Dion's face, and he nodded with understanding.

"Forgive me," he sounded pained, "my arrogance overwhelms my common sense. You've been injured." I should have been healed by now, but something about Coraline's toxins messed with that process. I pinched the spongy flesh, and a clear liquid excreted from the wound where her teeth dug in. Somehow, I needed to get the toxin out of my system.

"I thought you changed me into your shirt?" I accused pointedly. He would have seen my injury then, I thought with irritation and a lifted brow for him to deny it.

"I did," he admitted with no shame. "The injury appeared minor, with no bleeding." I wanted to scoff at how this was anything but minor. The mermaid literally chewed a chunk of my flesh off. Bleeding or not, it was flayed and gross.

Dion leaned in while I was focused on my shoulder, and he ripped his borrowed shirt to get better access to the wound. Scanning the hall, I worried this wasn't the best location to be feeling vulnerable.

"Hold still," his voice was soft. A hand laced behind my head, and I stared up into his dark blue eyes. Heart thundering in my chest, his lips parted above me, his nose brushed against mine, and I suddenly forgot all about my injury. All my thoughts were focused on his inviting mouth, and how I wanted it to consume me. His eyes glowed with power, and an ache built in my sternum.

Then a weight lifted from my chest that I didn't know was there. Pressure pushed up my throat, and then I gasped with the cleanest air I never knew I needed. Salt water streamed from my mouth in a magical stream between us, being sucked up and out of me towards Dion. He pulled away from me, his hand gently releasing my hair as the water danced and sparkled between our lips.

He had pulled out whatever remaining sea water clogged my lungs, and then his hands clapped together. Circling and guiding the water in his palms, he pushed it back towards me, wrapping my shoulder in the warm liquid. Sharp pain shuddered through me, making me shake. I launched back, pressing myself against the gilded wall behind me to keep myself upright. Only all the energy was being sapped from me, and my knees weakened until I was sliding down, slumping to the floor.

I gritted my teeth, and watched as the water was thrown from my shoulder slamming to the other end of the hall.

Panting, I stared at Dion. He kneeled down and scooped me up into his arms. The ache in my shoulder eased, and I turned my head against his firm chest to see my wound was knitting itself back together. My blood was finally healing me. He had removed the venom.

"What was that?" I whispered into his neck, letting my muscles relax in his arms. I felt safe with him, and I couldn't explain why.

"I'd put too much faith in your own ability to fend off the toxins. My apologies, little goddess, for not assisting you sooner." My blood heated with the kindness in his voice as he called me a goddess. No one had ever given me such an endearment before, and I found it doing odd things to me, giving me a fluttery feeling in my belly.

I had to remind myself that he was my prison guard, and his kindness meant nothing. He was just doing a job, but then why did he make me feel this kind of way?

"How did you know?"

"That you were healing yourself?"

I nodded into his chest, my nose rubbing into his suit and I could smell the sea on him.

"You weren't bleeding when you crashed into me."

I snapped my head to look up at him. "Crashed into you?"

"I didn't find you. You found me."

"And you took me to your room..." I stated shyly, trying to figure him out. Why was I not in a dungeon? Not that I wanted to be in one, but not knowing the rules, or the why of things, worried me. If I wasn't being executed, then what did they want with me?

Dion's blue pools darkened, and I tucked my face into his hold, not sure what that meant. But his grip on me remained gentle as he walked back the way we came, towards his room.

"I did."

"Why?" I insisted. I didn't know what kind of answer I was expecting, or hoping for, but held my breath for it either way.

"It was my right."

"Your right...?" His right to what? What did that even mean? I thought about wearing his pajamas and lying in his bed. Panic was setting in, and the dungeon was sounding better every second. My muscles tensed up. I may have found him attractive, but I wasn't ready to cross that line, and it certainly wasn't his 'right' to do so. I felt sick.

My brows narrowed, beginning to fume when only moments before, I felt safe and comfortable in his arms. I wiggled to remove myself from his grasp. I could walk on my own, at least I thought I could, though part of me knew I was still weakened from healing myself.

Clamping down to hold me to him, he prevented me from squirming free.

"By Atlantis law, the sentinels are given the right to detain and weigh in on the decisions pertaining to those they bring to Atlantis," he explained with amusement.

"Oh." I felt flushed for at having 'other' thoughts about what rights he had. I jumped to conclusions, and it may or may not have had something to do with my own thoughts about my designated sentinel. He loosened his grip once I stopped fidgeting, and a big ol' smile was plastered on that smug face of his. I could only pray that whatever he thought I was thinking that got me riled up wasn't too close to the truth.

"You chose to keep me in your room?" I lifted a brow, trying to bring the conversation back to his decisions, not on my own guilty mind.

"I did," he repeated. I waited, using the silence to try to pry out more information from him. Watching him pointedly, he finally caved. "Until we know more about what you are capable of, it was too risky to leave you in the dungeons. I'll remain at your side at all times."

My mouth fell open. Again, not where I thought this conversation was heading. Was I just a lovesick teenager? Why did I keep thinking we had some sort of connection? Because he was pretty? Because he showed me some kindness?

"Of course." I nodded, averting my gaze ahead of us now. I couldn't keep getting lost in those beautiful eyes of his, when it was obvious that he was focused on his job. He didn't know what kind of magic I had, and that made two of us. To him, I was a flight risk that he had to watch over at the expense of his own free time, and his girlfriend that

I stole a dress from. I pursed my lips in sourness. "How long until I'm transferred to the dungeons?"

I wasn't in a hurry, but embarrassment made me overly eager to be uncomfortable in a way that I understood. Whatever this tightness was in my chest, it wasn't waterlogged lungs anymore, and I didn't like it one bit. At least in the dungeon the comfort, or lack thereof, was something I could handle.

"I've seen the look in Triton's eye. You may be seeing them sooner than you'd like."

My heart thudded anxiously. Why was I always surprised that his answers were the opposite of what I wanted from him? He had no reason to care for me, or to wish for me to stay with him. So then why was I so upset that he didn't keep me in his room because he cared if I went to the dungeon or not?

"You'll let him." I was practically begging for him to disappoint me again.

"I could press my rights to prevent it," and a small bead of hope dimpled my cheeks with a smile, "But you would be better off if I didn't." And that smile faltered just as fast. I shook my head.

"What does that mean?"

"If the king suspects you care for a guard, even his top adviser, above him it will only invigorate the quest to claim you, and potentially lead to sending me away from Atlantis."

"I'm not–" trying to be his consort, but he stopped me from finishing the thought.

"It was a smart play, and I did try to help you by informing him of your virtue."

I choked on my own breath. "My what?"

"Your virtue," he repeated plainly.

"What do you know of my virtue?" I tried to push away from him again, this time he let me, and I regretted it immediately. Feeling the loss of his body heat and no longer being held by him wasn't as gratifying as I had anticipated. I held on to my indignation, and glared at him to help hide the sudden tingling of his absence.

His lips thinned as he watched me. I must have been a sight with my torn white shirt, which was his, and a long, elegant dress with a plunging neckline, and high slit showing off most of my leg. I was pretty much a hot mess as my sister would say.

"I did not violate you, if that is what you are insinuating. I have no need to force myself upon anyone. Your virtue is obvious in the childish blush you wear upon seeing any bare chest that is presented to you."

I balked at his agitation with me, and his insult that was very clearly jabbing at the way I ogled the exposed abs of King Triton. I'm not sure why that seemed to upset him when Triton was a god of the sea. I highly doubted there were many that didn't gawk at him. What Dion didn't know was that more often than not, even standing next to a god, I was watching him more. Which made me even more riled up at Dion. He had no right to be jealous, and then I stopped myself from thinking like that. I shook my head of the confusion. He was doing it again. That thing where I thought something was there, and in the next moment he would say something that made me feel foolish for thinking it. He was definitely not jealous. This was my imagination all over again. Maybe this had to do with caring about the king. He was irritated that someone that had killed the king's daughter would have the audacity to try to seduce him. Well, I wasn't.

"Maybe I wouldn't have to insinuate anything if you actually talked to me instead of making me imagine the worst!"

Dion's blue eyes blazed, and he took a step towards me. I found myself backing up at the advance. He spoke coolly, "Some time in the dungeon would probably do you some good, but he wants you to know how bad it can be so you are more grateful when he rescues you from it. You're supposed to be desperate enough to forget he's the reason you'd be there in the first place. Grateful enough for his kindness that you give yourself to him. Is that what it would take to earn your affection? Do you wish to squalor in the dungeons, petite goddess? Do you wish for me to treat you as the enemy as the king so desires of me?"

I gulped, watching him inch closer to me, rage in his tone. I was shaking my head no without realizing it, and he gripped my chin between his fingers. I was expecting it to hurt, but he was gentle, merely lifting my chin so I would not turn from him, so I stared up into those intense eyes. He may not have been the king, but he was just as lovely even now when I should have been frightened.

"That is what the king had asked of me before I escorted you away. He wishes for me to abdicate my rights to him. For you to be treated no better than a monster so that you look at me the way you are now, fearful. Do I scare you, my goddess?"

I nodded, but that was not all that I felt for him. Why did I feel sorry for him, when I was the one being held captive?

He released my chin and stepped away turning from me.

"You should be. I didn't become the king's first sentinel by accident," but there was no venom in his words, simply stating what he believed was fact, "I will not send you to the dungeons tonight," he said after a tense silence between us. I stared at the back of his silky black hair, and then he walked forward not turning to see if I was following, but I did. There was nowhere to run just yet, and I was still processing what had just happened.

What had just happened?

Did he just agree to risk being sent away from Atlantis by defying the king and keeping his right to decide my fate? Keeping me from the dungeon, for now.

We reached his room, and he opened the door for me. He stayed in the door frame, not entering the room.

I stopped, and turned to watch him. Curious as to why he wasn't coming inside with me, but not willing to break the silence.

"I must send for the fates. You will need to stay here until I return. I'll have food sent down." He was making an effort to explain what was happening, and I couldn't help the smile curving the sides of my mouth. I had just yelled at him for making me guess, and here he was now offering information without being prompted. He seemed uncomfortable with the effort, and all that did was make me smile more, until a chuckle escaped, and he narrowed his eyes at me. Though I could swear there was a glimmer in them that assured me he found the circumstances just as amusing. The guard making accommodations for the prisoner.

"Thank you," I said softly.

He nodded and before he could shut the door to leave, I asked, "How long will you be gone?" I already noticed that the lock to his room was on the inside, not like a prison cell. This wasn't a traditional holding room, this was his room, meaning he was trusting me to stay here until he returned. How long would I have to figure out the layout of this place? I didn't have any real hope that I'd be escaping today, not if this place was truly a sunken city, but I could do some recon and figure out my surroundings.

Dion paused to consider my question, then quirked a brow in assessment. "You'll want to stay in the room or the next time I see you it'll be in the dungeon." Was I that transparent? He grinned at me. "I'm not the only sentinel that has chosen to live in the palace's estate. Should you find yourself wandering unescorted, you may find yourself under another's care that may find the king's incentives more agreeable." He gave the door a final tap of his palm, then left without another word. That seemed to be a habit of him, patting the door. I rushed to the door and opened it.

Not locked, and I searched both ways down the hall. He was already gone.

Chapter 5

Fishing

D ion left me free to leave his room, but with a warning that 'if' I was caught by someone else I'd be in the dungeons. The king wanted me there anyway, and I figured that isn't much of a threat considering he was a king, and he'd find a way around my sentinel's rights if he really wanted something. I might as well gain some knowledge about where I was before that happened. I couldn't pass up this opportunity. Knowing the palace grounds could be the difference between escaping or not in the future. Convincing myself to step out of the room was surprisingly more difficult than I thought.

There was going to be food sent to the room. My stomach grumbled at the thought. I was hungry. Should I stay until the food came? Then go exploring after the food? What if I left before the food, and the person bringing it told the king I was no longer in the room? My cover blown before I have a real chance at discovering the lay of the land. Clenching the door latch, I struggled to make a decision.

I put one foot outside the threshold, and then I gasped at someone else's boots in front of me. Staying in it was then.

"I didn't think you'd be that dumb," she said. "He told me you would, but I didn't believe him." The woman was in a similar suit to Dion's... a sentinel. Her brown hair was pulled back and braided like a Viking warrior.

"Excuse me?" I still had my hand on the door, and stepped back, so I was firmly inside the room again.

She sighed. "Dion is too soft on you. He told me to follow you should you leave, but I'm not a babysitter, or a secret tour guide. Do you understand?"

"Got it." Kind of, but I wasn't telling her that. Not sure what she was told about me or what she 'was' going to do. I itched to slam the door in her face, but there wasn't much keeping her out of the room except for the lock, and I didn't know what kind of magic she had to become a sentinel. I'd seen what Dion could do, control the water from my very lungs. What could she do?

"Why he didn't just tell you there's no point in trying to escape is irritating. He's not even here to enjoy catching you in the act or getting a good laugh when you realize the only way out of the palace is with the king's chariot, or a sentinel escort to the main city." Keeping the disappointment from my face was difficult to do, but made easier if I believed she was telling me the truth. Then she saved me the effort of wandering. And here I thought Dion and I were evolving, with him giving me more information instead of letting me flounder. He had played me again.

"But not you," I surmised. She wasn't interested in my humiliation or condemnation from being caught without an escort.

"Again, not worth my time."

"But you're here," I said defensively.

She glared at me, matching my annoyance. Her hand twitched at her side, near what looked like a blade at her thigh. Was she going to attack me?

"Dion is the First Sentinel. Right-hand adviser to the king. I won't let you make him look a fool by being caught, even if he was expecting it."

"Do you plan on guarding my door, then?"

"No, I'm not your personal entourage."

Were we at an impasse? What exactly was she going to do then? We awkwardly stared at each other before she groaned. "Come with me."

I inched back into the room more, and closed the door a bit, before her hand swung out to stop it, boxing me between her and the door frame.

"I won't ask nicely again." As she smiled her teeth sharpened into rows of jagged razors. She was a merlady, just like Coraline. Scales appeared on the side of her neck that fluttered with her controlled breathing.

I nodded.

"Shall we?" I said nervously.

"We shall." Her sharp teeth gleamed at me before she waved her hand in the direction of the large hallway. Her other hand clamped over my own, still clutching the door's handle, and she eased it closed behind us. So much for staying inside his room.

"Where to?" I tried to keep things light, even though I knew I was on a slippery slope with this lady. Her teeth disappeared into regular pearly whites, and she licked her tongue over them.

"We're going to show you what you're up against, so you can release your dreams of escaping, and accept that you'll probably end up dying here, or wishing you had." How encouraging, I mocked in my mind, that I would be given an escort to find the exits only so that my hopes are crushed. Such a charming woman.

"Is that typical of most prisoners?" Death? Or wishing you had died?

She grabbed my arm and tugged me down the corridor.

"I've never seen Dion watch a prisoner so closely before, if that's what you're asking. There's always the occasional nymph that thinks they can get out of punishment by seducing their sentinel, or the king, but it won't work."

"That's good to know," I snarked back. Why was it that everyone thought I was trying to seduce someone to live? Not that I'm above a little seduction for the sake of living, but I wouldn't really know what to do. I'd be going off of over dramatized movies that I've watched with my sister as reference, and I didn't really think any of that applied to sea gods, or merfolk. For all I knew, they had a thing for tails, sharp teeth, and scales. All of which I did not have.

She quirked a brow at me. "Not interested in delaying your judgment with a bit of clam slam?"

I choked on the sudden use of the phrase, clam slam. Aside from it sounding absolutely ridiculous, it was also closer to a thing she might say to a friend, and not a prisoner.

"Excuse me?"

"Clam slam," she repeated seriously, like that phrase was normal, and regularly used to refer to sex. Maybe it was with fish creatures, but for someone raised on the land, not so much. "You know, clasping the cloaca, fishing for fins, plundering for pearls, tickling tentacles. Touching all the sensors that make your nerves feel on fire."

"You mean sex," I offered, hoping I was catching all the suggestions correctly. I may not have done anything like that before, but I've had plenty enough fun myself to get the point.

She shrugged.

"If you must get all emotionally attached like that, you may call it that."

"Uh," I cringed thinking about the possibility that merfolk didn't 'clam slam' the same way humans did, "can't say that I'd prefer to 'go fishing' with someone that intends on debating whether I was better off alive or dead."

"There are plenty of fish in the sea, so offering what can be easily caught by another will never earn you what you're worth," she contemplated before adding, "It's what my mother would always say, and why I trained to become a sentinel."

Softening to my new guard, I smiled at her, and she quickly turned her gaze and cleared her throat. Clearly uncomfortable with the moment of camaraderie we shared.

"Better to find another way to stay alive."

"Agreed."

Then she shoved my arm. "Also, leave Dion out of it."

I rubbed my bicep to distract myself with anything other than thoughts of Dion. I didn't think that was really an option, and now that she said it was off the table, I didn't know if I could stop thinking about it. I kept silent, unable to bring myself to agreeing once more.

"We're here," she brought my attention back in front of me. A large aquarium you could fit multiple football fields in bubbled out. A shadow passed by my side, and I turned to see a shark pass by a film that was a wall between us. The whole area was an air pocket within the sea, and in the distance, beyond the passing fish, and rocks full of sea creatures, was a city in a similar bubble as this one.

It was amazing to finally have proof that we were still under the sea, and the city within the water was gorgeous. Pillars of marble, circular roofs of varying sizes made of what appeared to be gold glinting in the water, layers of civilization lit up with an otherworldly glow.

"How do you get to there?" I took a step forward, and my guard's arm went up to stop me.

"You don't want to enter the room," she warned. "Only the sentinels have the blessing to come and go without waking the creature."

"What creature?"

"Don't say I didn't warn you."

My legs took me deeper into the room without a second thought. I turned in place taking in the underwater scenery, mystified.

"So, this is the only way out of the palace?" I asked in wonder, still awe struck.

"Usually, people are brought in by chariots guided by a sentinel when they come to the palace. With a sentinel you could be brought safely to the city, but–"

My attention was taken away from listening to her when I saw a large octopus descending from above. Its tentacles surrounded the dome of air and made the water sprinkle through the barrier like a stormy rain. Suction cups could be seen from all sides, and some were the size of a human standing tall. One of those suckers could trap me without any effort. Avoiding one of those tentacles would be like racing against a mansion falling from a tornado. I was more likely to be flattened into sea dust.

How had I missed it before? How could it possibly hide from view and then suddenly appear?

Backing up into my escort, she guided me back to the hallway we came from, back into the palace.

"How?"

"How do any of us exist?"

"It came out of nowhere, but it was larger than the dome..."

"He's always there protecting Atlantis. You won't be able to leave the palace without Krall knowing. If you aren't with a sentinel or in a chariot, you're not part of the oath that keeps him calm."

"I thought he was going to fall into the room and flatten us."

"That's too much work. He probably would have just swatted at you with one of his tentacles like an annoying copepod." She was always so full of positive vibes, I internally mocked.

We made it back to Dion's room, and she gave a final warning before leaving. "You're on your own now until Dion returns. I wouldn't recommend leaving since I've wasted enough time as it is making sure you understood what you were up against." She opened the door to usher me in, but she made an effort not to actually enter, though her eyes lingered to take in the space. I had an inkling there were laws against entering a sentinel's room against their wishes, and she was careful not to actually cross the threshold.

"Wouldn't want to keep you from your duties," I hinted towards her continued awkwardness at the door. Her eyes were captured by something behind me, and I followed her gaze to the kitchen where a tray of food was left out while we were away. A slab of raw fish fillet, prepared and served fancy sushi style, sat next to a small tray of dried seaweed and some condiments. Uncooked meat wasn't really my thing, but my guard seemed transfixed by it.

"Hungry?" I offered.

She licked her lips and debated the offer for all of about two seconds. "Dion always catches the best fish." Eyeing the food one more time, she took a deliberate step inside, and then rushed to skewer one of the pink slivers with her extended nails. She didn't even chew the morsel, slurping it down like a pelican, and then digging in for another. After a few, she audibly sighed, and then narrowed her gaze at me. "Why aren't you eating?"

Clearing my throat I broke my stare at her eating habits. "I guess I assumed you were a merperson, and being half fish didn't seem respectful to be eating fish in front of you?"

She nearly choked on a lump of fish flesh that was sliding down her throat before she belted a laugh. "What nonsense is that!"

"You're not a merperson?" My eyes widened at my assumption, and she reared back in another belt of laughter.

"It's too much! Stop!" She held her belly, and I was the one narrowing my eyes now. I didn't find much of my circumstances that amusing.

"Of course I am," she finally answered through labored breathing, trying to control her humor, "But why wouldn't we eat fish? It's the cycle of the sea for us to eat what is provided for us. Do the sharks only eat the kelp? Most of the sea is full of carnivorous creatures. Why do you assume we, with our sharp teeth, do not eat the meat of our ecosystem?" She shook her head and patted my shoulder like we were friends. "I see why Dion chooses to protect you from the worst of your fate." Her eyes were warm, and up close I could see there were specks of green swirling in her brown orbs. "You really are quite virtuous, full of an innocence that lightens the mood of late. I don't know why I thought you were trying to seduce either of them. You poor thing, either of them would devour you." She was laughing once more and clutching her side. "Priceless," she choked out, and I did not share in her joy at my expense.

My face flat, I folded my arms to wait until she was finished. As a sentinel, I didn't think I'd stand a chance fighting through her for my freedom. I could wait. When strength was not your weapon, timing and holding your tongue could be just as effective.

Blood rushed to my cheeks thinking about how even though she now agreed with me about not trying to 'go fishing' with either of my captors in exchange for my life, it was somehow just as bad that she found it ridiculous that she even thought me capable. Something about being told I wasn't good enough for something, even if that something wasn't appealing, irked me the wrong way. Plus, I got all hot and flustered at the thought of Dion devouring me. My ears burned, and I bit the inside of my cheek to think about anything else.

"Name is Ray," she offered me her hand, smiling at me, "I hope you survive your judgment. Coraline was a bitch, anyway. King Triton has been cleaning up after her messes for centuries." Tentatively, I shook her hand, and offered her my own name, "Aless."

"Alice," she repeated with a nod, "You should eat the fish. Once the fates arrive, Dion's rights could be overruled. The king will use whatever they say to make Dion step down. Don't tell the king, but Dion catches the best fish. And whatever the king has planned for you, you won't want to be weak for it."

I grimaced, eyeing the fish like it was vermin. My stomach grumbled. Ray wrapped a chunk into a seaweed roll and nudged it toward me. Smiling tightly, I picked up the offering, and quickly popped it in my mouth whole. The bulge in my cheek showed Ray I hadn't swallowed yet, and she laughed again. She slammed her hand onto my back, and I reluctantly choked down the raw fish from the shock of the jolt.

"There you go, my little crown-of-thorns," she crooned.

Choking, I coughed until the scratch in my throat at being forced fed raw fish eased. I'd always avoided raw fish on principle, but even now I didn't really get the chance to discover whether or not I actually liked it. "Why are you 'helping' me?"

She leaned back in the bar stool, and thoughtfully answered, "Dion helped me become a sentinel. He sees something in you, and I don't think you're here to destroy Atlantis. Coraline probably had it coming. She's been crossing the line with mortals for a long time now, all in the hopes of having a child. The girl's been barren for ages, and it's not from lack of trying. And I do mean with anyone... and everyone." She wrinkled her nose to whisper, "Tricked the king into a round of rocks, and though he isn't open to turn down a bit of fun, he doesn't like being manipulated and cursed her to keep her merform. Not nearly as fun to slap scales with a tail." She shrugged at the story, Coraline's fate already decided and done. Made sense why she was so desperate to have my legs. Who knew how long she had been stuck in merlady form? I was grateful for the knowledge, and it confirmed my suspicions about the king. The only way I'd get out of this is if he decided it, and tricks wouldn't work to make that happen. I had to find another way.

"Guessing you don't have any advice on how to survive this, then."

"Oh, the same advice I already gave you that my mother gave me. Give him something useful that he can't get from anyone else. That isn't manipulation in the strictness sense. Even kings bend willingly when given what they want." Ray hopped up from the stool and made her way to the door. "Eat the fish, stay strong," she paused assessing me one last time. "Don't leave the room."

Easy enough for her to say. She wasn't the one awaiting the fates. I had nothing useful I was willing to give to the king, and I had every intention of risking my chances with the octopus. Who's to say I don't just wait there for a chariot to come, and steal it for myself? The chariots are given freedom to come and go. Even if it's not controlled by a sentinel, the octopus could be confused long enough for me to ride that wave all the way out of here. After all, Ray said it herself—the octopus never leaves Atlantis. I was willing to bet my life that I only had to get far enough fast enough for the guardian of the seas to realize one escapee wasn't worth leaving his duties. After all, I wasn't harming Atlantis, and I was one person.

I smiled at Ray as she closed the door behind her. Picking up a slimy fish, I sucked it down whole, and found I actually enjoyed the sushi. Dion had great taste, and I was sad I wouldn't get the chance to tell him.

Chapter 6

Recon

Taking a strip of the already torn shirt, I made a belt to cinch in the waist of Dion's extra sentinel uniform. I was done wearing this evening dress, and it didn't matter that I was swimming in extra material, and had to fold up sleeves and hems. They were comfortable, and from a distance might trick someone into thinking I belonged, and I'd be lying if I said I didn't enjoy the scent left in the fabric that reminded me of when I was being held in Dion's arms.

Taking inspiration from Ray, I braided my hair, and then took a deep breath to steel my resolve. This was it. I was as ready as I would ever be. Then I left the security of Dion's room.

The palace was huge, but having recently been led to the exit, it wasn't that difficult to find my way back. I'd passed a few people that watched me curiously, but they were not sentinels, and must have been guests of the king from Atlantis, one of the many who were gathered in the throne room earlier I presumed. They didn't stop me, but I had made quick work of avoiding eye contact, so they didn't recognize my face. My heart pounded against my rib cage, adrenaline coursing through my veins at the thought of being caught, of someone saying, why is your uniform so big?

In record time, I finally made it to the room with a view. Scanning the space, I didn't see any chariots around, but that didn't mean there weren't any. I pressed my hand to the barrier, the watery wall to my side. My hand sunk into the cool water, and when I pulled my hand back it was soaked, dripping on the floor. There was one question down, could I leave the barrier without help, and the answer was yes.

I stayed to the sides of the air pocket, following it down, hoping to find a carriage, while still remaining as small as possible, staying out of sight should anyone arrive. The whole area was like a welcoming sea garden. Magic seemed to keep the sea life alive within the air bubble as if it were underwater, but it wasn't. Even the kelp swayed in the air, as if rippled by my movement beside it, a wave of gentle water making a ribbon floating free, nothing weighing it down.

Then with a yank, I was on the other side of the barrier. The kelp ripping in my grasp, and my eyes were wide in shock at being submerged in the salty sea. Maybe staying too close to the barrier was a bad idea, and a shark had found its meal? I didn't feel any pain from being chomped.

I whirled around and found a man with the blackest eyes, and deep black hair glinting purple in the light of the garden staring at me. He wore nothing but the surrounding kelp we were hiding in to cover him. I pressed my lips together with a blush and quickly turned away. I'd let him swim in peace without an audience, I thought to myself, and made my way back to the side of the garden with air.

On my hands and knees, I breathed in, letting my drenched clothes soak the ground beneath me.

Then his feet entered my field of view, and I didn't dare look up.

"You," he said, "are not a sentinel."

He was very astute for a skinny dipper. I cringed, ringing out my blonde braid. Why wasn't he being slapped around by the octopus? I covered my eyes and stood up.

"Closing your eyes will not make you disappear," he continued, like I was turning away from him because I didn't wish him to see me. Did he not have any decency to cover himself up? I was trying to give him as much respect as I could, given the circumstances.

"I know that," I grumbled.

"Then why do you hold your face like a child playing hide and seek?"

My ears got hot at the thought of peeking through my fingers. I couldn't do it. Squeezing my eyes tight into a squint, I removed Dion's jacket and held it out to the man.

He chuckled before grabbing the offering. "You can open your eyes."

Partly still squinting, I opened one eye to check, and seeing a flash of the black jacket fabric, I deemed it safe to open the other. The jacket wouldn't have been enough to cover him if he wore it normally. He tied it sideways, the arms falling wrapped at his right side, and the main flap covering both the front and back like a toga.

I breathed a sigh of relief.

"I must say, I was not anticipating your return so soon, and certainly not such a shy reception."

I blinked several times to let his words register in my brain. Return? I stared at him dumbly.

"Will you be trying to leave?" He lifted a brow, and the seriousness in his tone told me that, however I answered this question, would change the course of our conversation.

"Eventually," I answered as honestly as I could. Something in me warned lying to the magical sea creatures here wasn't advisable.

"Not now?" he pressed.

I gulped.

"Not now," I repeated, knowing that it was true. Not now that he was here. I'd obviously have to wait until he was gone to resume any escape attempt.

"You know this is the main entrance to the palace, and guarded by the Krag at all times. This is not the safest sea garden to stroll through on the palace grounds." He made it seem like there was another 'safer' sea garden, or perhaps even another entrance to the palace that wasn't the 'main' one. This was either the best possible person to run into, or the worst. Was he going to turn me in for impersonating a sentinel? Or was he going to reveal a safer way out of the palace?

"You were swimming here. It can't be all that bad," I remarked, trying not to seem too desperate for him to continue talking about other palace exits. We'd get to that, eventually. I'd just casually ask him to show me where the safer option was after he convinced me this one wasn't fit for a stroll. I smiled at my plan, and when I met his inky black eyes again, he might have misinterpreted my excitement at another exit for interest in the practically naked swimmer before me. If it helped me get out of here, he could think what he wanted. I squeezed out some more water from my clothes.

"Not afraid of the sea monster?" He watched me for any signs that I was playing him. He wasn't letting my failed escape attempt go without seeing if I would get nervous, say something that would make him turn me over to a sentinel, and thus directly to the dungeons.

"There are scarier things than running into a guardian protecting a lost city." I couldn't help but search the sea around us for the elusive octopus beyond the bubble. How was it that such a enormous creature could hide out of sight? I lifted a brow,remembering this whole place was magical, so maybe the octopus had some sort of reflective skin that made it disappear in the deep blue water? Magical camouflage?

"A guardian?" He grinned at that. "Most call him the Krag, monster of the sea. He's capsized ships, crushed bones and muscles to sand, and taken the lives of any who are not protected by the blessing of the king. Does that sound like someone protecting the city, or someone that is terrorizing any who cross him?"

I watched the waters with a wary eye before responding. It brought my attention back to my first impression of the fancy guests in the throne room and all the subjects of Atlantis. Were they really free here? More and more it seemed like they were being kept in, just as much as the sea creature kept dangers out. My mouth thinned, and I wondered who this swimmer was. There was no uniform to tell me if he was another visiting subject or a sentinel guard.

"Sounds like someone with the worst job ever." I swung my wet hair over my shoulder and readjusted my makeshift belt that had loosened with the water. Ray was so certain that the octopus was always there to protect the city, and there was no way to escape. And if that was true, then the sea creature was just as much a prisoner as the city it protected, or terrorized as my naked interrogator suggested.

"You feel for the creature, then?" He studied me.

I shrugged. "Sounds like it's not the creature's choice at all. Why blame the octopus for doing its job? Shouldn't you be calling the king the monster for ordering the guardian of the city to only protect those that have his blessing, and not all of his subjects?" There had to be a reason Triton was keeping a close hold on his subjects. I averted my gaze, uncomfortable with having revealed I wasn't a fan of the king to a complete stranger in my irritation at how this whole place was being run. "Not that the king is a monster," I backpedaled, "but whatever you name the sea creature is a direct reflection on the one that controls its actions. So," I quickly added, "wouldn't the creature be the guardian of Atlantis, and not the monster of the dark waters? Or would you have me believe you think the king is the monster?" I accused back at him, muddying the conversation so much as to hope the man was confused about who actually called the king a monster. I wasn't in the best position to add treason to my list of offenses, and I couldn't trust this man with such opinions.

After all, he was the one that called the octopus a monster, and I was the one that called him a guardian, so maybe that was enough to cloud the issue of whether the king was also a monster or a guardian himself.

"Guardian it is then," he let my slip fall from the conversation, and I finally breathed again. Whether or not he believed me didn't matter as long as he didn't turn me in for treason, or my attempted escape. My life was very much in his hands, whoever he was.

Like he was reading my mind, he introduced himself. "You may call me Mavron."

"Aless."

"I know you are not a sentinel Aless, those are not your greaves, and no one from Atlantis calls it the lost city," I sucked in a breath realizing my slip of the tongue as he explained it, "You are the Conqueror of the Coral Sea that everyone seems to be abuzz about."

There was no use denying it. Should I run now? I turned to look at the forest of sea kelp on either side of us. He understood I was contemplating a final attempt at escaping. He was only one man, and he had to be just as afraid of the guardian octopus as I was. Would he chase or let me go?

"I found it odd that they did not decide to keep you in the dungeons, but upon seeing you, it makes more sense." He followed my sight to the kelp in the salty water beyond the thin barrier. "The palace is just as much of a prison as the dungeons and they would want someone as pretty as you to make the mistake of trying to escape so that when you were sent to the dungeon it would be your own fault, forcing their hand so that when you were saved from it once more you would be most grateful," he contemplated the scenario out loud, and he made no move to approach me so I made no move to bolt, just yet.

"Why are you telling me this?" It wasn't the first time someone had told me that was the king's plan; even Dion had said as much.

"I want you to realize who you can trust and who you can not," he took a step forward then, and I instinctively took a step back in kind towards the water.

"And I'm supposed to trust you?" I inferred from his tone, though if anything, all he did was make my skin prickle.

He shook his head. "You were tricked, little conqueror. This is not the only exit from the palace. It is merely the largest, and the most protected. When you left the throne room, the king informed everyone to leave you alone, and then doubled the patrols of every exit."

My mouth went dry, and I squared my shoulders in defiance.

"You're part of that patrol, then?"

"No." He was grinning then, his black eyes sparkled making me nervous. I felt the water barrier at my back, my clothes soaking up the liquid once more, it dripped down my legs. "Do not try to escape," he warned.

I pressed my lips hard to prevent myself from screaming, and control my desire to jump in the water and take my chances with the sea creatures than be sent to the dungeon.

"In your haste to seek freedom, you've trusted whoever led you here to 'dissuade' you from escaping. I'm under oath to turn you in if you are leaving. The king left his orders open for interpretation. Some may consider the act of you being here an attempt at leaving, and therefore reason enough to detain you..."

"And you?"

He shrugged. "Maybe you're just enjoying the garden. I can't know your intentions for certain, can I? You are still within the palace grounds." He let that thought trail, leaving out the knowing thought of how close I was to doing just that.

"Right," I whispered.

Was he trying to help me, or intimidate me? I couldn't tell, and my heart was hammering so hard I could hear the pounding in my ears.

"It is a very nice garden," I choked out, trying to sway his decision to let me go. If he was looking for an excuse not to bring me in, and still keep his oath, I'd give it to him.

"It is, isn't it?" He agreed and then added, "Yet so confining for such a large display." His words were very pointed considering how trapped I felt pressed against this thin membrane between me and the sea. Ray had led me to this exit on purpose, and not just to dissuade me from leaving, but luring me to the most secure exit should I have chosen to try to escape anyway. I really couldn't trust anyone, not even this naked guard. His muscles were coiled and taut, ready to grab me if I made a move outside of the garden to activate his oath to bring me in. What reason did he have to delay and allow me to head back to the room? Or better yet, go in search of a smaller, less secure exit?

"What do you want from me?" He had to want something. Why else was he deciding to swim naked in the kelp instead of guarding the exit? This was just horrible luck that he spotted me at all.

"Do you have something to offer?" He cocked his head in amusement.

"Not really," I admitted.

"Not yet," he corrected. "You want to leave, and so do I."

That was a surprise. My eyes grew wide, and then I narrowed them in suspicion. Was he trying to get me to say I was leaving? I would not add to his case for taking me to the dungeon.

"If I wanted to bring you in for 'leaving', I could convince myself the oath was met merely by observation alone. You are soaked in sea water. I could say you already tried to leave."

"You pulled me in!" I objected.

"Semantics, others would have brought you in for less. Merely being in the garden without an escort would be enough. But drenched as you are..." He let me fill in what was being unsaid, and he was right.

Carefully, I replied, "You want to leave?" Leaving out the obvious that I was doing the same, and we would then be on the same page, if he was telling the truth.

"Not permanently, but I don't have the same privileges as a sentinel, so leaving would require breaking an oath. Many here are unable to leave Atlantis without first having their memories removed, and their immortality stripped."

So, that was what kept most of Triton's subjects here? That was quite the cost for leaving, and he certainly wouldn't be able to return if he didn't know Atlantis existed. Giving up immortality was probably the easy part. Not many would give up their past for an unknown future.

I remembered the people washed to shore lately that had memory loss—were they from Atlantis?

"You want to leave without losing your memories?" I inferred, contemplating whether or not I could trust him. How was I supposed to help him do that? He must have thought I could, or else wasn't he wasting his time?

"Among other reasons," Mavron conceded, "You are in a position to help me do that."

"How?"

"I can get you out of Atlantis safely, but only once you've tricked the king into releasing me from my oath," he saw my disbelief that I could do such a thing and he continued, "You have no fealty to him, as long as you do not swear an oath to the king you are in a position to bargain with him."

"What do I have to bargain with that he would agree to let me live, and release an oath?" I was just a twenty-two-year-old girl that recently discovered the gods existed, and weren't just stories my sister and mom liked to use to scare me.

"You'll figure out something Conqueror of the Coral Sea. You must procure my release, and then I can swim us both back to shore."

"Why do you want to leave so bad?" Was his life in danger?

"Apollo spoke of a prophecy of Poseidon's return after the death of the seven seas. Prophesies are filled with nuances, too many to rely on taking the words for their face value. Return does not mean he will return to Atlantis, and he must return. I intend on making sure he comes home, and I can't do that from here."

"You want him to return? I was getting the vibe that it was a bad thing for the powerful sea god to come back."

"Maybe for the king, that is true. He's grown comfortable with his power over the trident, and Poseidon's return would threaten that. Many gods have found it entertaining to target Poseidon, and those gods have made Triton's life a fearful one. He keeps everyone, and himself, trapped close to Atlantis to prevent interference from the gods. He has lost much."

I hadn't thought of it quite that way before this, and the sadness in Mavron's voice made me sympathize with the king. Maybe Mavron wasn't the traitor I was making him out to be. He wasn't escaping Atlantis to escape the king and his prison. He was trying to help the king somehow by bringing Poseidon back, but the king doesn't agree with that method of saving his people. Or he wouldn't have to go around him to release his oath.

"You're willing to defy the king to bring back his father?"

"Triton has lost sight of what Atlantis really needs. We need a show of power, an offensive plan that ends the war between the gods, and brings peace and freedom to the sea."

"And Poseidon will do that?"

"Not alone. The prophecy has said he will not be alone. This is the chance to change history repeating itself. To end the cycle of hiding or fighting."

I nodded. "What do I need to do?"

"Get the king to release me from guarding the palace, and then we can leave. First, you will need to get closer to him, and that will not happen protected by your sentinel."

"What are you suggesting?" I folded my arms.

"Go to the dungeons on your own. Don't wait for the king to force what he wants. Give him what he wants."

"The dungeon isn't what he wants," I contemplated out loud. "That's only a means to an end."

"Find the end then."

And I would, eventually.

I didn't know if I could trust Mavron, but I didn't have a better option either. If he was a merperson, he could breathe in the sea just fine, and he might have been my only hope of getting out of here. I can't stay conscious under the water for long, and he could get us a chariot and steer us out of here. If I trusted him.

Chapter 7

Tools and Monsters

Mavron let me leave, but really, it was returning. He was right. I couldn't let the king manipulate everything. I had to find a way to get in front of this. What exactly did he want? He wanted me to help him against the gods that supposedly sent me to kill his daughter. Not sure I could give him that, but he also wanted more control over my judgment. Dion still held rights that somehow superseded the king. What kinds of laws does Atlantis have?

There were too many questions and not enough answers, but what I did know was I couldn't wait around for my fate. Even if my end was already written, I'd meet it head strong. I had control over that much.

Mavron gave me enough information to know why no one I passed by bothered me and why none of the sentinels were in sight. They were all waiting for me to incriminate myself so I could be sent to the dungeon.

Something in the fabric of the uniform helped it dry from water very quickly. I was without Dion's jacket, but only my hair was wet now. After taking my time to make mental notes about where things were in the palace, I'd found the entrance to the kitchen, a few side gardens—that I didn't dare enter—and the entrance to a bath house. I saw a few people enter wearing only robes, and I debated entering to get the sticky feeling of dried-on salt from my skin, but I didn't want to lose my nerve and get too comfortable. This was merely the illusion of freedom.

Pressing my back against the wall to a double door with golden etchings of some historical picture story, I tried to manage my breathing. In and out, my lungs filled and emptied in quick succession. My blood pumped and my chest tightened, but I was having trouble making my feet move. Closing my eyes, I tried to psych myself up with a pep talk. You can do this. You're already going to the dungeon. Do it on your terms. This is your life, and if you go to the dungeon it's because you decided not to play pretend anymore, not because someone set you up.

I nodded firmly and forced myself to push open the door to the throne room. It was a large space, more like a ballroom, where people mingled and socialized. Many guests of the palace still lingered off to the side, and chatted to themselves while eating their lunch or dinner, whichever it was. Time wasn't really easy to gage here.

I made my way through the room. People hushed as they parted for me. More and more eyes watched me the closer I got to the throne. I searched the raised dais for the king, but he wasn't there. Then again, he wasn't sitting on his throne the first time for a formal meeting either.

"Where is the king?" I wondered out loud.

"He's retired to his rooms," a man behind me spoke. When I turned, he had a stunning shade of green hair similar to Coraline, and I flinched at the memory of her sharp teeth and claws digging into me.

His hair was long and slicked back and looked expensive, like the rest of the guests.

So much for my plan to confront him. All that built up adrenaline buzzed under my skin, and I heaved a heavy sigh trying to relax from the let down. Seeing what he might have thought was disappointment, but more like being terrified of trying to make myself go through this all over again, the man offered, "I could bring you to him?"

That was possible? You'd think the king would have better security than to let anyone have an audience without an appointment. I mean I was barging into the throne room where a bunch of people were mingling, and guards were regularly posted throughout the room, but going to his private rooms seemed unbelievable.

"He isn't expecting me," I gave him an out, and watched him carefully.

Waving his hand to display the surrounding room, he replied, "Sentinels are only posted outside of the palace. The only guards inside are off duty. If someone wishes to see Triton all they need to do is know where he is. Most don't venture to have his company unless they need something they are willing to trade for, have an offering, or wish to gamble their life on his whim. Which are you?"

"Maybe a little of everything."

I guess the plan was still on, but I hadn't thought far enough ahead to know what I had to offer him. Was my blood even something I should be offering for trade? All the myths spoke of how greedy gods could be, and what if my blood to heal or to poison was something that kept me prisoner longer instead of bargaining for my release? I'd have to keep that to myself for now.

"I will pray that everything isn't too much of a price to pay then," he gave a small bow, and lifted his arm to escort me, "for some, the price is too high."

Like the memories of their past, and their immortality. The price the merpeople had to pay to leave Atlantis.

Behind the throne dais, there was an inset wall. From a distance, it all appeared as one solid surface, but now that we got closer, there were two halls on either side, hidden in plain sight. My guide veered left, and then we ascended a set of stairs made of sea water illuminated by eels, and various fish that glowed in rotation as we stepped on each platform, circling higher and higher. I clutched my escort's arm tighter, unable to fully wrap my head around what was possible here, and he patted my hand.

"If he didn't want anyone to visit, the stairs wouldn't be here." He misinterpreted my reaction for fear of Triton, though sure that should have been what it was if I let myself focus on what I was actually going to do. Bargain with a god.

We reached the top, and he released my hand with a small bow. "This is where I leave you. May the gods favor you." He left down the stairs, and yet again I had to force myself to open the doors in front of me. Should I knock? I thought about going back down the hall to find my escort to ask what the protocols were, but then I didn't know if I would come back if I left. I bit the inside of my cheek. This was it, the final threshold. Placing my hand on the door, I thought about knocking, and then it cracked open before I could.

Triton's voice carried with his commanding tone, "You ask for too much to end this feud."

Then a female answered him back, "Your father's burden should not be your own anymore. Do this, and you will have the power you need to keep the trident in your grasp, and start a new family stronger than your last, born in love, raised with care, and destined to thrive." Her voice was melodic, hypnotic, but how could she offer him something like that? That kind of guarantee was impossible, and not without consequence.

"I am my father's herald, his power is already my own." He tried to sound uninterested, but I could hear the surety in his voice waver.

"Which is why you stay in his rooms, rule over his subjects, protect the seas, and one day with the right match be greater than your father ever was."

"Hera, you will make me an enemy of Zeus with what you speak of."

She laughed heartily. "With what I speak of you will not need to overthrow your father to have it all. Poseidon was always toeing the line, trying to be faithful to both his brothers, even pretending to be on my side while he secretly planned to undermine everyone in the process.

"You can't possibly wish for his return, now that your daughters are no longer keeping the trident hidden," her voice lilted. "You protect the sea, and your father interferes with business that is not his own. You can succeed him completely. He has stepped down before; he can do so again. You can convince him; you are the only one who can. He may not have loved your mother, but he would give up everything for you."

"If that were true then we would not be having this conversation," he dismissed her, "We would not be forcing his hand, nor would you be trying to force mine."

Triton was going to overthrow his father when he returned, and I was snooping on a conversation between two powerful gods. This was not good. The door swung open, catching me off guard. The room was like a rooftop view of the sea, and the city beyond, full of priceless artifacts, gilded furniture, and precious stones. Things that were lost to the sea, and recovered by the king. But, what caught my attention was the watery form in front of the king. His back to me, the form watched me, the water moved with her, reforming fluidly with her flawless features.

She didn't say anything to the king, who seemed to be too distracted to notice me just yet. She smiled, a ghostly sight that had me speechless.

"Do not debase yourself with nymphs any longer Triton." She narrowed her eyes at me, disgust in her tone, "With a goddess at your side, you can be strong enough to no longer be bound to the sea. Join the rest of the Olympians, and still be able to protect your people."

"There's always something in it for you. Will you bind me to a goddess that does not love me, as you did my father? So my children will see the disappointment in their mother's face at being reminded they were nothing but an obligation forced upon her by the demands of their queen?"

Hera clucked her tongue. "That was so very long ago, and I merely bless marriages now. I'll have Aphrodite find matches that are destined for true love. Attraction is half the battle, really, and love blooms through time, and attention. She would be your choice, of course."

"My choice," he parroted unconvinced, "You've tricked most of my consorts to seek out their death so that my loneliness would weaken me. I keep no favorites because of you, and yet you call upon me to sacrifice for your ends." His temper was rising, and I sought to close the door and leave before I was caught between two warring gods.

"What I ask of you is no sacrifice, and I have always cared for you when your father could not. Your daughter's deaths were not at my hand, but by those who seek Poseidon's return. Blame Apollo for his prophecy, not me who has protected you from Athena for your choice in courting virgins to ensure your offspring are pure. Your nymphs all chose to deceive you, every one of them traitors. That is why they died. Do not blame their weakness on me!" Now it was me she was pointing to, and with a sudden burst of power the door slammed shut, with me still on the inside, caught in my silence of listening to their private conversation. Triton's bright blue eyes sought me out, and the water of Hera's form splashed to the ground.

In seconds he was on me, his large frame towering over me, cornering me with his mass and the door. His hot breath on my cheek, "Tell me Conqueror of the Coral Sea what would you do if you were me?" Catching someone spying on the gods? I turned my chin from him, and his lips brushed my ear. How could I answer such a question that would only indict me further? He wished me to the dungeons. He would have it now, and not the way I had intended. Did the gods always win like this? Could I not even have this small dignity to control how my fate unraveled?

"She does nothing without a reason, but she is bound to never betray Zeus directly ever again," he took a step back, and watched me, "The only thing you can trust is that she will find a way to support Zeus, but also harm him. So the question is, what part is helping him and what part is meant to seek retribution?"

My mouth gaped, wondering why he was including me in this debate. I had thought his first question had to do with my fate for spying after murdering his daughter, and he was talking about what he should trust about Hera's offer.

"I've only known about gods existing since meeting you, and it's still very disorientating."

"Half true," he remarked, "even you do not believe yourself." How did he know? I'd known about gods all my life, but it was about avoiding the gods' attention. But I didn't truly believe they existed. Did I? Maybe now I did?

"If you know that, then you know if she's lying to you, too."

"She protects herself," he frowned, and paced the room. "Zeus wants my father to return, that much is certain. For what end, is unclear."

"Maybe the why isn't important." I thought of what Dion had said, "She wants you to marry a goddess. Maybe it has nothing to do with you, but the goddess she wants you to marry?"

"I will never marry a goddess of her choosing," he growled. "We must hear from the fates and find why Zeus sent you to begin Apollo's prophecy. Hera did not recognize you, you are not part of her plan—"

"You knew I was there..." I put the pieces together. He wanted Hera to see me, to see how she would react to me. That is why the door opened.

"I couldn't have planned it better. You coming to me was unexpected, and it pleases me that I was wrong about your attachment to my First Sentinel. He means well, but believes I'm much too vulnerable with you around, as we still do not know what gift Zeus gave you that could kill a goddess of the seven seas." He paused, taking a step towards me again. I pressed myself flat against the door, unable to go anywhere. "As you heard from Hera, I've been betrayed by nymphs before. Do not fear me," he brushed a strand of blonde hair behind my ear. His touch was soft. "Dion does not believe you can harm me physically, as the other nymphs were foolish to think they could. I am the sea. So," he traced a finger down my arm, the sleeve of Dion's uniform. "Tell me, nymph, how else can you harm a god? Is his concern warranted? Should I be sending you to the dungeons instead of keeping you at my side?"

Were those the only choices? He was trapping me into staying with him or staying in the dungeons, and that wasn't why I came here. I had surprised him by coming here, but he easily turned it in his favor and used me to glean more information from Hera. He was smart, and he was charming. And he was manipulating me even now. How much of his words could be trusted?

"How did they die?"

"My consorts?" He pondered, like there were other deaths to explain, and there probably were. That thought terrified me.

I nodded. The question made his eyes light with a kind of mischief. He seemed happy that I asked, and his smile was making me squirm. It was the kind of smile that could bring enemies to their knees and lovers to their backs. I forced myself not to look away. He was testing me. Everything was a test.

"Each one was different, but all of them intended on taking the trident in some way. Some of them wished to overthrow my rule with an heir, others for themselves promised a seat at Olympus should they acquire it. I was a means to an end for them, and if I am honest with myself, they were one for me. I did not love them, nor them me."

My heart thundered in my chest. He wanted love? It's what Hera offered him. She wouldn't try to sway him unless she had something he wanted. I shook my head. I couldn't offer him that. Ray's advice haunted me. Give him something no one else can. What? What could I give him? What did I have? Why was he telling me all of this?

"I don't want your trident," I pleaded with him. He still didn't tell me how they died, merely why they had, and only vaguely at that. I was just another nymph to him, and I had my suspicions that they died at his hands for betraying him. That's something I could give him... true loyalty, but not at the expense of my freedom. Loyalty didn't thrive in captivity. Any one of his subjects, even me, even his consorts, would betray him for that. Did he not realize?

"What do you want, Alessandra?"

The way he said my name made me shudder.

"My life, my freedom, my choices..."

"What will you give up to have it? What will you do to get what you want?" He paused, pinching the collar of the borrowed shirt I wore. "What will you risk? How far will you taint your virtue?"

I flushed and then glared at him. Defiance steaming from my very ears, turning them bright red with anger. I was tired of everyone assuming I'd willingly offer my body to someone weighing my life in their grasp. Anyone who is considering my death wouldn't just let me live because they had my flesh with a round of 'fishing'. If that was all I could offer them, then they already had it, and there would be no reason to keep me alive. I was as good as dead anyway, if that's all I had of value.

It was my turn to do what I came here for. I would not be giving him my virtue in any form, but I would change the narrative of this assault. He thought to intimidate me with my innocence, by brushing my cheek, caressing my arm, and his body so close I must press myself against the door, praying I would melt into it. Not anymore. I pushed from the door and closed the gap between us.

Lifting my hardened features to his face, our noses a molecule away from touching. My eyes blazed, burning with determination that if I was getting sent to the dungeon I would take my moment of dignity while I could, before it crumbled beneath his feet. I laced my hand behind his blue-white hair—a god had no reason to fear me, so he had no reason to pull away—to hold him in place while I pressed my mouth to his ear, a snarl on my upper lip.

"True virtue is not trapped between one's legs, and it will never be yours if you try to capture it through force. If your consorts betrayed you, it is because you betrayed them first," I hissed.

Triton's hands weaved into my golden hair, and untangled the braids, while keeping my cheek to his. He had to bend to meet my height, and I was much too frightened by what I had said to him to move, much too cowardly to meet his eyes, to see how he would kill me. At least I would pray it would be quick in a surge of emotion, but as my waves fell behind me, he kept me secured to his half naked body, his warmth radiating into my skin.

"I will not make the same mistake again. Have I betrayed you, Aless?" He used my nickname without me having to tell him, and it wasn't unpleasant on his lips. "Have I betrayed the messenger of Zeus's will, who has killed my only daughter? What betrayal needs a remedy before it is paid in kind to whence it came?" He was threatening me, his voice cold and heated all at once. How could I compete with such power? What could I offer someone so devious to spare my life and let me free? His silver tongue spun a web so captivating I didn't stand a chance. In one smooth response, he both pretended to be merciful and just, while turning it back on me, to take full responsibility for my predicament. He didn't send me to the dungeon yet, he hasn't harmed me yet, and yet I was not free, and he twisted my actions into being the first one to betray whatever this was. It was his daughter that attacked me, and if he was right about Zeus then it was by his influence that I had my unfortunate timing to run into Princess Coraline.

I was the victim.

But then... wasn't he as well?

Against every common sense, he had somehow done what I thought was impossible. He made me sympathize with him, made me feel for him. The man that lost a daughter by my hand, but had yet to seek his revenge on me. The man that lost all seven of his daughters, and who knows how many other children by the influence of other gods, because of his father's decisions. He didn't appear old, but he had lived ages of being used, and played with indirectly. The man that lost every relationship he had to betrayal... had he killed them?

He must have, I tried to tell myself; he had to have. I couldn't let him get under my skin. He was the one holding me here. I was his prisoner. He wasn't the victim here. My hands fisted straight at my sides as he held me to him.

"I may have been the tool that killed your daughter, but I am not the monster here," I gritted out.

He released me, and as suddenly as he was there, he was gone in the mist that was left in his wake.

His haunted words echoed in the room, "Monsters are born from betrayal. Even tools are shaped by those that wield them."

Was he calling me just as much a monster as Zeus? Or was he warning me to be careful how I'm used in the future? By a monster or him? What if he was both?

What if my sister was right about the gods, and it was better not to be noticed by any of them? But now that I was... what was I supposed to do to disappear again?

Chapter 8

What the Nymph?

Triton didn't send me to the dungeons, but he didn't have to be the one to issue the order for me to end up there. Ray was waiting for me when I finally made my way back to the throne room below the King's suite.

"You didn't stay in the room," she finally spoke once we were alone in the corridor leading down a set of damp stone stairs, the least impressive of the palace, cracked, and covered in algae that smelled of rot. I knew where we were going, even if she didn't admit it out loud.

"I didn't get a chance to plead my case to the king," I explained casually, like it was no big deal. Then ended with a shrug, because I had expected this outcome.

Ray gave no indication of the personality she showed before—the oddly familiar and 'instant friends' vibe gone. Nothing remained but her job. Then we made it to a large, empty stone room, where water dripped from the ceiling, and through the grates below us. I could hear a few moans in the distance echoing off the walls. We were not alone here.

"This way," she guided me to the wall on the right. On the way, I stepped across a grate and fingers grabbed at my ankle. Jerking my leg free, I watched in horror as the cells were in the ground filled with water like a sewer system, but prisoners were inside with only a foot worth of air between them and the floor. This was a different kind of torture I was witnessing. I crouched down to help the man, once the shock of being grabbed passed.

"Why are you in here?" I asked, but what I really wanted to know was why were the dungeon cells submerged in water?

He gurgled from bobbing in the water, then gasped. Ray grabbed my arm, and the man's slick hand slid from my hold. She led me back to the far wall and pushed open a stone scraping against the floor, revealing a hidden room where I assumed they kept the prisoners they didn't want just anyone to have access to. Or perhaps to add a layer of isolation torture in your own special underground water hole away from talking with others.

"He was a smuggler, bringing mortals to Atlantis without permission. Most of the prisoners are smugglers or murderers..." She let that last word hang in the stale, moldy air as we approached a specific grate in the ground. Taking the short rapier from her thigh, she jabbed it into a slot in the ground, popping the rusty cell door open.

I stared down into the murky water, true understanding creeping up my spine that if this water wasn't somehow connected to the sea, I wouldn't be saved from drowning once again. It was hanging on to the bars until my strength wore out... or sink. She would do this to me? Sentence me to death even after earlier when she wished I would survive?

"How long?" I asked instead.

"Until the king is informed, or Dion returns," there was a pained crease around her eyes, "This is best for both of them, and even for you. Many of the highborns have seen you wandering," she paused, "in uniform, no less." She shook her head, finally cracking and needing to explain herself.

"The king chooses to ignore that we have spies in our city, and even the palace. The smugglers haven't just brought mortals, but those fealty sworn to other gods. Spies will tell the gods you were not killed yet; that is certain, but what kind of message does it send to have you dressed as a sentinel, informed by the king himself to leave you alone? You must stay in here until the palace believes you are being treated as a prisoner. Do you understand? If even a small part of you wants Atlantis to survive whatever war is coming between the gods, you will accept this horrible treatment with grace and use this time to train yourself."

My eyes widened at that last bit. Train? In a small watery hole?

"You," she continued with resolve, "are not mortal, though you were raised as one. Learn to access what is inside you. The nymph within. Triton and Dion are both much too proud of their own abilities to accept that you don't need their protection, so if they wish to keep you alive... as it seems they do, then start acting like the conqueror you are, and quit running." The green in her eyes lit up, making the surrounding brown brighten and she flipped her braid over her shoulder. "Going to the king took guts, but what you need now are claws."

I was pretty sure I was the only one in this dungeon to have a motivational rally before needing to plunge into my cell. Was I going to accept that I wasn't mortal? My blood was proof enough of that, wasn't it?

Ray was either the smartest sentinel in Triton's army, or I was the most gullible, because I trusted her. I hardly knew her, and yet I was going to willingly dip into this gross looking water because I believed she was doing it for Atlantis. Not for me, perhaps, but did it matter if the motivation could benefit me, anyway? I guess I was betting it would.

With a fist bump to her bicep, I gave her a weak smile. I didn't have to like what I was agreeing to, but I'd repay her for the bruising punch to my arm at breakfast. She was right again. I would need the strength of the fish, my last meal. Did she already suspect this was what was going to happen? I think she did.

With a firm nod—she didn't smile, knowing that wasn't what I needed right now—she helped lower me into the water. It was colder than I expected. I'd never been affected by the cold of the sea before. Maybe that was my answer. These cells weren't connected with the sea outside, cut off from whatever magic normally warmed me? Magic. I shook my head, and my mouth bobbed in the water. It wasn't that long ago I wouldn't have believed a seer if they told me about my future.

The grate was slowly clicked into place, and I tried to save energy by linking my elbow through the bar to hang on, only my head fit in the air pocket in between.

Ray reminded me once more before leaving, "Don't waste your time; figure out how to breathe under the water. Every sea nymph can do it; it changes your voice when you're successful. It's harder the first few times unless instinct takes over."

Instinct... she meant unless I thought I was drowning, unless I truly thought I was going to die. And no one would be here to pull me out if I failed.

If I was a nymph... then I'd do it. If I wasn't, then I wouldn't be surviving this whole mess anyway.

I unlinked my arm and dove down beneath the black water. It was nothing but darkness, and the tunnel walls widened the deeper I got until I couldn't feel the walls within reach any longer. A tightening in my chest told me that if I didn't swim to the surface now, I might not make it in time to avoid a lung full of water.

This was my chance.

I tried to stay under just a little longer, long enough that my body will be on the verge of drowning by the time I could make it to the surface. Regulating how much carbon I released, I knew as soon as the last of the gas was pushed from my lungs it would be seconds before they tried to fill themselves again... but with water instead of oxygen.

Muscles twitching, I forced myself to swim as fast as possible, desperate to make it to the air above me. Pitch black, and unable to really know how far away I was from making it back, there wasn't a bright enough light in the dungeon to lead the way. Would I make it?

Struggling, I wanted to feel the walls that told me I was close, that the cell was narrowing, that the oxygen was seconds away. Nothing. Only water.

I couldn't tell if my vision was blurring, not in the darkness, but the wooziness in my body was a good indication that I would pass out soon. Then I couldn't hold my breath any longer. Out of my control, I gasped, taking on the salty burning water. Choking, I sucked in more, unable to stop myself from doing so. My whole life I've always been able to hold my breath for a long time, but I had purposefully waited until my breaking point to reach the surface again. It was the only way to know for certain if I was a sea nymph, if I could breathe under water without the sea helping me.

Everything stopped, my body seized and went limp. I didn't make it. Was this it? Was this...

Next thing I knew I was coughing up water, and then accidentally drinking it back in, all in succession. Flailing, my hands scraped against corroded metal, and I felt my skin tear. It stung as it hit the salty water again. Then I grabbed hold to lift my head between the bars. Water spilled from my mouth, and I couldn't get a full breath even if I wanted to. Water still cramped my lungs. I tried to heave, to choke it up, but I'd just had to wait for my body to force it out on its own.

And it did, painfully, it did. I clung for dear life, hanging from my elbow laced through the bars once more.

I was not a sea nymph.

That was near death if it weren't for my super healing.

I may have been a nymph, and the sea may have saved me from drowning before, but after this, I couldn't believe I was a nymph from the sea. Or if I was, the magic was long gone from being raised on land too far away from the sea. I wouldn't be doing that again.

The dull light filling the room was only enough to see in front of my nose, whatever lit up the room when I arrived disappeared, along with Ray.

Wedging my other arm up through the bars, I tried to secure myself so that even if I passed out, I'd stay above the water line.

Then I waited.

Sputtered for air when I slipped and regained my hold. My arms and hands torn from the grate in ill repair, only to heal once more. I'd never been so thankful for my hidden talents as I was then. Sometime during my struggle I had lost the over-sized pants, and only wore the swim bottoms I had under my wet suit when I first arrived, reminding me of my life when I yearned to feel the calming hold of the ocean all around me. That seemed like lifetimes ago, and it was only a few days.

What was Theo doing right now? Would she send out the coast guard to find me? She would have known I went to the water against her warnings... my phone and clothes left on the beach like a ghost.

How long would they search before my sister told our mother? Before they considered me lost at sea? Dead?

Self-pity filled me, a resignation that my family would move on without me. No one was coming. All I had was myself.

My tears disappeared in the water trickling from my hairline down my face.

Had I tried to take the easy way out? Knowingly sending myself to the dungeons to hasten my death? And now that I was here... I knew I couldn't follow through. I would miserably fight to live. Hang here until I couldn't hold on another moment.

Try to survive.

Fight to survive.

Until there was no more to give but my life.

Chapter 9

Scraps

Scraping noises startled me awake, and the room glowed with light once more. Someone was coming. How long had I been down here?

Not enough strength was left in me to pull my face up to see who was there. Boots clanked on the stone, and then a loud thunk landed near my cell grate. A guard leaned over, not someone I recognized, and she kicked the bucket over, making me gasp for air as water splashed over my nose and mouth. The water was murky... tainted with brown, bloody water. I gagged, spitting up what might have been swallowed. Chunks of guts and flesh were chummed with the bucket.

"Breakfast," the woman grumbled, and she used her booted foot to catch the handle of the bucket. She took care not to get too close to my cell, and didn't dare bend over lest I grab her.

"Wait," I choked, not wanting her to leave, "When will the fates arrive?"

They were my only hope now.

"Spies like you don't get blessed by the fates. They never stay in one place for long, and by the time you're scheduled to face judgment, they'll be long gone."

"They're already here?" I read through the lines… they were here. Now. "How long have I been here?" She said breakfast, but I didn't really know what meal the fish Dion prepared was dinner or lunch. Maybe a day?

"The chart says you've been down here for a few nights and are scheduled for judgment in a few weeks. You shouldn't waste the scraps. We only come down here every three days." The fish heads were floating to the surface, but the chunks of minced raw flesh were already sinking below me. My lips curled in disgust. I wasn't that hungry. But I was thirsty. Surrounded by water, and none of it fresh.

"Water?"

She nudged a cup across the ground at the edge of the bars with her foot.

"Does Dion know I'm down here?"

She snarled. "He has better things to do than waste his time on you."

"Does anyone know I'm down here?" I could hear the whine in my voice, the desperation. I wouldn't last weeks down here.

"Everyone is aware you're here," she said finally, and my heart sunk.

Did part of me think if the king or Dion knew I was here, they would release me? Was I that delusional?

The guard approached, and I stuck my hand out to reach for the water, making her back up.

I had killed the Princess of the Coral Sea. I was dangerous. Not to be touched. She kicked the bucket over so she could pick it up without getting too close.

"The king is wrong about you." She snatched the bucket and left the way she came. Slowly, the light in the room, which I now noticed was from the algae dimmed once the light of the other room was closed off.

What was the king wrong about? What did he say? I struggled to carefully lower the cup of water to my lips, spilling most of it, but quickly getting the hang of it to gulp it down my raw throat.

The algae glowed around my hand, and I flinched away. Sinking into the water again, my skin painfully puckered at my toes. Lifting my legs up, I shoved them through the bars up to my knees to allow them to dry out, resting my back and head at the top of the water. I'd switched positions many times over the hours that passed, waking up when my buoyancy failed. Spitting and choking, I pressed my shoulders against the wall to help wedge myself in place.

I'd lost count how many times I'd gone unconscious. I'd undone Dion's over-sized shirt, wrapping and knotting it around the grate like a sling to hold under my neck, keeping my face above water as my legs linked above me. Under my knees were bloody, where the rusty bars dug into my softened flesh.

The smell of bread and buttered fish woke me, a welcome difference to the rude awakening of almost drowning when my body moved too much and slipped from its position. Slowly, I adjusted from my sling to follow the scent. My muscles too achy and weak to be fast. I cracked my neck back and forth, wincing. Whatever ability that healed me before had stopped working long ago, along with my energy reserves. The rusty bars scraped my legs, and I'd noticed how much longer it took for them to scab over where my waterlogged feet would crack and bleed, unable to do even that much. I wiggled my toes to make sure I still had blood flow; multiple times, the feeling had been pinched off painfully coming back to life when I moved again. Something crinkled with my toes, not that I heard it, too much water in my ears, but something felt different.

Gritting my teeth, I adjusted my legs through the grates, and in the small glow of the algae could see my feet had been wrapped. Not just my feet, but my calves as well in a strange tar-like substance. There was also a plate of fish, a loaf of bread, and a cup of water next to my cell.

Not wanting to ruin the bandaging on my legs, I debated how I would eat the food without losing it to the depths below or knocking it away from where I could reach it. I had to bring my legs and feet down and pull myself up to get the right angle. It had to be done. Like a dead weight, my lower half crashed back into the water, and the bandaging kept my feet and calves dry, unaffected by the water. Relieved, but curious how the guard was able to fix me up without waking me I slipped my arms through the grate, stuffing my chin and face through the bars up to my ears, but not wanting to risk getting stuck I never went past the ears. One arm clung to the bars and the other brought the fish to my lips, the butter making it difficult to keep in my wet, shaking fingers. Only a few scraps made it to my mouth, but it was heaven to my chapped lips, rubbing the residue over them, and licking them clean just to confirm I wasn't dreaming.

Trying again, I scooted the plate along the grate to scoop the food into my mouth. I got a few bites in before my grip faltered from exhaustion, tipping the plate. Distraught I tried to recover it, but the corner broke, sending it, and the food into the water.

Sinking into the water with it, I swiped to recapture the food. I didn't care that it was in the same salt water I've been urinating in. The fish fell apart between my fingers, much too delicate to withstand the water and my desperation.

"No, no, no, no," I croaked, growing more and more upset. Sputtering, I had to reach the rusty bars again, and found myself unable to hang on without sinking into the water again.

Algae glowed around me as I took my final breath before my muscles went limp, not responding to my commands.

Water swirled, and raged within my cell, lifting me to the surface once more. With every last ounce of reserves, I clawed at the corroded bars, willing them to crumble. A hissing sound filled my ears as one bar loosened against the wall. Leveraging my shoulders against the wall, and clinging to the other bars, I flung my feet at the weakened spot, sending the bar clanging across the stone floor.

Disbelief threatened to freeze me in place, but I knew without daring to say anything that one bar was all I needed to shimmy out of the cell. They would have been better off leaving more of a gap between the water and the top of the cell, but their desire to torture their prisoners was why the bar was corroded by salt water, and why I'd been able to lift myself out.

I collapsed on the algae cushioned stone next to my cell grate. The water left out for me overturned from my escape.

Blonde hair clung to my face in wet clumps, and a single yellow snake slithered next to me. If I weren't so exhausted and drained I would have screamed, or jumped, but all I could do was stare between strands of webbed hair, panting.

Something warm wrapped around me, and I couldn't keep my eyes open any longer. The ground was the most comfortable I'd felt in days.

"I've been waiting for you, little goddess," I imagined Dion's voice soothing me to sleep. I smiled to myself. I liked how he called me a goddess. No one's ever called me that before except for him. Somehow that made me feel powerful, like I could get through this, that a goddess could escape one day. I'd escaped my dungeon cell, but I wasn't strong enough to attempt leaving this underwater city. This was as far as I was going to get today, and that was enough for now. Not drowning.

"Why didn't you come for me?" Why did he leave me in the dungeons for days? Did he have the right as my sentinel to choose where I stayed until my judgment? Did he want me to die here? Why did I think he'd care?

I didn't expect a response; after all, he wasn't really here. He wasn't here holding me in his arms.

"I did come for you," he said. It felt like my hair was being pushed from my forehead, lifted by the water itself when he continued, "as soon as the fates allowed."

"I'm not a sea nymph..." I confessed to my fake Dion.

"You are something so much more. You shouldn't be possible."

Was he trying to say I shouldn't be alive? That seemed right. I didn't dare open my eyes lest I lose the comfort of my hallucination. So, I let myself hold on to the illusion the algae cushioned floor was the merman I thought it was.

"None of this should be possible," I murmured.

"Rest now," he soothed, "you've done your part. Let me do mine."

My sigh of agreement muffled into his chest, "Mmm."

I let my fate rest with my imagination.

Chapter 10

Law Bound

"She can not be sent to the dungeons again!" King Triton thundered. "How was I not informed of this?"

"It was unexpected for her not to have an affinity for breathing underwater," the other guard I saw in the dungeon earlier remarked unapologetically. Unexpected didn't mean remorseful.

"She could have drowned," Triton growled. That was news to me, I thought being a nymph made me immortal. But if Triton's exes were any indication, that didn't make them invincible. Suddenly I was very much having a moment of shock from nearly dying, because I could have drowned, and Ray had even suggested I try to in order to train my inner nymph.

I had trusted her... again.

Trust no one.

"She didn't," the guard sounded disappointed.

Groaning, I tried to adjust to where I was. Opening my eyes, I found myself staring into the dark blue pools of Dion's eyes.

Sitting up abruptly, I scurried back against the headboard made of a large seashell.

King Triton turned his head to watch us, his serious features softened, and then returned to his conversation, a lightness to his tone, "How fortunate for you that she didn't, or I'd be questioning your loyalties, Brin." A lightness that didn't match the severity of his words.

Brin's face paled as her muscles tensed.

"In the name of the sea, my king." She bowed low, bending at the hips. He waved her off dismissively.

My neck heated, and my attention was brought back to Dion standing beside the bed. He stood there at attention eyes now staring straight ahead, not concerned with me in the least. His black hair was perfectly sea swept, but his sentinel uniform appeared rumpled, as if it were the same uniform he wore before he left to gain an audience with the Fates. His extra uniform was ruined by me when he left, so it would make sense if it were, but I could have sworn there was another set.

While he appeared to be a sexy kind of disheveled, I was pristine. Sniffing my sleeve, it smelled like heather, a woodsy, mossy kind of fresh scent on the silky, pale-blue fabric. I didn't feel sticky from salt, and I ran my fingers through my blonde strands confirming it was clean and soft.

Images of Dion gently combing through my hair as I soaked in a bath of clean water with scented oil made my ears burn. Did that happen? I thought I was dreaming when he picked me up from the cell floor.

My mouth went dry as I twisted the comforter in my hands before looking up to see the king watching me. I flinched.

Brin already left the room; now it was just us three. Triton sat on the edge of the bed, wearing nothing but a pair of jeans to complement his white-blue rocker hair. If I wasn't trapped under the sea, I'd say he was a guitar player in a band. All he needed to complete the look would be some tattoos and some piercings.

Not daring to sneak another peek at Dion, I forced myself to say something so Triton would stop staring, "I thought sea nymphs couldn't die from drowning..." Way to start things off on a positive note, Aless, I thought to myself.

"Many can't, but not all nymphs are the same. And though nymphs are immortal, they are not invulnerable."

"But I didn't drown before..." I thought to myself. Well, not to death anyway. It certainly felt like drowning over and over again.

"You are a subject of the sea," Triton agreed, "but the cells in the dungeon are designed not to connect to the sea, cut off from its song to prevent any kind of comfort. Even a nymph can drown in the dungeon if they don't metamorphose. Some choose to become the water themselves, though they can rarely regain mortal form after."

"I was down there for days..."

He grabbed my hand clutching the comforter and squeezed.

"I shouldn't have left like I did." Was that guilt in his voice?

Easing my hand from his, he expertly followed my movement like I had meant to move our affections to my lap. He used his other hand to clasp over and run circles with his thumb over my fingers. All the while, I was remembering why he had left in the first place.

Narrowing my eyes at him, I wondered what he was up to. He had insinuated about my virtue and what I would be willing to give up, to live, to have freedom. And now he sat there acting like he was the reason I was safely placed in this bed and not back in a dungeon.

I held myself above water for days.

I was the one that propped myself up with a makeshift sling to prevent myself from drowning.

I kicked the corroded cell grate.

I lifted myself out of the watery death trap.

None of that was him.

"You'll have me believe you were gone for nearly a week?" I asked sweetly, though my own insinuations were obvious. He was the king. He could have freed me any time that he wanted. He had to have been waiting until I was good and uncomfortable, on the brink of breaking, to swoop in to 'save' me.

"I let my shame get the better of me." He kept his composure, even going so far as to sound sincere and caring while he said it. Those bright blue eyes glowed and captured my own with a certain kind of attention that made me want to squirm.

"When I returned, I thought you would need more time before I summoned you. I avoided asking of you so I would not see this kind of distress on your face. Time can muddle the memory of poorly executed conversations, but I fear my shame has delayed understanding the true reason for you not barging into my rooms sooner."

As if being in the dungeon would be the only reason I would be avoiding him. Triton had a way of twisting his words and actions to form his own narrative that casts him in a more positive light. He made it sound like the time away from him was the issue, and not having been thrown into the dungeons, or nearly dying.

He was so convincing. I had to admit I was really thinking about if he would have retrieved me sooner if he'd known I was there. I shook my head of the cobwebs. How could he not have known I was there? He was the king for sea god's sake!

Triton brought my hand, held within his, up to his bare chest. His muscles were firm, and certainly lived up to the standards of gods. He was otherworldly in his beauty, and he wasn't afraid to use it to his advantage.

I cleared my throat and tried to take back my hand. This time he let me.

My attention drifted back to our silent sentinel Dion. He was still staring straight ahead, purposefully avoiding the king, and me, eyes glued to the doors.

Feeling me watching him, he spoke, "The Fates have been summoned. They came only on the conditions that I pay for their services first, and they speak with Aless, alone. Their payment took longer than anticipated." His words were directed to Triton, but the way he ended his statement felt more like a plea for forgiveness. It was almost like he was apologizing to me for taking that long to return and finding me collapsed outside my cell.

But that couldn't be right, could it?

"What did they want?" I asked, and the interest Triton showed made me believe Dion hadn't yet told the king about his time away further than getting the Fates to agree.

"We aren't the only ones seeking their guidance—only one would agree to see us."

"One?" Triton growled, and he quickly pushed from the bed to pace the room.

"She wishes to have a tour of the city," Dion continued.

"Her payment?" He lifted a brow at that.

"A condition of seeing Aless outside of the palace," he confirmed, but left out the unsaid, that it was not the only condition that was made.

"Outside?" I perked up at that.

"It'll have to be done discreetly." The king didn't bat a lash at me leaving the palace.

From dungeon to city, I thought gleefully. It would be my chance to actually escape, but now I knew that they thought I could drown to death. I needed to find a smuggler to help me. Because that was simple, I mocked. Easier said than done.

"My guard said the Fates already arrived," I added, though she didn't use those words exactly. I read between the unsaid lines, assumed.

"A few days ago, the Fates responded to the summons saying they were to be expected, and where to collect them for escort," Dion confirmed.

"So, she didn't arrive yet?"

"Zeus hardly lets them out of his sight," Triton sighed, "I'm honestly taken with how quickly they were able to answer our summons. The death of the last of the seven seas has piqued their interest, as it was predicted by Apollo, and confirmed by Morta that the threads of the Poseidon line were melted by Zeus's thunderbolt, making our lives, and potential deaths, less predictable. Probably his way of preventing any offspring from becoming stronger than him." Triton ran his fingers through his hair and rubbed his neck to work on the frustration.

"Hera had wished to cut Poseidon's thread with a dagger made from the tooth of Chronos, and dipped into the River Styx. It was Zeus's thunderbolt that stopped her by melting the threads with those close by, including all original Olympian usurpers, hiding the individual threads into one entwined rope of them all. Stronger, thicker, and now protected by all the gods due to the mystery of which god would be affected by attempting to meddle with fate," Dion corrected.

"You know your history, Dion," Triton lifted a brow at that, "Though your story lacks a bit of context. Hera did cut Poseidon's thread with the dagger but was only able to nick it. Enough to make him vulnerable during a small section of his life. Not satisfied with waiting for whenever my father would be weak enough for her to seek her vengeance on him, she convinced Zeus to help her, hoping his thunderbolt would be powerful enough to do more damage, but it backfired on both of them. This is why none of the Olympians can seek vengeance on any of the gods directly. They must go through their children, and those they care about."

Both stories seemed plausible, though how either of them could be certain which one it was I didn't know? The only ones who knew the answer to that were Hera and Zeus. Never thought I would be saying anything like that with all seriousness. Talking about gods like they were more than myth, but real beings capable of affecting my life.

"How do you know?" I asked.

"Know what?" Triton asked absently, still staring at Dion like he could read all of his secrets if he just looked hard enough.

"How do you know which story is correct? All you know is that a dagger was attempted to be used on a fate thread, and Zeus struck the loom with a thunderbolt that melted the gods' lives together. The motivations behind the actions could go either way, couldn't they?" They both watched me like I grew a second head. Did they never think about this before? How was I the first one to bring it up?

I explained, "If you heard the story from Zeus, he has motivation to tell you the story in a positive way where he was helping. If you heard the story from Hera, she has reason enough to say Zeus was the villain, but what motivation does she have to cast herself as a villain with him? Unless she's bound by oath not to go against Zeus, then she could convince herself that she was only doing what Zeus wanted, so she's still the unwilling victim..."

But how does this history help them decide whether or not to trust Hera and Zeus? If anything, all it did was breed distrust.

Does trusting either of them help them with making the decision to keep me alive, and potentially allowing me to go home?

There was a whole war between gods that I didn't know enough about to figure out my next step.

I needed more information.

"Both Hera and Zeus have spoken of the story of the day all the gods' fates were destroyed so even the Fates couldn't control them. The attempted murder of Poseidon and Zeus's heroic effort to ensure no other Olympian would be at risk of Fate's intervention," Triton mused.

"Do you have to trust either of them?" I wouldn't recommend it, but Zeus is the leader of the gods according to myth. Could Triton really go against their wishes? Not directly, but what would it even look like to defy the gods and still be safe from retribution?

The best thing would be to find a way to remove myself from the equation, preferably still alive.

"It's not a matter of trusting them," Dion advised. "It's how do you do what they ask without giving up your own interests."

Triton smiled brightly at that. "That is the game." He seemed more pleased by the predicament than I would have thought appropriate given losing a daughter and being the focus of two powerful gods.

"How do I fit into this game?" I folded my arms and stifled a groan.

"Uncertain," Dion answered simultaneously with Triton saying, "Perfectly."

"You were chosen for a reason, and whatever it is, they wanted you dead. And normally I would be happy to oblige them, but they didn't account for my close relationship with Apollo. You are enrolled in his university, are you not?"

I nodded. How did he know that? Duh, he's a god. He has his ways.

"As such, I've given you the same rights as any subject of Atlantis, even without your fealty."

Like the right to have the sentinel who found me weigh on my judgment for my crimes. Or not slaughter me in front of a throne room full of people? Not letting me die in a dungeon...

"How kind of you." I couldn't prevent all of my mock appreciation from seeping into my words. Like I was supposed to be grateful to him for not murdering me because his daughter wasn't able to finish the job.

The way his blue eyes twinkled, I knew he recognized my sarcasm, and yet he was amused, not angry. The sea god was as unpredictable as the sea itself.

"I like a woman a bit on the wild side. Be careful how you tease me," Triton flirted, and I balked, flattening myself against the headboard. That was one way of getting compliance from a prisoner. How was I supposed to take that kind of comment?

I'd definitely be more cautious about my defiance if he took it as alluring. I'm sure many women threw themselves at the gorgeous sea god, but I didn't see any good coming from being involved with him longer than necessary. Especially if his enemies decided they wanted to target anyone close to him because he was too difficult to attack directly. His daughter was evidence enough of that.

"You'll be giving her judgment to the arena, then?" Dion interrupted the intense stare Triton was giving me that was making my insides squirm uncomfortably. Like at any moment he would come pouncing on me, and my body betrayed me by feeling a bit excited by the prospect. But it was a different set of blue eyes that replaced the image in my mind.

I was disappointed once more when Dion was still preoccupied with a spot on the wall towards the doors instead of me.

He was just doing his job.

Was it wrong of me to have secretly wanted to see a bit of jealousy from his king's flirtation with me, or the satisfaction at my reaction to his advances instead of his apathy?

Of course it was. I had some kind of sick Stockholm syndrome at the small kindnesses he'd shown me while fulfilling his duties to Atlantis, and his king. And twisted as it was, his lack of interest only made me think of him more, because he wasn't trying to take advantage of my imprisonment. If he would just blatantly try using his charm on me like the king, maybe I could stop myself from feeling this kind of way towards him.

Turmoil was evident on my face, but neither of them would know what caused it. The king's next statement was confirmation enough. And Dion wouldn't even bother to notice.

"She is hardly trained for such a trial." Triton approached to get a better view of me, assessing, "You've grown cruel over the years Dion, I would not have expected such an advisement from you."

"It is a right every subject can choose."

Triton considered this and then nodded. "An honorable one, but she must know what she is agreeing to. The arena is a sought-after profession, and the ones that enter do so after years of training, a love of the sport, and loyalty of offering to the sea. Many lose their lives, and many of those sent for judgment do not choose to enter as they are unfavored by the gods, and highly likely to fail."

"Excuse me," I choked out, "Are you suggesting I sign up for some sort of death match like in ancient Roman times? Like spears, swords, wild animals, chariots, and a crowd full of blood lusty voyeurs?"

"Of course not," Triton feigned shock at the suggestion, "we don't use weapons, that would be quite unfair. Only your natural gifts are allowed—as well as anything available in your surroundings."

Because that made it better? It didn't. That was worse. My eyes widened in horror. I wasn't sure that being bludgeoned to death with a rock was better than skewered by a sword. How was any of this honorable?

And the more pressing question was, why would Dion suggest it? Hurt crept into my heart squeezing within my ribcage.

"Let's see what the Fates have to say first, if you are favored then you may choose to have your judgment by arena, but there are better ways to be judged for your actions that aren't so archaic, and much more enjoyable," Triton's insinuations weren't missed, and I highly doubted that avenue didn't come with equal if not more risk than the arena.

Dion remained silent during our exchange. Not that I should want to hear him speak again, since his contribution to the conversation was to put a battle to the death on the table.

"Will I get to return to the University of Apollo after my judgment?"

"If that is what you wish." And I had this eerie feeling that how I returned there was undetermined. Like one of those last will testaments where my remains are scattered to honor my wishes. I shivered.

"The Fate has requested you be present for their arrival. You'll be escorted to the city this evening, and then return to the palace." Triton walked to the door. "Dion will discuss with you any questions you have about the arena. You can give me your answer about if you choose it as your judgment at dinner."

And with that, I was left alone in the room with a statue in the form of Dion. As soon as the doors closed, it was like relief washed through the room, and Dion relaxed only long enough for me to yell at him.

"Are you trying to get me killed?" I fumed.

"You're doing a fine job of that on your own," he snapped back, "every time you stare at me with those giant evergreen emeralds of yours, I can sense the coil of Triton's patience grow closer to snaring you, and me. Do you have no sense of preservation?"

I blinked back my shock at his very detailed, and quite flattering, description of my eyes. He was so rigid I hadn't thought he noticed me watching him, and I found myself smiling now that I knew he had. Was that a hint of his attraction to me smothered beneath his efforts to protect me? I shook my head, no. He had offered me up to a death match. *Get your head in the game, Aless.*

I snarled back at him, finding it relatively easy to find and harness my own anger at this situation, and towards him. "You're the one sending me into the arena to die, not Triton!"

"Triton would sooner devour you than let you go! Don't you see the way he tends to you? It's gone too far," Dion walked away from the bed in frustration, "I don't know what you did or said to him while I was gone, but this is different than the other nymphs he's lured to his bed. If you continue to push him away, he may resort to other means of procuring your affections." He turned to stare into me, directly to my core. "Not even Triton, whom was gifted with a calmness over the sea, is immune to the call of the rage and wildness of the sea's passion. He's lived a long life," he explained seriously, "and with that comes immense loss, and a history of taking what is not freely given to fill the chasm within his depths."

I gaped at him. What was he trying to say to me? What would Triton do? I didn't want to know, not truly. But what he said was both scary about what the sea god was capable of, but also there was a tenderness to what Dion had to say about his king. He thought of him as reasonable and calming. Pity for everything that was taken from him by the gods, and viewing my refusal to give him what he wanted as yet another thing taken away from him, was sad. I felt for the lonely king, but not enough to open my arms to his advances. Wouldn't that be worse? To lie to him about how I felt?

He needed trust more than he needed my love.

"I won't do it," I huffed.

Dion lifted a brow, and for a moment I thought I saw him smile before his stone face returned.

"Which is why I offered the arena," his voice was firm on the issue. I wasn't following. He saw my confusion and continued, "Triton isn't a full god, though he would have his subjects think differently."

"What?"

He waved off my interruption and pressed on, "His mother was a nymph of the ocean, powerful, but making him only a demi-god. He is bound by the laws of Atlantis as long as he is king, and as soon as he allowed you to be considered a subject of those laws he is bound to accept the outcome," Dion paused and revealed his plan, "including accepting the privileges that the arena offers. Should you survive the trials, you are granted freedom no matter the crime. Should you win," he added, "you are given the honor and favor of the gods which will allow you one request of the king that he must honor, which you can use to return to your life before, unharmed, and without objection. He will set you free."

"You think I could win?" That seemed like an unbelievable feat, because, as the king had said, I was untrained.

"First, we must consult the Fate," I smiled at the way he said 'we', like we were in this together, "then we train." How did he make joining an ancient death match sound so appealing? It was as if my victory was assured as long as he was in my corner, and that I could have everything with that win. My freedom, my life, my future without the fear of being hunted afterward. If anything, the gods were known for honoring their oaths and those that passed their trials. Even at the expense of the one asking for the oath.

I remembered the bedtime story my mom used to tell of the sun god's son that asked to ride his chariot, even though he knew it would kill him. Or the maiden that asked to see her lover's true face, even though his true form would be too much for a mortal to live through. There were many stories where the god's honor of their oath was more valuable than life.

Even if I won the arena, I knew better than to ask anything of the god's favor, even if I used to think mom's stories were fiction.

And I still had a better option than submitting myself to a blood bath. There was still an escape; that sounded more appealing by the minute. Mavron offered me a way out.

I merely had to convince the king to release Mavron from his oath, and the best way to undo an oath is with a new oath that overrides the previous. Then get the hell out of here before I'm committed to being slaughtered in an arena.

Dion was still trying to help me, in his own twisted way, and I would have gladly chosen to go out in a blaze of glory than be imprisoned for life. That was if I thought I didn't have other options. As handsome as Dion was, I would skip out faster than a blink if it meant the smallest chance of living through this without being tied to any of them.

Under different circumstances, I would have fallen over myself to have a date with this man who was confident enough in his abilities to make me victorious. He did, after all, train Ray, and she became a sentinel, one of the strongest warriors of Atlantis.

As I stared into those dark blue eyes, like the deepest of the ocean waters, I was half compelled to agree with him. I could win. I could have everything I ever wanted and more. I could be an honored hero of a god's trial of virtue and strength. There was a fire in his gaze that spoke of power, power that could be at my fingertips if I only reached for it. Stayed with him.

My mouth was dry, and I licked my lips. Coming back to my senses, I knew I would have to keep up pretenses until I could escape. He may have wanted my freedom, but at what cost?

Mavron wasn't asking me to risk my life any more than he was risking his own to help me, and he was still planning on returning to Atlantis. What Dion was asking of me... was too much. It was a last resort, and I wasn't out of options.

So I lied to him with the strongest kind of lie, one buried in truth.

"I'm not a nymph. How can I win?"

I didn't say I was going to choose the arena directly, but why would I ask how to win if I wasn't? I wasn't a nymph, and it did pose a big disadvantage to joining the arena by not being able to breathe under the water. Or have claws or sharp teeth. They didn't need weapons; they were the weapon.

"You are more than a nymph, Aless," Dion said resolutely. "Triton is beginning to have his suspicions, and he is waiting for the Fates to confirm it for him. When that happens, your options will narrow. What," he sat next to me on the side of the bed, "did you do while I was away?"

I knew what he meant, and I stood up clenching my fists. Was that why he was acting so cold before?

"I told him the same thing I'll tell you. I am not the monster in this game, and if you feel betrayed,consider who was the first betrayer." I tried to save someone from drowning, and then am almost murdered. I am no conqueror of the Coral Sea. I was a survivor.

He will not make me feel bad for what I've had to do to survive, even if it was some tryst with the king. Which it most definitely was not, but that's none of his business.

How the king looks at me is not my fault. If anything, I'd been pushing back, not reeling him in.

I scoffed.

I would have stormed off, but I didn't really have anywhere to storm off to, except the bathroom. So I did.

Huffing over the polished stone sink, I stared into the mirror, repeating the mantra in my mind—I am a survivor.

A knock at the door pulled me from my trance, and I whirled around ready to tear him a new ear hole. But he didn't barge in. He waited.

"What do you want?" I growled in annoyance.

"I don't think you're a monster," Dion sighed, then continued, "You deserve better. Better than Triton, and better than me in your corner."

Dion paused, and when he was certain I wasn't going to respond, he tried again.

"We are. You know, in your corner. In different ways. Triton isn't as ruthless as he's made out to be. He prefers the reputation to help protect his subjects–"

"You just said—"

He cut me off like I did him to try to explain. "I know. And that's all true. He is capable of destroying an entire city in a tidal wave. Capable of sinking ships, and islands, but he was made to quell the rage of the sea, not feed it. He can forget it is his temperance that gives him power, not vengeance. He should leave the rage to his father, but," he saw me about to interject, "I've seen this look about him before. He will forget himself with you. And I fear you will never forgive him."

Closing my mouth, then opening it again to start, I finally responded, "Why do you want me to forgive him?" Out of all that he said, he confused me all the more with how he was both defending and warning me about Triton. Two conflicting opinions, and then to end it with an almost plea to be on good terms with him, to forgive him. While also warning me that he may do something unforgivable, and Dion doesn't want that to happen.

Whether that's because he doesn't want anything bad to happen to me, or because he doesn't want me to have an irreparable opinion of Triton, I couldn't tell.

Dion turned away from me to answer, "In the past, I thought I was beyond consequences. No one would dare do something to harm the ones I cared about. No one but me." And that's all he said on the matter. This wasn't about me at all. This was about himself, I thought. Of his past. Somehow, if I was unable to forgive Triton, Dion himself could never be forgiven for whatever he'd done in his past.

What exactly had he done?

Did he care so much about forgiving Triton... or forgiving himself? What did I need to forgive Dion for?

"Okay," I said softly.

"Okay?" He repeated.

"Okay, I'll try things your way," I acquiesced. I'll try to forgive you both for keeping me against my will if I make it out of this alive. And if he happened to interpret this as agreement to join their arena of death, then so be it, I thought to myself. I'd figure out a way of getting Mavron on my side. I just needed Triton to agree to Mavron being oath sworn to help me, and by proxy negating his previous oath to stay in Atlantis. After all, if he truly wanted to protect me, then he better get me the hell out of here.

I smiled sweetly at Dion, hiding my plan of escape under a layer of offered forgiveness. It wasn't a lie. I would forgive them both. I just won't ever see either of them again. If it were left up to me.

"Then we have work to do," Dion said excitedly.

Yes, we do, I thought victoriously.

Chapter 11

Defender

Suddenly, it made sense why I hadn't found a carriage in the garden entrance before. They were all outside of the air pocket, though all was stretching it. More like two, and without asking, Dion added, "We only keep one emergency carriage at each entrance and have all the rest called in when needed. And of course, the royal chariot held at the throne room."

The golden bucket opened, and Dion waved his hand, forcing the water to push itself away from the transport. It wouldn't have mattered if I found the way out of here earlier. There was nothing to pull it or propel it.

The half-naked guards that flanked us were not sentinels, but they marched into the water on either side of us until they were in front of the chariot. Each one assisted the other in harnessing themselves... and then it made sense why they were only wearing loincloths.

In the water, their legs swirled with a vortex of water, and then calmed, revealing dolphin butts. Even their forearms had fins, and there was webbing between their fingers.

They were the motor for the chariot. Effectively removing all hope of escaping without help. Maybe Mavron was a dolphin hybrid? He had said he'd be able to get us both out of here.

Dion offered me his hand to step up, and like a waterfall, the chariot was pulled back into the sea. Yet I didn't get wet. Back erect, Dion stood at the helm of the small golden cart. He guided me with a sweeping motion to sit on the cushioned ledge next to him.

Before I could sit, the chariot darted off. The half man half dolphins, cut through leaving a trail of white foam behind us. I stumbled at the velocity change and squeezed Dion's hand while mashing face first into his arm. He adjusted and pulled me into his chest to keep me steady.

I had a firm footing now, but I didn't move. And he didn't break away.

With my cheek resting against him, and his arm around me, I watched as the city of Atlantis became larger, and off to the side the shadow of the giant Krag hovered in the distance.

Our escorts circled around the city, giving us a tour of the sunken island. I'd never seen something so beautiful. The chariot veered up and the film over the city was almost like an oil slicked rainbow shimmering with magic as we ascended beside it.

Tapping his foot, Dion whispered, "Look down."

And as I did, I squeaked while clinging to him, unable to prevent myself from the shock of standing on nothing but water. The bottom of the chariot was completely see-through, gone. He chuckled, and before I could tear my gaze away to be upset with him for terrifying me. I was in awe.

The view was breathtaking.

This was Atlantis.

This was magic under the sea.

Then we dropped, sinking into the water. Whatever magic making the chariot floor solid water gave way, and we submerged, watching the carriage disappear above us. I flinched into Dion's grasp, remembering the cold of the dungeon, but the sea was warm, welcoming as I had grown to know it before stumbling upon mermaids and gods.

Dion's arm wrapped around my waist, aiming us towards the city.

My eyes were wide, but he remained focused on diving like a torpedo through the water. He used his control over the water to propel us through without sprouting a fin or tail.

A large bubble of oxygen bubbled out from my lungs, and I struggled not to suck in water.

His hold on me tightened, and he pulled me against his chest. Finally, his blue eyes met mine, and I stilled.

I saw nothing but him.

Nearly forgetting breathing.

And his lips were on mine.

For a moment, my heart soared, pounding in my chest like a rock band, and my hands laced into his black hair pulling him closer.

Then air was forced into my lungs.

This wasn't a moment of passion, this was keeping me alive. He was doing his job, I reminded myself. Mentally, I flogged myself for getting lost in the buzz of the touch of him on my lips, and the pressure of his arms around me.

As Dion's lips left mine, I hid my inflamed cheeks in his jacket as we soared through the water. Not sure what to do with my hands, I kept them wrapped around his neck for leverage. You know, to keep myself from slipping from his grip and floundering in the sea. I felt firmly pinned in place, but I wouldn't admit that.

"Ahem," someone coughed to get our attention. I was suddenly aware that we had an audience, and we were no longer moving.

Slowly, I lifted my head from his chest, and Dion's blue eyes stared at me. Not shifting his attention to whoever was there he responded, "You'll have received the order from the palace by now?"

"Yes, my team is aware of the need for discretion First Sentinel Dion." The way he said the title was with a kind of scorn. I gulped and tore my gaze from Dion to see it wasn't resentment towards Dion's rank that caused it. The vehemence was clearly directed at me, and most definitely had to do with my proximity to him.

I tried to pull away, but Dion squeezed my shoulders to him, and smiled directly at the fellow sentinel, wearing a similar uniform. Water pooled at my feet, drenching my new outfit. Luckily, Dion had brought an outfit that was less fancy than what was available in the closet Triton had prepared for me. He said I would blend into the crowd better, but I couldn't help but think that maybe he knew it would make me more comfortable.

The sentinel noticed the gesture and frowned, but continued regardless, "The Fate is expected to pass by on a cruise ship in a few hours and retrieved by a chariot as discussed."

"The king's chariot would have been faster, but she insisted on making a vacation of it," Dion explained, seeing the incredulity on his fellow sentinel's face at the prospect of the Fate arriving this way.

"What's the difference between the chariots?" I mean, the only way it could be faster is if what was propelling it was better, but couldn't the fastest escorts be assigned to either chariot and be equally as fast?

The other sentinel's mouth flat-lined in response to me speaking.

Dion smiled at the question and decided to humor my curiosity, "The king's chariot is blessed by the sea, and is the only chariot capable of summoning Pegasus from the stars other than the lost chariot of Poseidon."

My mouth gaped. And all I could think of was, isn't Pegasus a winged horse? Not a sea creature?

Dion seemed to read my mind.

"Pegasus is a daughter of Poseidon. When summoned to the chariot she has the lower half of a fish, and her wings glide through the water faster than even Poseidon himself. She is magnificent," he recounted, as if reminiscing fondly. Dion glowed thinking about the horse, and I was pretty sure I remembered the myth saying Pegasus was a 'he'. I'd save that question for after the scowling sentinel was gone.

This world I found myself in was continually amazing and leaving me in awe.

"You're earlier than expected," the sentinel ruined the light mood, and we followed him through a tunnel underneath the city.

Dion returned to his all-business tone, but kept his arm around me, nonetheless. "I never did trust a Fate to do anything as expected, so we must also be prepared as much for a timely arrival as an untimely one. The Fates have a way of twisting their meanings or layering them deep into subtext."

The sentinel nodded in agreement; their face was only moderately less severe. Maybe that was just their face, and I was reading too much into their displeasure at my company.

It was hard not to take their glares personally, but maybe that was how he was with everyone.

Our escort waved to a ladder, and Dion dismissed it, guiding me and him past it.

"The instructions were very specific from King Triton to take you to his personal estate."

He had another estate in Atlantis when he already had an entire palace? Of course he did, I scoffed.

"We'll join him there after the Fate arrives. My instructions were also very specific, and he will understand the deviation from his when it involves an agreement directly with the Fate herself." Dion never missed a step, and the sentinel obviously respected his leadership because that was the end of any objection he might have had.

"Will you be needing further backup?"

"I can take it from here," Dion insisted.

"I'll leave you to it." He bowed, and gave me one last glare of disapproval before climbing up the ladder. There was no denying it was personal, and that wasn't his resting face.

I bit my lip, more than a little agitated. Dion's hand massaged my shoulder. The tension had lifted them, and his action kept it there, but for very different reasons.

When we were far enough away from where the sentinel left us, I finally spoke, "So, Pegasus is a girl?"

"You have a way of depressurizing a room little goddess," he chuckled, and when he realized I was serious about learning more about Pegasus, he added, "It wasn't common to use the pronouns available today. He was used for all references, female or otherwise, and because she was commonly depicted in her horse form, the pronoun was never updated along with the re-tellings of her story."

"Did she go into hiding like the rest of the Olympians?"

"You must not be a scholar of Greek mythology," he mused, though it wasn't condescending, but more of a thoughtful note to himself about being more aware to fill in where needed, "Most who grow up with abilities, which I'm sure you—"

"I didn't," I lied quickly.

He smiled tightly, almost a grimace, "Most," he repeated, "are told of the true bard's tales of their history. Yours being the sea. Pegasus was captured by Zeus after her mother's," he cleared his throat unable to say the words, instead passing over that part, "She was used to capture the finest lightning bolts, as service to stay in Olympus. But one day, she had decided to take her mortal form, no longer merely a horse with wings, but a goddess in her own right. The very depiction of an angel," he spoke as if he had seen her himself, love in his eyes, and a surge of unwanted jealousy made me regret asking about this story.

Dion couldn't possibly be old enough to have been alive during the time of myths and legend, so I had no reason to be feeling this way about a woman, or horse that he might have feelings for. He so obviously had feelings for her, even if it was just admiration of her story. I took a breath, waiting for the rest of the tale.

"Zeus had found her, and she didn't stand a chance that he would simply let her continue her job without wanting more from her. She was too beautiful, and what god would not bend to her heart after seeing the truth of how she culled the power of lightning, forming it with her very hands and distilling it for him, and only him? He was taken with her," Dion sighed, then rubbed his face.

"I didn't mean to bring up something so," he stopped me before I could let him off the hook.

"He is a powerful god, and it's difficult not to be drawn to him. I've found it almost impossible to refuse him myself, and she was no exception. Strong in her own right, she had no intention of making a habit of their affair, but she was a conqueror like her parents. She would have him, and then she would move on."

"What happened?" I couldn't help but be sucked into the story, and we'd been stopped at another ladder for a few minutes now. Soon, I'd finally be in the city of Atlantis, and not in its underbelly.

"Hera happened, and Zeus did what he always did with the ones that he protected. Sent her to the stars," he got a hold of himself and finished the story abruptly. Then he hoisted me onto the ladder and followed closely behind.

I guess he wasn't interested in reliving that part of the story. When we made it to the surface, it was in an alleyway between two houses. Not the kind of impression I was expecting, given the spectacular view from the chariot ride. From the distance, the city glowed. From here it was just a city made from stone and mortar, cobbled streets, and open windows with curtains flapping by artificial wind. It was a humid heat, but the breeze morphed it into the perfect temperature. Sunny above, there was a point of bright light, similar to the sun, but it obviously couldn't be. When my eyes adjusted it was clear it was merely the tops of the buildings gilded in gold that gleamed across the city, creating daytime in an otherwise submerged city. The sky, if you could call it that, was a deeper blue than the pale blue of a surface city, reminding me of Dion's eyes.

If you grew up here, in this aquarium of a city, it was beautiful, and it didn't feel as if you were trapped in a bubble at all. As long as you stayed away from the edge of society, you may never feel the claustrophobia creep up on you.

The hairs on my arms lifted, and I turned to see Dion watching me take in the city.

"How is this possible?"

"The wind, if you can believe it," he lifted his hand as if to grasp it, "is created from the movement of the sea's waves. Subtle and perfect.

A calming caress of our surroundings that turns to a breeze once the movement reaches the barrier."

I could feel that power, the calmness of being touched by the sea with every gentle sway of the wind. It even smelled like standing by the seaside. Fresh, salty, and reminding me of the very reason I liked to sneak off to wade in the water before all of this.

Finally, I closed my eyes to take it all in, and said, "It's magical."

"It is," he agreed. "I'm glad you like it."

I opened my eyes at the last part and lifted a curious brow. It was almost as if he was holding his own breath for my approval, waiting to make sure I liked Atlantis, and when I did... relief was in his words.

Deciding it was my own imagination, placing intention where there was none, I ignored this warm fuzzy feeling growing in my belly.

"What were your instructions from the Fate?" I tried to change the topic.

"There weren't any," he admitted. "I just didn't want you to spend your whole time in Atlantis being cooped up in the Royal Estate. The heart of Atlantis doesn't live there."

I flushed. He was playing hooky with me. He was trusting me not to be locked up in Triton's home.

This whole thing felt very much like a... date.

I smiled awkwardly, not knowing what to say.

He grabbed my hand, laced his fingers with mine, and guided me into the bustling street market where performers of all talents showcased, fishers displayed their catches, even bodies were lavishly flaunted with abandon. Speeding up I tucked myself closer to Dion as one of them tried to pet my hair.

"I can show you the way to Olympus," he called out seductively.

Dion narrowed his eyes at him. The man waved his hand dismissively and winked before pursuing the next potential customer.

"Some heart of Atlantis..." I mocked the seediness of the kind of vendors soliciting us as we passed.

"Not yet." He smiled, pulling me forward playfully. I couldn't help but forget, for the moment, why I was there, and his attitude was so contagious I smiled along with him.

"Where are we going?"

"You'll see," he replied with a cheeky quirk. It wasn't how I would have imagined him acting as a high-ranking sentinel, but here he was acting like a kid without a care, without a job to do, and... with me.

Through another alleyway, there was an end to the buildings popping us out in a field of wheat. We were away from the city, and into the farmland, and then I saw them.

The horses.

Not a single one like another, but all of them grazing, running, nudging in play with their snouts.

"Aren't they magnificent?" He watched them in wonder, rubbing my hand absently with his thumb.

"They're free..."

He nodded, but he wasn't watching the horses anymore. He was watching me.

"Freedom is an illusion, don't you think?" He took my hand, and without realizing it a horse had approached us from the side, placing both our joined fingers to rest on the nose of a great steed with a deep black coat.

Warm breath huffed on my palm, and his tongue came out as the horse lifted its head to slime me. Dion laughed a heartfelt rumble from the depths of his ribcage. True happiness filled him. I could see that.

"She does not like to share. I call her Lia after her father, but most here call her Black Water, as she is fast, strong, and as graceful or stormy as the sea herself. She is free here. More free than most mortals are, no matter where they've decided to roam."

His hand stroked down her neck, and he nuzzled into her mane.

"Do not mistake leaving this place as freedom. You could be free here as well." He sounded eager, almost pleading. I could practically hear the unsaid words of here... with him.

I cleared my throat. Only moments before, I had been enjoying his company, forgetting why I was here, and then it came crashing right back to me.

Pulling my hand back from the horse, I stared at him. He was as magnificent as the horses, beautiful, and there was a kindness that surfaced as he cared for the horse that I really didn't want to want for myself.

"And if you were told you couldn't leave? How free would you feel?"

This was not what he had wanted to hear, and his blue eyes sobered.

"To be almost murdered, jailed, threatened, and told you'd never see your family again... but you'd be 'free'?" I questioned incredulously. My muscles tensed up, and I could feel my emotions welling up, preparing to burst, all the while backing away from him.

Dion patted the horse, and it trotted back to the herd as he sat down on the mossy grass. He didn't make a move to try to stop me from leaving, simply sat. And waited. I found it more difficult than I thought it would be to leave him. He was giving me the chance now. I knew he wouldn't chase me, but I couldn't.

So, I sat.

Next to the man that was assigned to guard me.

He spoke after a while of us sitting and watching the horses, "I could go anywhere," he paused, "but nowhere was outside of the reach of the gods. I could have stayed with my family, but I found the closer I was with them, the more danger was stirred.

"In the beginning, it was a thrill to feel anything, even chaos, fear, and those things only made me more invisible. But I realized that it was my invulnerability that made those around me targets. Everyone wanted something from me, and though I could go anywhere... I was trapped.

"I am more free now than I have ever been, and yet I go nowhere," he finished.

"What happened to your family?" I asked softly. There was a pain there, and quickly I added, "You don't have to tell me, but you know... if you want to... I've got nowhere to go." I joked, but wasn't it true?

He looked up at the deep blue domed sky above us. Dark shadows like clouds passed over, probably whatever sharks or whales lived nearby.

"I was married—"

"Oh," I couldn't help my shock, and I was equally surprised by the tinge of jealousy I felt.

"It wasn't love," he amended quickly, and I sighed before he continued, "She was in danger. Marrying her protected her from a life she didn't want, but it also didn't allow her the kind of life she wanted." Dion rubbed his face.

I kept silent, not wanting to interrupt. There was still so much not said.

"I've never really felt comfortable talking to anyone about this. Not sure why I'm compelled to now, after all these years. I'm ashamed to admit loneliness made me believe I could learn to love her, and even she tried her best before seeking another."

She had cheated on him. I wouldn't have thought, but then again, I wouldn't have thought he was married before either. He seemed so young to have all this history, all this hurt simmering under the surface.

"It's okay to feel lonely," I was speaking from experience myself. Part of me thought I understood him better now.

He shook his head.

"Had I waited, had I found another way… things would have been different—for both of us." He blamed himself for something, that much was clear, but for what he still wasn't willing to say. A mask filtered over his face, and what was once raw and open had closed up and hardened into a kind of resolve.

He stood now and offered me his hand to do the same. Then he promised me in terms that were certain to him, but so fluid and elusive for myself, "We'll find another way this time."

Was he talking about me… or his ex? Was that why he was helping me in his own way? Because I reminded him of his wife… or worse, another woman that he'd let down—that he loved. My chest clenched up thinking about how this wasn't about me at all.

But that didn't stop me from taking his hand.

It didn't stop me from getting lost in those ocean blue eyes. So many secrets hidden beneath the surface. Would he share them with me, like he did today? Or would that be as far as I swam in his madness that seemed to grab me and not let go?

As much as I should, I couldn't let go.

I nodded to him as I squeezed his hand maybe too hard, maybe too desperate to keep this feeling building inside me.

He made me forget he was my guard, and his duty wasn't to protect me for my sake… but for the sake of the king, for Atlantis. He was my prison guard in a very beautiful cage, and I doubted I'd leave even when the gates opened as long as he was by my side.

I couldn't keep this up.

Not if I wanted to be free.

Somehow—some way—he couldn't be there when it was time to go. I couldn't stare into those eyes and turn away. I knew that much.

So the next words I said surprised even myself. "We will."

We, together. How had that happened? When had I thought of us as a 'we', when did that change? I hardly knew him, and yet ever since we met I've felt this connection with him as if reuniting with someone I'd known forever.

Lia, Dark Water, returned to snort air at my neck, nuzzling into my hair.

"She would like for you to ride with her," Dion interpreted.

"I've never been on a horse..." Let alone one without a saddle.

"You don't need to know 'how' to ride a horse with her. She isn't asking you to control her. She's asking for you to join her. She'll lead you."

Stroking the mane of another horse that trotted up with silvery gray hair, Dion whispered into the mare's ear. She snorted and kicked up dirt with her front hooves, neighing.

"This is Lia's mate, Moon Glider. I call her Luna. She said she'll be joining us."

"That's all she said?" I watched him skeptically. If he was actually talking to the horses, then Luna certainly said more than a few words. Joining us was a fairly short remark, and she had quite the long string of neighs and snorts, and a few head bucks for added measure.

Dion cleared his throat, "Ahem, yes, well, she is equally headstrong as Lia, and seems to be jealous that you won't be riding with her. She was insisting we switch, but Lia has already ignored the request."

"You got all that from her snorts?"

Luna bucked her head and scuffed her hooves. I got the impression she didn't like my description of her snorting. It was snorting though, and she was probably happy she wouldn't be giving me a ride now.

"That was pretty self-explanatory." Dion smirked.

"Yah, don't insult horse talk. I got it." By now, I was petting Lia's cheeks and neck. She didn't seem to be insulted the same way Luna was.

"When you connect with a horse, they give you everything. They trust you with their very lives, and that honor should not be taken lightly. Lia feels compelled towards you. It is a great honor, and one I have never seen her give another for centuries."

I pressed my forehead to hers, closing my eyes.

"Take care of me," I pleaded with her. Silently, I wished for her to take me away.

Her head dropped from mine, and she kneeled down for me, allowing me the ease of climbing on her back. Nervous, I traced my fingers along her neck and stroked her back before slowly easing my leg over. With a buck of her head, she adjusted me all the way on while pushing to stand again. I clung to her neck, and my fingers gripped into her mane.

Her lips flapped in a horse raspberry sound.

"You can relax a bit. She says she won't let you fall."

My eyes were squinted closed. Opening one eye, I saw Dion mounted on Luna, looking like a dark contrast to the light-colored horse.

"Like this." He demonstrated his light hold on Luna's mane, above her shoulders, and leaned down. She lifted herself on her hind legs, neighing in an excited cry for release. That kind of action would have sent me flying, but he moved with Luna gracefully, and as she landed, he hadn't budged at all. Instead, he had a big cheesy smile plastered all over his face. He was happy.

"They'll show us around their home."

Still much too uncomfortable to smile fully, I tried my best, but all I could manage was a grinding teeth mash. Not wanting to hurt Lia I did loosen up my grip on her mane and switched my hold to lower down where I saw Dion do so on Luna.

Like that was Lia's cue, she too reared up, and I screamed, clutching her hair like my life depended on it. I swore I might be tearing her hair from her neck, but Lia continued on to gallop beside Luna like it didn't matter.

"Oh my gods, oh my gods!" I clung to dear life. How was I even still upright? We whirred through the field, and met up with the other horses that circled and then joined us in a rush across the land.

Suddenly my terror turned into exhilaration, and a high like I've never felt before. I finally understood what Dion was saying. This was freedom.

Something came over me, and I released my hand. Just one up into the air. Then the other, my thighs clamping down to steady myself as Lia rode.

Then I screamed.

I screamed into the vast land before us. Releasing all of my tension out of my lungs. Forgetting that Dion was riding among the horses with me. Then Lia joined me, a loud neigh like a warrior's cry in battle.

Closing my eyes, I yelled out again.

It wasn't only Lia that responded; it was the entire herd of mares that shared my hurt, my frustration, my call to action. Did they feel like me, so touched by this moment of freedom that it only made me crave more?

I felt it then, this surge of understanding and power. They did. I felt them through Lia.

Tears wiped away in the wind of our gallop. I knew it in my soul, that they would always come back here to this home... but they wanted more.

Home was a place to come back to, not a place to be trapped.

Loving a place didn't mean losing that longing to explore.

Then I heard him.

Dion.

He screamed with us, and I knew he was just as trapped as the rest of us.

Would he come with me when I left?

Because I would leave here, no matter how beautiful it was.

In a rain of arrows, the horses scattered around us before grouping back together to protect Lia and Luna, the alpha's of the herd. The sound of whirring projectiles wasn't all that unpleasant, almost melodic, before the pained cries of the horses hit by their impact.

Someone was attacking us. Attacking the horses. And I didn't know where it was coming from. Over the hill to the left they appeared. The sentinels, in uniform, marching towards us.

Over a loudspeaker, one of them called out in a familiar voice, Ray's voice, "Return to our custody or be given immediate judgment!" I was pretty sure that was the diplomatic way of saying these arrows wouldn't miss next time, though they didn't miss all of the horses during their first assault. Dion had already jumped from Luna and was pulling an arrow from one of the mares. His hand pushed pressure on the wound while Luna gathered the rest of the horses to line up for a charge against their attackers.

Turning in a rage, Dion ran and leapt back onto Luna's back calling out, "You've betrayed the amnesty agreement! You will leave the herd out of this. She is already in custody, stand down!" Luna ran up next to Lia and me, then he jumped from her back to sit behind me. His arm wrapped around my middle, pulling me against him.

As if the sentinels didn't hear him, they nocked their arrows for another round. Dion patted Lia's neck.

"Hurry," he whispered to her, and then she was off, leaving her herd behind so they wouldn't be caught in the crossfire.

She was fast. Faster than I could feel her hooves on the ground, faster than the whoosh of arrows flying after us, but Luna wouldn't leave her. Pacing just out of reach beside us, Luna followed. My heart was racing, and my mind tried to catch up with what was happening.

What was happening?

Why was Ray shooting at us?

Why wasn't Dion bringing me in? Why was he running away with me?

Lia took a sharp turn, and an arrow thunked where we were. It was like she had a sixth sense to dodge projectiles. How were the shooters so accurate to get so close to hitting their mark? When the mark was Lia, and she was so damned nimble and swift, there shouldn't have even been that close of a call.

Then I heard her.

"Protect him," Lia commanded. I knew it was her, without ever hearing her voice before; I knew. Then a warmth spread through my limbs and burned at my back. It was like Lia's energy was bursting through me, commanding me to act.

Protect him.

A golden glow emanated from my hand until what I was looking at was no longer a hand at all, but a claw. Claws made of gold and armored feathers locking into place on my forearm. Instinct took over, and just as Lia could avoid the arrows with her speed, I let go of Lia's mane and flung my arm out beside Dion's shoulder. An arrow chinked off my hand, protected by golden armored claws.

Dion and I stared at each other as I leaned into him looking up over my own shoulder.

What was I?

Was this what kind of a nymph I was?

Lia reared up on her hind legs, stopped by the sentinels that had corralled us. She had nowhere to run now, and I understood why she hadn't dodged the arrow, and why she told me it was up to me to protect Dion.

Did he need my protection, and not the other way around? I didn't fully understand, but in Lia's herd, the women were the alphas, the leaders, and the protectors. Maybe it was as simple as that.

Then I saw the shadow above us... too many arrows blotting out the light. We couldn't escape this unscathed. So, I did the only thing I could do.

I made a choice.

A dumb one, but my body acted faster than my reasoning skills could object.

Throwing my body on top of Dion, we fell from atop Lia's back to the ground. He pivoted above me, and my eyes widened as his blue ones stared back at me from above. With his hand, he tucked my head into his chest and I screamed, muffled, into his jacket.

Whirring arrows collided around us, and I felt the impact of several feel like they were puncturing my arms, but my arms were held against Dion's torso. That would mean...

I couldn't bring myself to admit what feeling an arrow embedding itself in my own skin would mean. I choked on a sob. Dion had stayed on top of me, and my eyes were squeezed closed against him. My own arms were aching, but everything was now silent aside from the hooves scuffing around us.

Relief followed once I heard his voice. He was alive. That much was certain. For how long, I couldn't know for sure.

"Impossible..." he stammered. His hand stroked the top of my head before lifting his body from mine to evaluate the damage.

Squinting, I did see an arrow sticking out of his abdomen, but he wasn't searching himself. He was checking me. His hands roamed over my body, even over my arms.

My arms, my unmarred arms.

My jaw hung open, unable to comprehend. They were still covered in golden feathers and my claws. I was fine.

"Who are you?" Dion asked before I noticed feathers falling around us in a remarkable shower.

He cringed, moving to shift off of me. Sitting up, I could see the feathers land like wings behind us before they blew up in the wind. With a snap, he broke the tip of the arrow off, and then ripped it out with a grunt.

"He doesn't know," Lia said and then a neigh followed up. I finally looked up to see she was flawless, and yet the ground was riddled with arrows sticking out like torches, still smoking from the impact.

"Neither do I..." I confessed to her.

"Your pride will be the death of you," Lia nudged Dion with her snout.

"I see you're still faster than an arrow. They've slid right off your coat." He grabbed at his side, and gave a strained smile. There were multiple arrows broken and scattered around her. She didn't dodge them... she ran towards them at just the right angles to stop them. The black coat was scratched up in places, creating a pattern where the arrows skimmed her skin.

"That was unexpected," Ray's voice interrupted casually. She stood there watching us as if she didn't just issue an assault of arrows that blotted out the sky to skewer us, including a fellow sentinel, and a magical talking horse. It might have made more sense if it were just me she was attacking, but my death didn't seem valuable enough for the collateral damage involved.

She tossed a canteen to Dion, which he promptly caught with little effort except for the grunt that gave away his injury. He uncorked it, and guided the water from the container out of its confinement and lured it over his wound, which I could only assume was a way for him to heal himself. That was how he helped cure my own injuries, from controlling the water within me, but I thought that had more to do with flushing out a toxin and less to do with the actual healing properties of the sea. But what did I really know about what he could do?

I didn't scramble to escape what Ray had in store for us, because there was a battalion of sentinels with arrows pointed in our direction, and nowhere for Lia to run between where they pinned us, and what looked like the shore of a beach not far off, the edge of the island.

But it wasn't me who she spoke to next.

It was Dion.

"I had my suspicions about you Dion, but I am glad I was wrong."

"Do you intend on killing me?" He stood and was now placing himself strategically between Ray and myself. Still speechless trying to catch up with what was actually happening.

"I wouldn't kill you in front of the sentinels now that they know who they've been aiming for. We don't kill our own. Now that we know you are who you say you are, it won't be necessary." She flipped her knife in her hand and twirled it around in a display of prowess.

She could throw it at either of us, and the threat of the possibility was pointed.

"You'd kill the one that trained you to be who you are today?" I balked at her lack of conscience.

Ray merely smiled and sheathed her knife. "Dion understands duty above all else, and I had a credible source inform me that the Dion I know and trust was killed. And replaced with a trickster. I was merely doing what's right by my honor and duty to test the validity of the claim."

"By killing him?" I couldn't believe my ears.

Dion lifted a hand to stop me from defending him, but it wasn't just about him. She could have killed the entire herd, and me along with him. Was this really only about Dion?

"I haven't been acting myself lately. If I had taken you straight to the estate this wouldn't have happened," he put all of the blame on himself. Running his hand through his ruffled black hair, now dusty with dirt and sweat, he sighed in a kind of resignation. I felt a distance grow between us as this pressure for him to turn to look at me built, but, somehow, I knew he wouldn't be giving me that relief as he walked past Ray, leaving me there.

Ray leaned over me, her tall frame hovering over my slumped form. "I wasn't lying when I said I hope you survive this, but leave Dion out of your plans. Whatever you were doing to manipulate him it's over now."

I couldn't even see her anymore, my eyes glazed over staring in front of me, through the spiky field of rooted arrows.

Not even Lia's calm voice could stir me as she said, "It's not over, Aless, please protect him."

Ray didn't respond either, and I had to wonder if all she heard were Lia's neighs while only those the herd trusts can truly hear their voices. Still I didn't move, weighted to my spot.

Lia nudged my head with her snout huffing at me. Slowly, I tilted my head towards her and closed my eyes.

"Why?" I asked her as I leaned into her cheek.

Ray responded first, confirming my earlier suspicions that not everyone could hear Lia's true voice.

"Some gods disguise themselves, and play tricks, or send spies. I was willing to lose you to save Dion. It's as simple as that. If Dion was switched with a god, he would have been fine no matter the result, but he would have been captured and returned to Triton.

"Dion can't die from a bunch of arrows. They're painful, but he would have survived no matter what, as long as he could reach the sea water. Every sentinel is carrying a flask of it, and we corralled you close enough to the beach that he would have been fine. I knew Dion would protect you, but I hadn't expected you to protect him. For that I am thankful to you."

I blinked up at her, confused. I hadn't protected him at all. He was the one using his own body to shield me.

I turned my hands over, my claws retracting, and the golden feathers molting from my forearms.

"You're unlike any nymph I've seen before. Now that you've learned to bring it out of yourself, I'm sure the king can find a use for you despite what appeared to be a failed attempt at escaping. You know wings can be quite useful, especially ones strong enough to withstand a deluge of arrows."

Ray picked a feather from the wind and tucked it into her jacket with a wink. Like I had her to thank for bringing out my nymph abilities, she waved for me to follow her.

"Let's get you back before Triton finds out what you've been up to. I won't tell him if you won't."

Shaky, I dusted off my pants and narrowed my eyes at the back of her head.

"You didn't have Triton's permission for this stunt of yours," I accused, remembering how upset he was with the guard that had nearly let me die in the dungeon.

Ray flicked her gaze over her shoulder with a bit of excitement to see what I would do next. This was entertaining for her. I could see that now. Her eyes glittered with anticipation.

"There wasn't time to get his seal of approval if that's what you're implying, but it would be disheartening for him to find out that you have been toying with him while joyriding and plotting to escape together with another man, his First Sentinel no less. I, however, returned you no worse for the effort, and will be happy to offer my support in rehabilitating his favorite sentinel back to his senses."

A light bulb went off in my head.

"You like him..."

"No," she corrected, "I love him. He is not only the best warrior of Atlantis; he is kind, he is just, and he will not be used by you." She took another step before stopping. Without turning around, she added, "I warned you to leave Dion out of it."

That was a warning... back when she was asking me about seducing the king?

She was not my friend.

"You're meant to be there when the Fate arrives, and at this rate, you're going to be late. For your sake, I hope she tells the king you play an important role in his future, or the next time you inevitably try to leave again... it will be your last. Dion trained me well, too well, but I'll make a deal with you."

I waited and after a long pause, obviously done to get my nerves on edge, Ray revealed her deal. "When I catch you again, and I will catch you. I'll let you go if you make an oath never to return to Atlantis."

She lifted a hand to stop any response I had without even seeing if I was going to object or agree. "No need to make your oath now. Best to never admit you plan on escaping again if you want to make it that far. And I want you to make it. Don't think just because of this," she waved to the littered ground of what could have been my massacre, "that I am against you. I'm doing my job."

Lia nudged me in the back with her snout to follow her and she whispered to me, "Your mother knew what you were capable of since you were born. Aless means defender. Only you can protect him now." Stumbling forward with another push of her head, she was acting like Dion was the one in trouble, not me. She wanted me to follow him, to protect him even when he abandoned me to Ray's custody.

How was my name reason enough to shoulder me with protecting a man that was the best warrior in Atlantis, a man that didn't need the protection of a doctor in training who didn't even have her first year of medical school yet?

"Make sure the herd doesn't interfere," Ray called out to the sentinel's and they gathered around Lia.

"They won't harm her will they?" I asked quickly, not liking where this was headed.

"There's a treaty in place. She'll be fine."

I wasn't convinced. "But you shot at her?"

"The treaty doesn't cover harboring a criminal yet to be judged. You're the reason why she'd be in danger." My chest tightened. It all came back to me. If I weren't here, Dion would be fine, and so would Lia and the herd.

"Defend," Lia said through a neigh as she was led away and I followed Ray back towards the city.

Ray whistled, and a few guards hidden behind the sentinels marched forward and transformed into centaurs that galloped to pick us up. Dion had long disappeared and was nowhere to be seen. Reluctantly, I climbed up and let the centaur, half-man half-horse, take me back with Ray to the royal estate of Atlantis.

Chapter 12

Cursed

"I'm struggling to understand why I am here, and she is not," Triton paced the ornately decorated room while Dion stood at attention, and Ray sat down, picking her fingernails with her dagger.

"The Fate sent word that her wishes were not followed for the nymph to be present at her arrival, so she adjusted her plans. She'll be at the arena for tonight's show and she's invited you to join her as long as you bring the girl," the messenger said while shifting uncomfortably. I didn't envy him the job of relaying news that wasn't ideal. This would be the second time Triton was stood up by the Fates.

Triton pinched the bridge of his nose.

"Someone tell me what happened?"

Ray kept her mouth shut, and merely switched which leg she leaned forward on, then eyed me with a smile. Taunting me about whether I would admit that my 'joyride' with Dion was the reason we were late to meeting the Fate at the designated time.

She was a Fate. She would have already known we weren't going to be there on time.

"Tickets to the Arena are always sold out," Dion enlightened the group. "If she is there then she already planned on going there instead of joining us for dinner."

It wasn't exactly an explanation of why we weren't there for her arrival, but there was no telling if she was even where she said she'd be, having known we weren't going to be on time.

"There's always the royal box seat left empty for you," Ray added.

"I was hoping for different circumstances before going to the Arena," Triton offered me his hand, a nervousness not accustomed to him giving him an odd glow. Gods apparently really did glisten, even their sweat was gorgeous on them. Ray narrowed her eyes at me, a warning to play my part and not cause any trouble. I took his hand and smiled at him, trying to forget that the only other circumstances I could think of that would have been different would be if I were participating in the Arena for my life. So, it was a bit more difficult for me to sympathize with the king's awkwardness at having to present me to the Arena as a guest of the royal viewing box instead of clad in armor and fending for the very breath in my lungs.

I gave his hand a bit more of a squeeze than intended.

"The Fate must think she has information worth enough to make up for the inconvenience of chasing her around," I assured him with a tight grin.

Triton patted my hand kindly, and it was difficult to remember this half naked man was a king who could kill me whenever he chose, instead of the man who recently lost his daughter, and is frustrated by the game he must play with the gods against him. His bright blue eyes were otherworldly and disarming. I couldn't help the blush on my cheeks as he held my hand in his, and he looked at me like what I had to say was a comfort to him, and as valuable as the Fate herself.

"I know she does," he agreed with me and then a soft laugh that could have made angels cry echoed in the room, "No other would tempt my ire at being led down a whirlpool without something that would make it all worth it. There is only one thing all of Olympus knows I would give anything for, and I am overjoyed at the prospect that after all these centuries, it will finally be mine." His skin was glowing golden, and he led me around him and into a twirl before leaning over to kiss the tops of my knuckles.

"Quickly, we will head to the Arena! My patience is at its end."

"Triton…" Dion warned his king. Some inside conversation played out between them.

Watching Dion, I couldn't read his expression; he stood stiff as stone. His deep blue eyes, which had once been so open and honest with me, were closed off and distant. He avoided eye contact with me. And I eased my hand from Triton's, discomfort growing exponentially with the contact.

Triton lifted a brow but chose to ignore the disappointment he might have seen in me.

"Your concern is noted, Dion. It matters not to me if she denies me this fate. I have long learned that even the Fates can bend, and she will not deny me what I seek."

Triton smiled at me, just me, while he spoke to Dion, "The Arena may be the perfect place to discuss the role of fate in this game we play. Ride ahead of us and ready for our arrival."

"Ray," Dion prompted. Both of them left the room, leaving me alone with the king.

"What are you planning?" I worried for the Fate. This didn't seem like a typical arrangement anymore. Something had changed, and his whole demeanor went from agitated at being stood up to being excited about what was to come.

His features softened, and he took a step toward me.

"It is true the Fate has disrespected my hospitality, but your fear for her is misplaced."

How did he know I was afraid?

"I have no intention of harming one of Zeus's favorite pets."

"What are your intentions?"

He took up my hand and placed it to his bare chest.

"I thought I had made that quite clear in my actions, Aless. You've awoken something inside me I thought long dead, and I now know why you were the one sent to start Apollo's prophecy."

I gulped, feeling his intensity grow, and the distance between us shrink.

"What is that?" I almost didn't want to know, not with that possessive twinkle about him, but his voice was so seductive, and I understood why gods had trouble accepting rejection. Who could say no to the power rush coursing through their veins at their touch, and the warmth in their bones at the way their eyes consumed you? It was hard not to want to melt into him and say yes to anything.

"My immortal enemy wanted me to destroy my own happiness with my own hands," he pulled me into him, and I felt my whole body shiver with his power flowing into me, "You are meant to be my wife, little angel. Do not think my sentinel's silence has hidden what you are from me."

Suddenly, I felt trapped in his embrace, afraid of what he meant by that. His wife...? I tried to push away but he held me firm.

"Do not jump to conclusions too quickly, my love. I would have married you even if you were merely a nymph, but I must admit I am much happier knowing you aren't. Do you know what this means?"

He asked excitedly but didn't wait to hear my answer. "I will not lose you as I have lost the others. A goddess such as yourself can stand by my side, defend the sea with me, and we can end this game together. The two of us. We can stand against the gods that wish you dead, and with you by my side, Atlantis will be free." Triton's chest was heaving with passion, and the cyclone of his thought eventually calmed for me to catch up to him.

I shook my head over and over. No, no, no, I thought to myself. This wasn't right, this was all wrong. He had it all wrong.

"I'm not a goddess," I objected, barely above a whisper. My shoulders stiffened, and I stared past him in shock.

"Hera sent you to me as my daughter's killer so that I would, with my own hands, destroy the one woman that was meant to be my wife. The only wife I was meant to have, the one that would lift up our kingdom, a goddess in your own right, bringing power back to the sea. Do you not see what you are? How you glow?"

"You're wrong." I pushed away from him, and he let me.

His blue eyes dulled, hurt by what was another rejection of the god of the sea. Unintended, but no matter how lonely I had felt before, or how much I nearly wished for a connection like what he was offering as I thought I was going to die, it didn't change that he was a king, a god, and I was just me.

Just me that had only a few bits of information to fill in the picture of who Triton was, and too much of the paint still red with the looming threat of imprisonment and death. Even as he proposed to me, which was what I thought that just was, a proposal included how someone had wanted him to kill me for murdering his daughter.

This didn't seem like the kind of foundation a strong marriage consisted of. He wanted loyalty, marriage... love, even, and that wasn't what was offered.

Power, most definitely.

Revenge, possibly.

But this was not love.

Whatever I stirred within him, whatever was awoken with my arrival, it wasn't love.

I didn't know why I was feeling so emotional over this, but I felt my eyes begin to water as I cupped his cheek in mine. Why was I crying? My lip quivered, but I forced myself to continue what I had tried to say to him, but only my body spoke. "This," my voice shook, "is not fate."

Triton tore his head from my hold with a groan, turning his head from me he then roared. His pained yell echoed through the dining room of his royal estate. I could feel his heart being shredded as if it were my own, and I then doubted my own words if this was what a nobody could do to a god.

Bent over the decorated table, his head hung, and he huffed to calm himself. His grip cracked the smoothed rock with his strength.

His voice was soft, barely heard, but there was no mistaking it. "I am a king," he slammed his fist, breaking the corner of the table, "Fate does not rule my future Aless, nor yours. If it had, you would be dead, and I would not have been born." The truth in his words resonated, and I flinched as he turned to face me. He stopped where he was surprisingly attuned to my fear, and his deep labored breaths showed me how torn he was between recognizing my needs and wanting to have his own.

Instead, he collapsed into a chair, covering his face with his hand.

Then he opened up to me, revealing a piece of himself to the woman that took his daughter from him.

"It was fate that my father would save my mother from Hera's vengeance on Zeus. If it weren't for his intervention, Zeus would have taken her, and Hera would have killed her. That is the fate of nymphs in our family.

"My mother was a powerful nymph, but still only a goddess by marriage. A god shares a bit of their power when they marry, making each other stronger–"

"Is that why–"

"No," he cut me off, as I did him, before I could confirm marrying me would make him stronger. Not that I believed that myself. I didn't feel powerful enough to make a god stronger. "My father would never admit this to anyone, but my mother's resentment couldn't pass up an opportunity to let me know the gods could not be trusted, even my father."

He paused, and this didn't seem like a conversation he should be having with his captive. This was the raw heart of a man that hadn't shared this story with anyone in a long time, if ever.

And I let him.

I should have ended it then, stopped him from giving me this piece of himself, but I didn't.

I listened, waited, and I honestly wanted to give him that bit of loyalty he never got from any part of his family. So, I walked over to the broken king at the broken table, and I sat next to him, squeezing his hand. Giving him the strength to let go of centuries of emotional trauma.

It wouldn't be enough, just this one time lending him an ear that wouldn't betray him, but I couldn't turn him away. Not like this.

Triton's wounded blue eyes swirled and watched me, at first confused, and then he gave me a sad smile.

"My mother knew Poseidon didn't love her, and his guilt, and possibly loneliness, made him try to make things work between them.

Being who he is, he courted his own wife until one day she finally felt something for him.

"The same day my sister and I were conceived, and the same day the fates revealed to Poseidon that they were the ones that told Hera he would one day find fated love with a goddess that would become more beautiful and more powerful than herself once they marry. Hera had insisted Poseidon marry my mother instead of merely courting because my mother was a nymph, meaning she would not be my father's fated love, and Zeus would no longer be tempted to stray from their own marriage. It was vengeance for both of them until my mother found out.

"Until my father pulled away from her, and my mother raged against Hera by informing all of Olympus that Zeus drove her from her home, and it was Poseidon and her that decided to get married so Hera couldn't have her killed in her jealousy. Everyone knows what Hera does to Zeus's conquests, but no one broadcasts it unless it's the way Hera wants the story told. It was then that Hera cursed my mother's male heirs to have all of their wives betray them, so they may experience what she had to endure because of her.

"So, all of my wives had betrayed me, and as they were all nymphs as my mother was, it is the curse of Hera that their betrayal should result in their death."

By his hand, I thought to myself as I held one of those very hands as it rested on the arm of his chair. I was torn between feeling sympathy for his loss and fear at what he was capable of. He'd had to deal with manipulation all his life. It wasn't a wife he needed; he needed someway to end Hera's influence over him.

"I don't believe in curses," I took my hand back, and leaned back in my own chair, not wanting to look at him lest I lose my nerve to speak, "My mom told me every curse, even ones given by gods themselves, are merely self-fulfilling prophecy, they are not as unbreakable as the words of a true seer, and even those words can be bent to your own interpretation." I shifted uncomfortably, feeling his gaze on me.

"She'd be pissed to know it was those words that made me ignore her and my sister's warnings to stay away from the sea. No offense, but this hasn't exactly been the best experience for me," I told him honestly, though I regretted it immediately after and cringed. What was I thinking being all open with the king that just yesterday was considering entering me into the Arena as my judgment for killing his daughter?

I groaned.

"It was Hera that lured each wife to betray me. And it was Atlantis's laws, and my oath as king, that forced me to fulfill their punishments. The curse, as you say, is indeed a self-fulfilled prophecy." My own words broke me as he said them, weighted with guilt. "I had betrayed my wives just as they betrayed me. I am the monster you think me as. I did not care for them enough to step down as king. I did not trust them enough to do right by Atlantis."

That was unexpected. I couldn't keep avoiding him. Watching him, reading his eyes as he bared his soul to me broke whatever resolve I had to hate him.

He was a god that needed just me. I could sense it in the way he spoke, in the very air we breathed, that what I said or didn't say next was important to him. It was my words that haunted him that night I called him a monster.

Finally, I choked out, "You would do that?" He would step down as king to stop the curse against him?

"Would you want me to?" It was like he was pleading with me to be his wife, and that same panic I had before came back tenfold. I darted my attention away once more, biting my lip and crossing my arms.

"What would be so different about me? You've had at least seven wives that I know of, and you didn't do that for any of them."

I could hear the shame in his voice. "I didn't. I'm sure if I had, I would have met you under different circumstances, and perhaps you'd view me differently as well. I cannot change the past Aless, though I would if I could, for you."

"Why?" He had no reason to care this much for me. This was a trick of the gods, all part of their game. It had to be. I found myself asking this question a lot lately, and each time I could hear Dion's silky, quizzical voice remind me that I may not be asking the right question at all. The why doesn't matter, I could hear him say, it's what you do next that does.

What would I do next?

"When you are young, there are too many distractions to read the signs exploding in front of you, to parse out the infatuation, the need to possess, and the greed from the very subtle ingredients that make up truth. I have lived a long life, and I can see our truth. From the moment I laid eyes on you, I saw the signs, but they were much too subtle to do more than give me pause. That pause saved my life."

Now he had me even more confused. Wasn't it my life that he had spared?

Gently, he hooked my chin with a finger and tilted it towards him. He had moved his chair and was leaning in close. His bright blue eyes were soft and comforting, like a summer night with the sound of waves lapping at the shore.

I didn't speak.

"Why do you think I was so upset when I found you had been sent to the dungeon?"

"To make me think you hadn't set up everything, so I was sent there to begin with," I told him the truth of his fancy lies. He thought I wouldn't know, that I hadn't been told by everyone he was just itching for me to screw up and be sent there. I wasn't going to fall for his beautiful blue eyes, and his charming, chiseled face with that dumb blue-white hair, and goatee looking like some sort of punk-rock star. Get a hold of yourself, Aless.

He shook his head. "I did want to send you there for a day, so Dion would be forced to stop keeping you from me, but I changed my mind after you stormed into my rooms. You made me acknowledge the monster inside of me, and I knew then that your heart was fierce enough to stand up to a god, and much too precious to be won by force. You were right about everything, and I want to earn your virtue, Aless. I want it to be freely given and one day I can be worthy of such a gift.

"You hold my life in your hands," he took up both of my hands and placed them on his chest above his heart, "Hera knows what she tried to take from us, and even still her curse persists by circumstance alone. I will not force you to marry me, but there are limited ways I can free you from the laws we've entangled ourselves in by way of our first meeting. Even should I step down as king, my successor would be bound to continue your judgment. What will you have me do, and I will do it." Triton rested his forehead against my own, and tilted to brush his lips against my cheek, then my other. My whole face flushed in color at how slowly his lips glided from one side to the other, narrowly missing my mouth, and his nose rubbing his warmth on me.

One twitch and we'd be kissing, and it frightened me how my lips parted, almost acting of their own accord, wanting nothing more than to bridge that minuscule gap.

Damn him if he didn't know what he did to me. This probably wasn't the first time he'd seduced a girl, and I certainly wasn't going to be the last, I reminded myself.

This wasn't real, and this wasn't some subtle truth. I pinched my lips tightly together against all the humming vibrations in my skin, and the tingles in my belly that begged for me to have my way with him, even if I knew it wouldn't last. I'd never had this before, this feeling, this closeness, this attention, and every hormone in my body responded to him.

He smelled like the sea, and brine, and... Dion.

My face flushed.

That was the opening I needed to finally pull away. Even so, it was slow, and I couldn't bring myself to pull my hand away from his chest. If anything, this distance made things worse. Now, I could see his eyes again, and they wanted me. There was a hunger there I recognized, and yet he let me lead how far this went.

All he had to do was kiss me, and I knew I wouldn't fight him on it. My heart raced, thudding in my chest. My butt is on the edge of my seat, as our legs were practically laced together at the thighs, my knee far too close to his golden armor breeches. Thank the sea, he was dressed in his armor, even if the top was a bit light on much more than a shoulder and a single breast plating that my hand was currently sliding underneath. Its cool metal was all I tried to focus on unsuccessfully.

I had to change the unspoken topic building between us, or I'd be lost.

Licking my lips to try to speak, I released a soft moan that was reciprocated with one of his own, confirming what each of us was struggling with. It couldn't have been easy for a god to deny himself what was probably freely given to him by literally anyone. And I was turning down an opportunity for my first experience to be with a sea god.

If I ever made it back home, I'd be sure to kick myself for this moment later. I told him the truth, "As long as I'm a captive to your laws here... this," whatever this was, "can't happen."

Triton took a deep calming breath, and pressed his lips to my forehead, heating my skin, and pulled away.

"I understand."

Then I surprised even myself, "What are our options?"

He gave me a broad smile. I had unwittingly given him an opening. I'd basically told him I wanted whatever this was, and how could we make it happen? What was wrong with me?

"I'm assuming marriage is something you'd like to reserve until you've sorted your own subtle truths?"

I coughed at his bluntness and the absurdity of his offer. Marry a god, I couldn't even imagine. And I certainly didn't want to become a queen of anything, let alone an underwater city that I couldn't leave without drowning. I wasn't trying to rule. I just wanted to go back to school to become a doctor and save lives.

"You'd be correct."

He frowned, but continued anyway undeterred, don't think I didn't catch his hint about until I discovered my own truths... about us, then of course I would marry him in his mind, "Dion is right about the Arena, but I don't feel comfortable with this solution. When you enter, your immortality is stripped, and even a goddess can be vulnerable. It is similar to the spells that prevent the sea's magic from entering the dungeons. And why I was so upset no one told me you were there. I had let my own shame prevent me from seeking you out sooner. For that, I must atone as you see fit. I feared you would never forgive me."

"I haven't," I clarified and seeing the hurt there I amended, "yet. There must be another option."

"An extended engagement," he offered hopefully, a gleam in his eye. That was exactly what he had wanted from the beginning, the sneaky god. First tell me what I don't want, then tell me something worse, then give me the pretend compromise that still gets him what he wants while luring me into a false sense of victory at hoping an engagement could postpone the marriage indefinitely, and I could go on living my life with my sister on real land avoiding ever returning to the sea to uphold that particular commitment.

Then an idea struck hold.

A bargain.

If Persephone could make a deal between the gods, then so could I, but preferably without the split custody arrangement.

"I won't get engaged without my family." I narrowed my eyes at him for good measure, and his skin glowed like he had somehow tricked me into agreeing to marry him. That wasn't what I said exactly, and my mom was very clear about never committing to any oaths that were too specific with a god. I thought she was a bit too religious at the time, but all that random information on gods has actually kept me sane during all of this.

"Of course not," he readily agreed.

Only a little bit more, Aless, you can do this.

"I can't stay here forever," I continued.

"People forget my father was not just a god of the sea, but also of the earth itself. I wish nothing more for us to enjoy the fruits of both the land and the sea." He was practically vibrating with power, surging off of him with his excitement at what he thought I was saying yes to.

He waited for my other conditions.

This was it; this was make or break. My hands dug into my thighs, and I watched as Triton's short spiky hair wafted in the invisible wind that only touched him in the room, as if he were underwater. I could sense the itch in him to scoop me up into his arms and claim his victory, but he held himself back, near to exploding. I almost felt bad at what I was about to ask for, and what it would mean.

I bit my lip.

Almost.

"You'd probably scare my mother if we don't handle this right," I began, and his jaw tightened, but he nodded for me to continue, "I'll need someone to go get them if I can't go back yet."

"By law you cannot be unaccompanied," he confirmed, his voice all business, but I heard what he wasn't saying. I wasn't allowed to leave here unless we were married.

I nodded politely, understanding. His shoulders relaxed after finding me agreeable. This was going to be harder than I thought. He was being rather reasonable, considering his position.

"I'd simply like to pick who goes, and tell them what to say, and where to go," I somewhat clarified. It was deceptive, I know, but what choice did he really give me?

"Consider it done, whoever you wish. If it is within my power, they will retrieve your family, but," My heart stopped right then, did he realize what I was doing? Was I caught? "The engagement will not wait for their arrival. We will announce ourselves tonight at the Arena."

"Excuse me?" I stammered in shock.

"I promise you the engagement will be as long as you'd like for it to be, until you are ready. We have plenty of time to get to know each other better, but I do not wish for you to be Atlantis' scaptive any longer, and I do not wish for the first time my subjects to see you after your arrival to be anything less than the goddess you are as their rightful queen. Please tell me you understand?"

It was strange having a god plead for me to be okay with what he literally just demanded of me. I couldn't balance the scale between the obvious control he was used to having in any given situation, and the sweet way his blue eyes watched me, and this melting feeling I got at how hard he was trying to do what he thought was right by me. Even if he didn't realize how he hadn't been giving me the only option that would be acceptable, my freedom.

No strings attached.

No marriage guarantee.

Just a trip with his trident to Florida's shores, and maybe, when I was certain I wouldn't be dragged back against my will, we could date.

I would have happily said yes then.

But he was right. He was cursed to have me betray him.

He'd already given me what I wanted.

I could have anyone go retrieve my family, and I said nothing about whether they were allowed to bring me with them.

Mavron, you better not let me down.

This was the only shot I had outside of the Arena.

"I understand."

Triton quickly scooped me up into his arms and spun us around with a joyful laugh.

"Thank the seas. You are meant to defend the seas, my Aless. It is written in the stars. Goddess of protection, understanding, compassion, and the very air I breathe. I will give you everything I have and more if it will make you glow."

My heart pounded in my chest, and his beautiful words had me wrapped up in the moment, thinking about what kind of a life this would have been if I had met him under different circumstances. If I hadn't been attacked by his daughter, and I hadn't poisoned her, and I hadn't become his prisoner. What kind of life would we have had?

My arms wrapped around his neck; I smiled up at him—this broken king of the sea. This god who thinks me to be his fated wife.

How could I feel so loved and so trapped all at the same time?

When he set me back on my feet water swirled around me, transforming my clothes into liquid blue silver. It sparkled like the stars, and dipped low beneath my arms, giving a bit of tasteful side boob, and the bodice wrapped up around my neck like a halter that draped in waves down my back.

I twisted and turned, trying to see myself, but it was Triton that said everything that I needed to hear, "You are magnificent."

Plucking a pearl from somewhere on his armor he pressed it to my forehead, and it grew, forming a circlet. I patted my head and felt the ornate carvings that were smooth and felt like lace with all of its weavings of swirls and etchings.

I felt like a princess.

But I couldn't help the dark feeling that rotted in my gut about tricking a god, and remembered what Dion had said about his past... There was no place on land nor sea that was safe from the gods once you've caught their attention.

Chapter 13

Too High

T riton's chariot was just inside an outdoor garden from his estate made entirely of gold, and formed like a crashing wave of water. The wheels were studded with pearls and precious stones. When you tilted your head just right, the golden water looked like it was moving, an active wave ready to take flight.

Offering me his hand, I stepped into the chariot, my foot sinking into the gold as if it truly was like surfing a wave. Falling forward into Triton's outreached arms, he tucked me into his embrace.

"Hang tightly, my love," he advised while keeping an arm around me. The other hand reached out, and the sky churned above us, or I should say the sea beyond the barrier of the city. Then a bright light burst forth like lightning caught in Triton's outstretched hand. His trident gleamed, still dripping with salt water and pulsing with power.

Tapping the trident to the golden floor of the chariot, a flash struck in front of us for each tap, forming what looked like a constellation in front of us, and then I heard the call of a horse. And the sound of flapping wings until a gorgeous white horse with stunning angelic wings stomped at the ground.

Pegasus.

We were riding to the Arena in the royal sea chariot, pulled by a mythical winged horse, and I was awestruck.

"We'll be making an entrance at the Arena, and Atlantis always loves to see you when they can. I thought you'd want to meet the future Goddess of the Sea and Queen of Atlantis," he spoke to Pegasus.

Pegasus snorted and huffed kicking at the grassy ground of the garden and over top of it I heard a musical voice object to his introduction of me, "As much as I am entertained by our chats, Triton, no one is foolish enough to marry you again."

Looking up, I saw his smile flatten, and I knew I wasn't the only one who heard her speak.

"I'll advise you to refrain from insulting my fiancée," Triton warned.

"I was insulting you," she corrected, "and she can hear me just fine, so she's aware you come with a curse that's killed anyone you've tried to keep."

Clearing his throat, he tried to stop Pegasus's rant. "I've not kept that from her."

"Really?" she asked, curious.

It was then that the horse finally turned her head to see me. Her eyes were as blue as Triton's. For a few moments she blinked, staring at me, then she bucked her hind legs back, pushing away from the chariot neighing and grunting, and shuffling around bucking her head in a frenzy.

"A ghost!"

"What is the meaning of this?" Triton demanded.

"She looks just like her," Pegasus panted. "How do you not see it?"

"Like who?"

"Medusa."

Triton squeezed me closer to him as if protecting me from what Pegasus was inferring. "Your mother died a long time ago. If she resembles her, then that's Poseidon's problem not ours."

"He won't let you marry her, not even Hera and Zeus will appreciate the reminder of what they allowed to have happen to her doppelganger. She could be her reincarnation. She deserves the chance to have a life not cut short by games and politics again. You would do that for me, wouldn't you, brother? Let her go, don't let the gods have her," Pegasus pleaded, and Triton looked absolutely torn.

"You would have me let go of my one chance at happiness?"

"Would you let your one happiness be targeted by the gods once again ruining her second chance at life?" Pegasus reasoned, her wings spread wide, and her head held high. She was powerful, beautiful, and Dion was right about her. I was glad I got to hear some of her story before seeing her in person. Even if she was convinced I was her reincarnated mother.

"You think I am–"

Pegasus cut me off, "You can't stay here, but you can not leave either..." Now, I was even more confused about what she wanted. I had hoped she'd help Triton realize he couldn't keep me here, and possibly let me go without any engagement or marriage.

"Aless," Triton lifted my chin, aware of my stunned state, "My sister has always been impulsive, and hesitates to pause long enough to let her reason catch up with her mouth. We should speak with the Fate before we try to hide from gods that already know you exist."

He was right. I got into this mess because someone already knew I existed, and leaving Triton didn't stop them from trying to find another way to kill me. I wished he didn't make so much sense, because now I was doubting my attempts at planning an escape when being with Triton was probably the safest place for me to be until I could figure out how to stop someone else from finding me again.

"That's why I said she couldn't leave... yet," Pegasus snarked.

"I don't recall a yet being thrown in there," Triton lifted a brow, and then he kneeled down before me, trident in one hand, and mine in the other, "We can run from the gods if that is what you wish," he waited and when I merely stared at him he continued, "or we can stand against them until they crack as even the strongest do under the constant tide of the sea."

The trident hummed with power, rising to the challenge, and even I could feel myself stand taller, firmer, and unable to shake the need growing in me to confront my enemies. But were they my enemies or his? Did it matter?

Bending over his face, looking into those large blue pools, I cupped his cheeks.

"There is no pride lost in knowing my own limitations. I am not ready to face off against gods, and I may never be."

He closed his eyes, and leaned into my hand, pressing his cheek into it with his hand cupping mine. Then he gave a short nod and then kissed my palm.

"They know you're here. Any number of gods could have assisted in your journey here, and Hera, not recognizing you, could be an act; or perhaps she had someone else handle logistics. It doesn't matter–"

"You still plan on marrying her?"

"Whether we leave or stay doesn't change my intentions," he said firmly and stood tall against his sister, whose wings made her look far more imposing.

"If you leave without dad returning, you'd leave Atlantis vulnerable," she pondered out loud.

"When have you cared about what happens to Atlantis or the sea?"

Pegasus snuffed. "You're a jackass. I was pissed off at dad back then for disappearing when he wasn't the only one that lost mom. I lost both of them, and Chrys... well, you know."

"You can't blame him Peg, Chrys was mourning your mother in his own way. He thought he could bring honor back by proving himself to Olympus, and joining the pantheon."

I felt uncomfortable being present during their personal conversation about the past, but curiosity numbed that part of me. A tightness in my stomach made me lightheaded as I listened to their family history. Lifting my hand to my head, I swayed until my hip caught on the edge of the chariot, and Triton stopped talking to help steady me.

"Tell me what you're feeling?" He sounded worried. I doubted it was normal for a goddess to nearly faint, and it certainly didn't make me feel as immortal as he believed me to be.

My throat clenched, and I grabbed at it, trying to breathe. I was having a panic attack. I knew it as it was happening, but I couldn't stop myself. Couldn't reason with myself.

"Can't breathe," I gasped.

"Bend over, I've got you," he soothed while he let his trident clang to the side, and he rubbed my back. He allowed his trident, a source of power to fall, more concerned with me. And then it hit me harder than I could have imagined that all those pretty words he gave me actually meant something. I meant something to him.

More than power.

More than his title.

More than Atlantis.

How was that possible?

Hyperventilating, I felt my breathing quicken at that realization. Triton cared for me. I saw it when I came out of the dungeon, the emotion in his eyes as he held my hand while I laid in bed. But he knew nothing about me...

Didn't he?

How could he?

"I've pushed you too fast," his voice cracked at the sight of my teary eyes. "We can stay here. We don't have to do anything until you're ready. Tell me what you need. Anything," he struggled with not being in control, not knowing how to fix me. I was just as broken as him.

Pressing myself into his chest, absorbing the comfort he offered, I finally steadied my nerves. His hands kept tracing soothing lines along my exposed back, under the draped fabric of my dress. Then a new sensation tingled through me as those fingers left a trail of heat in their wake that sent ripples to my core. I flushed at the thought of what was happening to me and remembered Peg was still watching.

Shoving away from him, my cheeks heated.

"I'm fine," I quickly excused my abrupt action. Even if I wanted to, I couldn't meet either of their faces for fear of what I would find there. That they knew why I pushed him away. That they could see how torn I was about what was happening.

Did it matter?

It did. Somehow, I had grown to care what he thought of me in such a short time.

"I don't know what's wrong with me." I wiped at my face. "I guess I've just been missing my own sister. This is the longest I've been away from her."

"Triton is right," Peg added, "You should see the Fate. She could help you both figure out what to do next. I shouldn't be telling you this, but I overheard Zeus talking about Apollo's prophecy. He seems to think that if dad doesn't return to claim his trident again soon that he could lose his immortality, and aside from losing a brother..."

he's worried it will make himself look weak and risk his rule over Olympus."

"Why are you telling me this? You know, without the trident, I'm bound to the sea."

"I know. But with the trident, dad could change that for you."

"Quit calling him that," Triton groaned, "he was no father to either of us. We don't even know where he is, and you said it yourself if he sees Aless—"

Peg sighed with a horsey huff. "Aless, if you're anything like my mother, then you'd rather disappear than be the cause of a war, or rather die yourself than let someone else suffer.

"If you want to survive the gods, you'll have to remind yourself that sometimes war is coming no matter what you do... and if you die, you weaken the ones you want to protect the most. If you're gone, if you disappear..." Peg turned her head away, her voice merely a whisper, choked with emotion, "who will defend the ones you leave behind?"

She was the one left behind. Her mother left her behind, and I looked like her. Something came over me as I listened to her, and this feeling was bursting inside of me to hold her. I had to hold her. I had to tell her it was going to be alright.

Wind wafted behind me, sending my hair flying. Feathers fluttered around me, coalescing until I found myself above the chariot. Triton's hand lifted with mine until he let me go, and I landed next to Pegasus, wrapping my arms around her neck.

Pressing my face against her long face, I knew then that I hadn't imagined things out on the field when the arrows had crashed down around us... the feathers were mine.

I had wings.

Pegasus transformed into her human form, wrapping herself into my embrace. With her own wings tucked behind her back, mine cocooned her now naked body.

Then I answered her, "I will." I will defend who was left behind, but I couldn't do that while I was a prisoner. I wouldn't run away, I told myself, it didn't matter what the Fate said tonight.

If the gods wanted a fight, they would have one, with or without me. Maybe Pegasus was right. With me, they were stronger... even if all I gave them was hope.

If her mother was anything like me, then she must not have thought she had a choice but to leave her behind. In my heart, I knew it had to be true.

A strange thought came to me then, something my mom used to say, "You win with your heart, not your sword. You don't have to bleed to gain power. Absolute power isn't forced absolutely." Then, in my own words, I knew I was here for a reason. "War may come for us, but we don't need to meet it with a sword. We need information."

"We?" Triton tentatively placed a hand on my shoulder. He sounded pleased.

Peg peeked from under my wing, her white hair similar to her brothers aside from the slight blue tint.

"I can get us more information," Peg added, "for you." She narrowed her eyes at Triton. The 'you' wasn't him, but me, and I gave her a squeeze before releasing her. My wings curled to protect her privacy once I remembered she was naked, and then I shoved Triton to turn around. I didn't like the idea of him seeing her like that. Too many Greek myths involved brother-sister relationships, and oh my gods... I was jealous... of his sister's beautiful body.

My hands flung up to his eyes like blinders, making him only have eyes for me. I blushed and averted my gaze, but through my peripheral I could see him smile at my reaction.

Immediately I felt the need to explain myself again. "We," I emphasized, "are going to be late to meeting the Fate again, and she may leave if we don't get going."

"Right," he placated, though it was obvious he knew that wasn't the reason I pulled him away, "Peg," he addressed without removing his blue eyes from me, making me squirm with heat, "We have a Fate to meet."

Then he leaned in, still smiling at me, he whispered in my ear, "Goddess," his finger traced my bare shoulder, then ran over my feathers making me shiver, "I have but only one desire, and it is yours."

I gulped down my extra saliva. Why did he have to be so charming?

"You don't even know me," I tried to reason with myself more than him.

My heart hammered in my chest at how close he was.

"I don't have to know everything about you to know who you are, what kind of a person you are. You're the lightning that stands up to a god. You're the tide that stays strong even after a storm. You're the sun that warms the hearts of monsters. You're the moon that shines even in the darkness, guiding the lost. You're the spirit that defends the weary, even when you have more reason not to."

"How can you know that?"

"The same way I knew you would not choose your freedom over protecting Atlantis. The same reason I know the sea would not drown you, but you still made a choice to swim towards Atlantis rather than away from it. You may not have known why at the time, but you were not captured by Dion... you found him and confessed while begging him to take you to Atlantis. You," he held me close, "Aless, chose to be a prisoner of Atlantis to protect it. I know this in my heart. That is the kind of person you are. And I look forward to learning all of the history of how you became that person in time, but I don't need that to know how I feel about you."

Peg snorted, neighing behind us, now back in horse form, "You're going to make me barf." But I could hear the sniffle in her tone telling how touched she was with what Triton said.

"No one's ever felt that way about me before," I confessed.

"I find that hard to believe." Triton kissed my forehead, then led me back to the chariot. The gesture was sweet, and I found myself wanting him to stay close. A hand brushing against my arm, his torso against my shoulder, but I found my wings flapping with nowhere to go. They wouldn't retract.

When they came out to stop the arrows, they came and went so fast I hardly realized they were my own. Disappearing in a flurry of feathers in the wind, I didn't get the chance to see them. Now when they came out touched by the loss of Peg's mother... they wouldn't go away.

Glancing over my shoulder at the feathery appendages, I hesitated before joining Triton in the chariot.

"They won't go away..." I mumbled.

It was Pegasus that chimed in on the subject of wings, "I've found that my wings never listen to me when my emotions are too stimulated," the way she said stimulated her voice lowered and became sultry.

"Stimulated..." I repeated, freaking out.

"Intense fear, anger, happiness... lust," she had to end on lust.

"What about nervous?" I amended, not wanting to admit anything else.

"Sure, that's part of it," she teased.

Keeping my focus ahead of me, and certainly not wanting to make eye contact with either of them I prompted, "We should get going."

Arriving at the Arena in the only chariot capable of flying with the assistance of Pegasus, Triton held his trident aloft like a rally cry, while I stood frozen, finally understanding just how massive the crowd staring at us was. Well, staring at a god and a divine flying horse. I prayed they were both distraction enough, where all those small forms of people below were not paying attention to me.

The chariot stopped above the mass of spectators, and Pegasus made a show of her wings while her two front hooves reared up in the air. Her white hair flourished as her slender head bucked up, and she neighed, performing for them. There were no clouds in a sky made of water, but even so, the atmosphere sparked flickering with her power.

Atlantians cheered at the display and Triton circled his trident and water swirled magically like a dance around us. From the sky, water from the sea splashed down in a tidal wave controlled by him, staying within form, never once crashing into the people below other than a light mist on their faces.

Suddenly, the crowd was quiet, a hush before they pointed up at us and the hum of growing curiosity ramped up again. I looked up to where they were pointing, and something sparkled and glinted in the water.

Murmurs became stomping of feet, and then loud boisterous accolades as the shiny object landed in my hands. It was a pair of golden crab claws, and I was even more confused by the uproar of excitement.

"This is my gift to you," Triton bent down on one knee, bowing his head with his trident at his side, "Please accept my mother's wedding crown. It will bring me great pleasure to see you wear it."

I wasn't sure how I was supposed to wear them, but knowing it was a crown of some sort at least told me they belonged on my head. There were too many watching us for me to turn him down in front of his subjects. This was much too precious of a gift for me to keep it, but I would wear it for now. Lifting the crab claws, I remembered I still had the pearl circlet on and nearly pulled away, trying to figure out how to attach them. Before I could, the claws snapped to the sides of my head and tucked behind my ears.

The golden claws seemed to make sound echo around me, making it difficult to concentrate.

I tried to focus on where we were headed, the royal box seating, and saw Dion and Ray standing there. I saw her lips move, and with precision her voice became clear, as if she were in front of me now.

"Good for her," Ray said. "Guess she found something valuable enough that he'd marry her."

My eyes flicked to Dion's lips, and his voice came into focus. This golden claw crown was more than just decorative, after all. "She doesn't know what she's doing."

"I'd say she knows exactly what she's doing," Ray countered. "When has Triton ever bowed to anyone other than Poseidon? She might be the first wife to survive him. I knew the tramp had something special about her. Look at those golden wings. I thought I was imagining them before."

"Enough," Dion growled, "She's watching us."

"What does that matter? They still have a few rounds of pumping up the Arena after that display. Atlantis wants to let the excitement linger for a bit after finally having King Triton present them with the first queen in centuries."

"She wears Amphitrite's crown," as if that was explanation enough, though for me it was. It told me that he knew I could hear him and he knew what the crown did, but Ray wasn't easily convinced.

"It pairs nicely with the pearl crown his previous wives wore doesn't it, lucky shark?"

"Ray," Dion said tightly, "when has any item given to someone by a god ever been just an item? The power of the sea was infused into the crown and anywhere there is seawater she can hear its call. It was said to be used as a way for Poseidon to talk with his wife no matter where in the sea he was, but in such close proximity it would act like an amplifier for anyone not just a god of the sea."

"You can't believe everything you hear about the gods. Sometimes they like to exaggerate."

"She hasn't taken her eyes from us. Is that proof enough for you?" Dion watched me carefully. "Aless," he sounded sad when he said my name, then he whispered, "little goddess, if you fly too high, how am I to reach you?"

"What are you mumbling about?" Ray waved at Triton and me before elbowing Dion in the side. I gasped as he doubled over in pain, still not fully healed from his injury.

My attention was brought back to Triton who was talking to me now, "My mother told me that when she wore her crown, she could stay in contact with my father no matter where he was, and the same could be done for me as long as I hold the trident. I wanted you to have this, so that you would always have a way of getting a hold of me, no matter where either of us goes."

I looked up at him, and his blue eyes seemed troubled. Did he know I still planned on leaving him?

"I can't keep these," I began, "they are much too important."

"You are important," he wouldn't hear of it.

I acquiesced for now, but I'd leave them for his true wife to receive one day before I left. It wasn't mine to keep.

He couldn't truly mean what he was saying, so I dismissed his sweet words and tried to find Dion again, only to see Ray by herself in the booth.

What right did he have to be upset about me being with Triton? He was the one that put me in this situation to begin with, and he had the nerve to just disappear when he said he would help me. That was the third time he's abandoned me.

Left me to spend over a week in the dungeon. One.

Left me to fend for myself with Ray after a barrage of arrows.

Two.

And again, left me to handle myself alone with the king of Atlantis while forced into an engagement.

Three.

I fumed, thinking about it.

"You seem upset," Triton observed, and kept his smile while waving to our audience.

"I feel manipulated," I admitted to him, an edge to my voice. "Why do I feel like your mother's crown means more to Atlantis than merely a gift from their king?"

He cleared his throat, taken aback by my blunt assessment. "That's because it does mean more. It's a show of my intentions towards you."

"Were you serious about leaving everything behind for me?"

"Of course."

"Even being a king?"

"If necessary," he replied carefully, "I have lived a long life, and just like my father did with me, I could appoint someone else to be the herald of Poseidon."

"It's that simple?"

He hesitated before answering, "Simple enough."

The way he said simple didn't instill trust that he would follow through, but I didn't need him to. And trust was hard to come by when I was introduced into this world of myth and legend with an attempt on my life and incarceration.

I had let myself dream for a moment that the warm feeling I got when he told me he'd sacrifice his power for me was real. That any of this was real. For a moment, I clutched at my chest at the swelling of a kind of sad happiness. If we were meant to be together, he wouldn't have to sacrifice so much to be with me, and I wouldn't dare ask it of him.

But wasn't that the point?

We weren't meant to be together.

I squeezed his hand and smiled.

For now, I'd just enjoy the moment.

And pretend that we were.

Chapter 14

Fate

Waiting in the balcony reserved for the king, we had the best view of the Arena. Triton lifted his trident in the air, and the large space filled with water. The Arena was like a fishbowl, and inside floated two gladiators. One dove down, and their lower body transformed into a shark, and their mouth filled with rows of sharp teeth.

Their opponent dove after them. She glided through the water without any obvious fishy modalities. Her black hair waved like ink about her before she faced off with the shark hybrid.

Keeping her eyes on the shark, she stroked the water in front of her like a dance. Circling the woman, the shark-person made to dive underneath and strike from below. She made no move to avoid the incoming attack.

Golden ribbons glided through the woman's fingers until she snatched one; surprisingly, with one tug, the shark froze, her mouth open. Slowly, the shark rolled, going belly up, and rose until she was within the woman's reach.

Her lips moved, and I focused in on her words to the shark-lady. "This is not an act. Zeus will not spare you when the Olympic Trials begin." Her golden eyes flicked up to me, like she wasn't just watching the crowd, but me, and only me, when she said, "Poseidon is vulnerable until his power is restored. The trident alone cannot save him. He needs a protector, but he is too proud... too hurt to accept it willingly, because he knows the truth.

"The truth is that protecting him, protecting the sea, joining the Olympians will begin your curse anew. Too beautiful, too powerful, and much too virtuous little goddess," she was talking to me, I thought, shocked. I didn't feel like any of those things, and yet her voice sucked me in, and I couldn't stop staring.

She reached out in the water towards me, and she grabbed another ribbon in front of her. Gently she wrapped it around her arm and lifted it up like an art form.

The ribbon changed colors from golden to black.

"Death comes for both of you." Another ribbon entwined with the black, a night sky blue, a deep ocean delved in shadows. They diverged, came together, and brightened, only to scatter into dust.

My heart raced, feeling dread overcome me at the beautiful display.

Sublime terror and dark divine wrapped into a single sensation.

"History likes patterns; yours was cut, and new growth emerges likening the same path it took before. Another war, another hero, another sacrifice. Embrace what is feared, and a new pattern will appear. Beware history will fight you, and many paths will act to correct what is not patterned with your fate, Gorgon's Angel of Terror and Protection. Two faces of a monster's truth."

Water swirled around her, and she emerged straddling the shark-being's back. The crowd cheered as the top human half completely disappeared within the whites of the wave until only the shark remained. Her body quadrupled in size, a large white shark with a dark-haired woman riding expertly atop. Ribbons surrounded them, wrapping and wrapping.

Then nothing.

They were both gone.

Shark and rider vanished.

I heard her voice again. "There are spies everywhere."

The crab shell crown was still pinpointing her, and as I searched, I found her again in the crowd pretending to cheer with the rest of the audience. She winked, and slid through the rows of people.

She knew that only I could hear her. She knew I would have Amphitrite's crown.

She was the Fate.

"She's trying my patience," Triton mused, "If it weren't for how happy I am in this moment, I would be chasing after her." He pressed his cheek to the top of my head, kissing my forehead. "What game do you suppose she's playing with us by avoiding our summons?"

He didn't hear her, of course he didn't.

This was her plan all along; to give me a message of my fate ensuring only I would receive it. There were spies everywhere.

Did she not trust Triton?

"I don't think she's avoiding us," I decided to reveal that much. He has to know that being isolated didn't mean Atlantis was impenetrable. "She's protecting us." Maybe not us, but me at the very least.

"What are you thinking, my love?"

"We have to give her an opportunity to meet us alone. There are spies in Atlantis."

"Yes," he agreed, "there are. I'll arrange for something more private."

He whispered into my hair, "You'll make a fine Queen," I tensed up, "when you're ready."

"Have you two ever thought about the fact that the Fates, all of them, are Zeus's pets? She might be luring you both into a trap," Ray advised, and I had almost forgotten she was there.

"I'll keep that in mind," Triton acknowledged.

"You should have a few sentinels posted for whatever you're planning," Ray added.

"Have Dion informed, we have a short window of opportunity before the Fate leaves Atlantis."

"Of course." Ray bowed and left the viewing box.

"I look forward to finding different ways of making your wings come out," Triton purred, tracing my now bare shoulder blade. Shivers ran down my spine at his touch. My skin on my hands rippled, and I had to focus not to lose control. I knew that if my feathered claws came out, so would my wings. He couldn't have that kind of control over me—this wasn't real. This couldn't be real, and I needed to figure out how to control this myself without his kind of assistance.

I changed the subject. "Can you trust your sentinels? Or who they may be overheard by?"

Back to things more pressing, like spies.

"No, that's why I sent them away."

"But you just–"

"I just gave us some time to find our Fate before she has time to plan an ambush, or a spy can intervene. Shall we?" He gave a short bow and offered me his arm, with his other hand readying his trident. The trident Poseidon needed to protect himself. Did Triton know his father was in danger?

Taking his arm, he commanded the water from the Arena to guide us from the viewing booth, and into the suspended fishbowl. I took a deep breath, and we dove to the bottom, and beneath where there appeared to be a tunnel where the water had come from to begin with.

When we popped up, we were surrounded by the gladiators of the Arena, who bowed at the presence of their king.

Water glistened off his chest and beaded in his blue-white hair. Skin glowing, his blue eyes bright and ethereal.

"Long live the sea," they hummed with their hands over their breast.

An older man stepped forward, head still bowed.

"We apologize for the unscheduled opening act, my king."

"Do not think on it, Sylvie. Fates have a way of manipulating even the best laid plans. It is me who must apologize that I will not be able to watch the remainder of the show."

"Act?" I wondered out loud. Show?

Triton merely smiled at my confusion, petting my hand as it held onto his arm.

"I do hope you'll come see one of our other performances. We have a few rising stars that have really taken the hearts of Atlantis with their talents."

"I'll leave that arrangement to Alessandra when she'd like to return for some entertainment. You've done a fine job in training the gladiators," Triton commended.

Another roar from the crowd above us could be heard.

"Viperess, don't miss your queue," Sylvie prompted, and a girl dressed in snake skins and long red hair stepped forward.

I nearly screamed before her warning glare told me not to.

"One of your new recruits?" Triton asked, and I panicked, trying to distract him by tracing a finger over his bicep. He turned his attention from her, and on to me, freezing me in place. I stopped, unsure of myself, and his blue eyes glittered excitedly. "I believe we have other matters to attend to Sylvie, if you'll excuse us."

When I searched for my sister, she was gone, and I sighed a bit of relief, but it didn't explain how she got here, or why she was with the gladiators. It was more imperative now more than ever that I knew what she got herself into because of me.

I took a moment to really take in what this meant. She found me.

Theo, what are you doing here?

It didn't take long for my common sense to catch up with reality. This wasn't merely an escape anymore. I couldn't leave here without her. This changed everything.

When Triton and I were down the nicely decorated staging hall far enough that the hustle and noise would drown our words from eavesdroppers, I couldn't wipe the concern off my features. He watched me and his expression changed from playful to matching my own concern.

"I do not wish to be with anyone else. I know my reputation is damning, but–"

"It's not that," I sighed, "I thought the Arena was dangerous, and gladiators... they die. It makes me uncomfortable."

He released his tension and laughed, "Oh, thank the sea. I thought you were punishing me for my past." Shaking his head he explained, when I glared at him for making light of the gladiator's fate, "It's true during the Olympics the Arena is very dangerous but on a normal day gladiators are actors, masters of performing arts."

I was trying to process what he was telling me.

"It is all staged for Atlantis. Most of them will never enter a real arena. They plan every move, and every counter for the best reaction."

"It's all fake?"

He nodded.

"And the prisoners?"

"Hmmm," he straightened defensively, "those matches are... not fake."

"Are they or are they not fake?"

"Usually," It wasn't a straight answer and something wasn't adding up.

"What aren't you telling me?"

"The gladiators are skilled at both their jobs, entertaining the city, and," he cleared his throat, masking the last part, "and executions."

Shaking my head, I couldn't process what that would mean for Theo. She couldn't possibly have become a gladiator if it meant she had to be an executioner. She wouldn't... she couldn't.

"There is a delicate balance to everything in the sea," Triton soothed. "When someone disrupts that balance, they risk all the life that remains. It is a small sacrifice for the future of Atlantis and the sea."

I hardened, my fists clenched.

"A small sacrifice," I repeated softly, counter to the storm inside me. I was a small sacrifice to fate. Did that make it okay? Did that mean I should accept that my pattern is set, and I will die if I protect the sea? Or should I even try to protect the sea when it sees me as a small sacrifice for its future?

I remembered how it barely kept me alive when I arrived. Constantly under the pressure of drowning. Was that how the sea treated all of its sacrifices, its protectors?

Small sacrifices only need small consideration and all of that, right?

Everything since my failed attempt at saving a drowning woman that was actually a merperson came crashing through me. It was like

I was running away the whole time, and only now did I stop to catch my breath.

My anger morphed into shame.

Had I let myself relax enough with Triton that I felt I could stop running for even a moment? That I could get angry with him without fearing for my life?

Gasping, I thought about how I yelled at him the first time we were alone together in his room. Had I always felt comfortable with him from the start?

How could I let myself feel this way with him? A god that accepted the sacrifices of lives for the 'greater' future. A god that accepted laws that forced me into an engagement or be punished.

My anger returned.

Triton noticed the change, and reading my emotion, he pulled his hand back reluctantly. An internal struggle between the need to touch me, and the accurate assessment of calming the rage growing within.

"If you treat them like sacrifices, then that is what they will become. If you treat them as monsters, then that is what they are... to you," I hissed.

To you, I remembered what my mom said about the gods. To them, we were nothing more than monsters. Things to be used in quests for the real heroes.

Triton narrowed his blue eyes, and straightened taller, commanding... a god.

"To me," he growled, "they have made their choices, even to their last breath. There is a monster in all of us, my goddess, and it is they, not I," his voice lowered, "that have chosen to embrace death rather than life. You will not pin their decisions on me, my love, nor will I accept that burden. Judge me for my own sins and I will suffer them, but not this. This, I will not suffer for."

He turned and left me feeling an aching absence where he once was, including a terrible longing to have it filled once more. Did I misjudge him? Was I too harsh?

Would I ever stop attacking him for things that may not be in his control?

Yet again, he did not punish me for my anger. And again, I have pushed him away. There wasn't the same kind of hurt in his eyes as the last time. Did that make it worse? There was a hardness there that I wasn't used to seeing directed at me. The softness he once had for me dissolved, and I feared I'd gone too far.

Would he return the same as he had before?

Did I want him to?

I didn't get to let my mind wander when I heard her voice again, the Fate.

"Every story has a villain. He doesn't have to be yours."

"You heard all that?" I shouldn't have asked. Of course she did. I didn't even turn to face her.

"I'm not omnipresent if that's what you're implying, but yes... I have a tendency to be where I need to be and hear what I need to hear. You can call me Mo, I hate that awkward moment when people can't decide whether to call me Fate, Fates, or even Destiny... can't stand it when people call me Destiny," she grumbled and then made a yuck sound, "reminds me too much of the days I used to work at the club."

Right, the club... because any of this reminded me of an ordinary club. Not that I've really been to one, too busy studying. Even a club wasn't really normal or ordinary, but this was a far different conversation than when she told me my fate while pretending to be a gladiator.

"You're going way up in your noggin', aren't you?" Mo sighed. "Never mind my name or my past. You over-analytical types are always so silent while making me carry the whole conversation."

When I turned around, she was lounged on a twin sofa, feet kicked up, and braiding her black hair.

How did we not notice her?

She was hard not to notice. She was unmistakable.

"How can he be okay with letting people kill each other?" Wasn't this the very definition of a monster, of a villain?

"He isn't."

"How can you know that?"

"Things aren't black and white, right or wrong. You used to know that. If you were listening then you would have heard him when he said they make the choice, not him. He is bound by laws, which he put in place as a measure to protect his subjects from himself, and anyone that would try to rule them. You know how the gods can get. He never wanted to be like that.

"When the gods make an oath, they are forced to keep it, to balance the power. Many gods have fallen victim to the whims of mortals. Many times, mortals have chosen, and even demanded something from the gods that would be harmful to them.

"Wanting to ride a chariot much too powerful for them to handle, see a gods true form, travel to realms their body can't sustain them in, yadda yadda, and so forth."

"How is it their choice to fight to the death?" It sounded very familiar to marry me or be punished. What choice did they really have? What choice did I really have?

Mo sat up and leaned in, scanning me over.

"This isn't about the prisoners," she lifted a brow, and laughed, "You think he'll kill you like the rest of his wives? Did you ever ask how they died? Pft, he probably wouldn't tell you just yet, touchy subject.

"He didn't kill them because they betrayed him. It is because they betrayed him that they died. The trident cannot be taken or stolen. It must be given or earned. Nymphs are not powerful enough to hold the trident, at least not the ones he married. His mother could."

"You're telling me the trident killed them?"

She shrugged. "Not all of them. One lost control and had to be stopped before she destroyed the city. Anyway, no one who battles a gladiator is forced to do so. Even the gladiators are voluntary, and usually just actors... until they aren't."

All this was doing was confusing me. What did it matter that it was voluntary, it was still barbaric?

"Are you here to lecture me on the definition of voluntary, or just to let me know I'm cursed to die?"

"I like you," her eyes sparkled, "no shits given, and did I say you're destined to die?" She weighed her hands back and forth like a scale. "Eh," she seemed to nonchalantly disagree with my assessment.

She didn't use those exact words. Death was coming for me—no for us—but dying was merely implied. Who escaped death?

"Right..." I doubted her sincerity. She did, after all, work for Zeus.

"You know when we cut someone's thread it isn't always to end their life," she mused thoughtfully, "sometimes it's to prevent their thread from unraveling, and give it a chance to grow again. Like plants, really. Some fight, some don't. That's our secret though," she winked, "when I cut your thread, you told me you'd fight, but it was your sister that tipped the balance in your favor. She's still fighting, it seems. Will you make her do it all on her own again?"

"What's that supposed to mean?"

"Nothing," she lied. Mo got up from the couch and gave a fake salute. "Your royal fishiness."

"How charming, as always," Triton mocked in return.

"Authority," she jibbed with an odd drawl, "always brings out the best in me." She gave him a winning, yet obviously forced, smile.

"I suppose we have that same rebellious nature to thank for why you're even here." He didn't approach closer. I watched him, and his gaze stayed glued to Mo, not one glance spared for me. Our previous conversation was still stewing between us.

Folding my arms over my chest, two could play this game. I didn't have to look at those solid muscles of his either; I fumed.

All of my irritation refocused on Mo.

She lazily switched between us both and gave us a knowing quirk of her mouth.

"By all means, you can both give me the stink eye."

"Moira," he warned.

"Fine, fine." She waved him off, and I had to stop myself from looking at Triton. "It's not my fault you haven't cleaned house of all your curiosities."

"Not all of us," he said pointedly for my benefit, "believe in the same cleaning methods."

They were not talking about cleaning, that much was clear. Triton hasn't killed his spies, and he doesn't plan to. At least, not yet.

"I didn't specify how you clean house," Mo dug into the core of the issue, and I could tell she was enjoying the double meaning in what she was inciting between us, "but I'll tell you what you already know. That is why you wanted me here, to give you the okay, the confirmation that it's possible. Am I right?" That what was possible? That what was okay? What wasn't she saying?

"If you can," he said numbly.

"She is who you know her to be, and yes, the path you seek is... possible. Whether or not it's okay, I won't weigh on. But," she paused to draw out the suspense, "every path will merge with Poseidon. This is fixed, this can not be changed, and like a Chinese finger trap, the more you struggle against this fact the tighter those threads will twine."

"I understand," Triton replied with a sternness. "What about the other thing?"

"Like father like son," she pretended to be exhausted by the issue, "I could spin a few threads here or there to weigh the scales," she paused for dramatic effect and added, "For a price."

"What did you do for him?" He was more concerned with what was already done than what could be done now, and I didn't blame him for it. I was also wondering the same thing. What had Poseidon messed with in my life? Because I was certain whatever he had done took choices away from me. I could feel it in my bones.

"Sometimes, what you want isn't what you think you want, and all that, but I grant it nonetheless. You both make the same mistakes. Maybe you'll do differently this time around?" She caressed Triton's chest, and I stiffened, before she pulled a golden ribbon from the air around him. Examining it, she grunted, and gave an absent shrug, then released it.

"I am not my father," Triton lowered his voice, signaling she was treading on dangerous territory.

"No," she perked up, "You're not," it was almost an insult the way she said it and I couldn't help putting an end to the underhanded jibbed between them both.

"I think we've dragged this on long enough," I quipped. "You already know what you're here to offer. Are you only going to rile us up, or are you giving us solutions?"

"Solutions, duh," she touched my golden blonde hair, and she looked over my shoulder from under those thick black lashes, "but," she stopped to take a step back from me giving Triton a cheeky look, "there's always a price to pay. You'll know it when you make the choice."

Mo took another step backwards, her gaze still fixed on us.

"Triton," she added, "sometimes fights are fought where your power can not reach. Inside an arena, only a few realize they have entered, and there are no winners or losers. Only those that are, or are not. And, Aless," she toyed with what I assumed was my own thread of fate, "they control many things, but your choices are not one of them. Don't let the difficulty blind you from seeing the possibilities."

Then she yanked at both of our ribbons, and I felt my whole world tilt. Sucking in a breath with a gasp, I reached out, and it was Triton that appeared when my vision cleared.

His bright blue eyes searched me for any sign that I was okay. Before he was about to pull away, I grabbed his hand to stop him.

"She's gone," he told me, like that was my main concern.

"I don't care about her." Staring at him, I tried to understand what I was doing, what I was trying to say, but I couldn't put it in words. How could I tell someone else what I didn't know myself?

He stopped mid stride but couldn't bring himself to face me. But neither did he pull his hand from mine, while his other planted his trident like a walking stick in front of him.

Triton squeezed my hand.

"I understand," he spoke softly, "Poseidon is not bound by the laws of Atlantis. He is the law of the sea, and if I give him the trident... I am bound to be his herald, his voice, and his action.

"I was young once, and eager to prove myself. Poseidon offered me power if I was willing to take responsibility for it. I made the deal. For you, I would make another."

"I don't want this life," I admitted.

"I'm counting on that." He surprised me. "It's why you're perfect for it, but just because you're destined to be the Goddess of the Sea, doesn't mean you must choose to stay with it always. My mother didn't, neither did Poseidon." It was rare that Triton called Poseidon his father. In the time I'd known him, he only used that title around Pegasus.

And I certainly didn't feel like a goddess, let alone the Goddess of the Sea, in the same rank as Triton and Poseidon.

Then it hit me.

That would mean to be a Goddess of the Sea that I... I marry him.

Fates, Mo, told me I was destined to marry Triton?

Then before I could say anything, Triton added, "Neither do I. As long as Atlantis is safe..."

"I can't ask that of you," I stopped him from making me even more confused. I need time. I needed to think clearly.

"I've never wanted anything more." He looked at me then, and the seriousness in those steely blue eyes shook me. "I've been trapped by Poseidon's grudges long enough."

"Is that really all that keeps you here?" There was more to being king besides protecting Atlantis from those who seek vengeance on Poseidon, wasn't there? Power, belonging, respect, and the sea... Not that the grudges against Poseidon were small by any means, and there was no telling if that would ever change.

Even if he wanted to, could he really leave?

"Let me show you something," he ignored my question. Instead of pulling me with him, he waited for me to take a step towards him, and when I did, his pace picked up until we were running through the corridors of the Arena's staging area. We had left Pegasus with the chariot, and I tugged back on his grip around my hand to slow down him down.

"Peg..." I looked back over my shoulder, and we were leaving her behind.

"She's been gone since we were dropped off at our seats," he answered quickly and picked up our speed once more.

That was a relief, but another tug pulled at me that I didn't dare voice. Where was Dion?

I shook the thought from my head and held on tight as we ran through the halls, and even barely missing a collision with a few gladiators along the way.

"My king," one said while backing up against the wall, still making an effort to show her respects despite the rush.

"I haven't seen him like that in a long time," one boasted to another.

"Just in time, if you ask me."

"Shhh, don't ruin this for him," they snapped back.

"He already knows," another agreed.

"What are they talking about?" I asked Triton as we turned a corner, now unable to hear the rest of their conversation unless I focused the power of his mother's crown. Though I wasn't fully aware of how the magic worked or decided what I was able to hear clearly, and when it stopped.

"They're talking about the smugglers and the rebels that don't want to have to choose between their life in Atlantis and joining the society of mortals. Many believe a new sea goddess will strengthen Atlantis enough that they no longer have to be so isolated."

"Is that why–"

"No," he stopped me from inferring about his motives for marrying me, "I'm well aware of the smugglers, and that some subjects leave, and others still come into Atlantis unlawfully. I let them. It keeps the people that would disobey the law to remain silent about where they came from. Having something be unlawful isn't always because I do not wish for my subjects to have choices, but that those who would choose to leave without going through proper channels are fearful of their own lives and must be careful with what they say. Sometimes, the only way for selfish mortals to do something for another's life, is to tie their own life to the outcome."

"So, you don't care if people leave, just that they do it safely?"

"Atlantis must remain a myth, or we'll have more to deal with than a few gods with grudges."

"What about the smugglers in the dungeon?"

Triton slowed down, the excitement in him for what he wanted to show me ebbing with our conversation choice.

"They took mortals without their consent. I've had to wipe their memories and scatter them on the shores if they did not want to stay. Too many as of late. I can only assume the influx is due to outside influences."

"You're the reason people have been showing up nearly drowned, with their memories lost..."

"They only think they were nearly drowned," he amended wryly.

I had him all wrong, I thought to myself. Smiling at him, a lightness filled me as the reasons for why I should hate him kept being chipped away.

"I'm sorry," I admitted, taking him in almost as if it were the first time I was truly seeing him.

"You have nothing to be sorry for," he rubbed my hand with his thumb, "I have a reputation for a reason. It's necessary to keep people safe."

"I'm sorry, even so." I bit my lip uncomfortable with this warmth spreading in my belly as he watched me. "You're not so bad," I joked, forcing a bit of sarcasm to avoid the growing awkwardness.

"So am I," he joined the apology train, "for not realizing who you were sooner. It's too easy to assume you were sent by the gods to torment me for merely being the son of a god that pissed them off."

"I might be," I joked.

"Torment me, my goddess. I welcome it." He swooped closer to me and took me in his arms. The conversation about politics forgotten as we stared into each other's eyes. I giggled and then we were both silent, frozen in the moment of realizing there was something heavier than air between us. A magnetism that I couldn't explain.

My breathing quickened, and his golden skin was warm against me. His lips were only a toe stretch away, and the smell of the sea on him was tantalizing. His hand slipped down my lower back, securing me closer as his lips parted.

A soft moan from his mouth nearly broke me, and a tension in my shoulder blades made me arch into him, sending my hips up against the hard armor of his greaves.

There was too much fabric and scales between us, and I couldn't help my own hands from wandering beneath the chest plate on one half of his body. I stopped just short of the need to tug at the straps that kept the armor over his shoulder and toss it aside.

The feeling built until my chest clenched, and every intake of air was labored. All we did was stand there, and all of my senses were overloaded.

Moving past the strap, up his neck and into his hair, I grabbed his crown and tossed it on the floor so my fingers could rake through the short blue-white strands.

"Aless," I never thought I'd hear a god beg, but my name on his tongue was ragged as he held himself back. For me, I knew he was holding back for me. I was in control over what I allowed him to do. And it felt powerful.

That mere thought had my fingers tingle, and I gripped the back of his neck. Pulling, I removed the distance between us. Feathers scattered around us, and I felt the tension burst from my back as Triton finished what I started. His lips pressed into mine, rough and needy, but slow.

Savoring the moment, he took his time massaging my eager mouth until I gasped. Slipping his tongue in, he lapped up my lower lip, suckling as he held me close. A clang hit the ground, and I knew as soon as his other hand grabbed me that his trident was tossed along with his crown. His skin rippled under my hands, and where his armor once was, disappeared in a splash of water that glistened on his golden flesh so he could press himself against me without resistance.

My wings spread out behind me, and my head leaned back in his stable hands, holding me from getting too far away from him, searching out for my embrace once again. As my vision came back, I watched the water wick from his hair.

White hair looked black as night, and those bright blue eyes turned deep ocean. The way his eyes looked into my soul made my heart clench within my ribcage. Who was staring back at me was no longer Triton.

"I'll come back for you," he whispered.

I gasped, seeing someone I wasn't supposed to be seeing. I shook my head, confused, and pulled back.

But when I blinked, he was gone. It was only Triton. He cupped my cheek and watched me concerned.

"What did you see?"

"Nothing..." I rasped. My eyes were playing tricks on me. He wasn't Dion, but why would I think he was? Even for a moment, why did I see him before I could kiss him again? My stomach churned, feeling sick that all it took was knowing Triton wasn't a completely bad guy to glue myself to his practically naked body.

And now that I was actually aware of what was happening, and a lot more in control of my hormones, I felt guilty.

I've never done this with anyone. As much as I wanted to experience all of these feelings and more, I knew there were expectations that came with accepting those things with Triton.

My wings flexed behind me, and as suddenly as they appeared, they shattered in a feathery haze around us. Dissolving the fairytale, I pretended there to be between a doctor with no training, and a king of the sea.

Caressing the side of my face, he tried to find what I've hidden between the unspoken words, the something behind the nothing façade. When I held firm with my lie, he reached out his arm to have the trident lift and magnetize into his grasp. Pointing the prongs to his crown, it too lifted and found its proper place on his head. Water rippled over him and his armor reappeared, as did the stoic expression of his features.

"Sometimes, after meeting with a fate, one can see glimpses of futures that are likely to happen based on current choices."

If that was true, then whatever path I was on led to Dion telling me he'd be back for me. And then he was about to finish what Triton and I started. I flushed at the thought.

"Whatever you saw, we can face it together." He wasn't accepting my 'nothing' answer. His tone made me think he thought I was scared of what I saw. But why I pushed him away had nothing to do with fear.

"It was nothing," I doubled down, only to see him narrow his brow at my lie, so I added, "that I can't handle."

But maybe I shouldn't be handling 'that' at all, I thought, now seeing Dion's bare chest again like the first time I saw him in his room wearing nothing but his pajama pants. What was I thinking? That couldn't be a glimpse into my fate. This was nothing more than a twisted fantasy that shouldn't even be happening when there was a god right in front of me. Now, perfectly irritated that I'd pushed him away again.

"Last time I gave you space, you were thrown in the dungeon when I returned," he brooded. "I won't be making the same mistake again. Push me away for now, but I'll be staying close by. At least, until your powers are more stable, and there isn't someone out there trying to orchestrate your death."

"Seems reasonable," I said dryly, if he was telling the truth about not knowing I was in the dungeon that whole time. How could I forget so easily that he wanted to send me there to begin with, all so he could be in more control over my fate here?

"When I need to reflect, I go to the cenote under Atlantis." As if he knew I was doubting him, he added, "It's where I went when I couldn't decide whether to execute you or convince you to be my wife."

"Charming," I mocked at the options.

Triton growled low, frustrated with my response. "You give me whiplash, my love." His tone softened and you could hear the hurt there. "Something holds you back from me, and every time I think we've moved beyond it, you wound me. I've spent centuries taking blows from the gods. I can take many more waiting for more of what you've shown me only a few minutes ago."

He pointed his trident to the ground creating a fissure that quaked near us, making me grab hold of him for support. I glared up at him, but he merely wrapped his other arm around me, and smiled. Only the ground around us was affected, and not even a ripple reached beyond where he intended.

Then he jumped, dragging me with him.

My scream was silent, too stunned to even make a noise. The air whipping my hair up, but the whole drop was measured, and even.

As we descended, our speed stayed the same, and there was a geyser of water beneath Triton's feet that guided him down.

As the darkness of the cave took over, and the light from above us closed, the colors of the rocks glowed, and there was a soft blue-green haze glittering about us.

When we stopped moving, there were sculpted pillars throughout the cave, and stone artwork scattered like a museum around the freshwater deposit.

One sculpture stood out from the rest, a centerpiece to the collection. She was sculpted from black rock, and precious stones. Gold made up her hair and wings. Her lower half was reptilian, a morphing between snake and bird. Even her hair was made up of green, emerald snakes intertwined with her gold hair. Eyes made of emeralds, skin from molten rock, and her hand lifted like she was holding something in her palm that needed careful consideration. No, something she was admiring. As I got closer, I could see emotion, longing, in her features. The detail was exquisite.

"She didn't have a face until recently. Nothing seemed to fit her. Every time I tried to finish, it was always missing something. It always felt off somehow."

I followed the direction of her eyes, and her hand to find the black rock wave, embedded with sapphires holding Triton aloft as he gazed back, but not at her, not at the sculpture, but at me.

"You made these?" I asked, astonished. Changing the subject was easier to handle than the way he watched me, so I walked towards the next closest work. I didn't want to admit that the woman's face did have a strange resemblance to me. Except for the snake thing.

"I did."

He still watched me from the stone wave he sat on.

The next sculpture was a severe-looking man. His hair was long and wavy, the black stone sparkled, and I noticed his skin was embedded with sapphire flakes, and his eyes were made of carved sapphire. His fist clenched at his chest, and as I walked around, I could see there was a hole for something he used to hold. The face reminded me of someone, especially in the eyes.

"They're beautiful," I stopped myself from saying my next thought out loud, and lonely. All of the sculptures were missing something. I ran my hand over the forearm of the smooth rock, leading up to his empty fist. The man was life size, tall, but there was a curved platform of rock that he seemed to be climbing, one leg bent, and water-like rock waves that you could walk on like steps.

"That one is Poseidon before he gave me his trident, and disappeared into what he claimed was his final resting place. He told me everything was taken from him, and he had no reason to stay."

Not even his own son. I could hear the sadness and the anger in his words.

"He trusted you with his trident, and the sea," I tried to defend Poseidon, and I had no idea why I even had the urge to do so.

I looked up into the stern sapphire eyes of the sea god sculpture, and it was like I could see something more there besides the coldness portrayed. I couldn't bring myself to turn my gaze from him.

He reminded me of Dion, come to think of it; maybe they're related?

Duh, of course they are, all of the merpeople were related to Poseidon in some capacity, right?

"You give him more credit than he deserves. Trust had nothing to do with it. I told you before I made an oath to take responsibility for the power he gave. I had no choice but to take care of what he left behind."

"Oh," I didn't want to press that family drama further, but I couldn't help myself. The fate's insight into knowing we would merge paths with Poseidon still lingered heavily between us. "How long has he been gone?"

"A few centuries."

"I can imagine that's rough to live up to the shadow of his legacy, but you've been able to rule the sea for centuries with past grudges and curses against you, and still you've held on to a kindness that most would have lost long ago. I'd say it's your father that comes back to his own son's shadow now."

"I've been cautious and reserved with my rule. Letting the gods keep their spies alive in my sea, because they would merely be replaced with another," Triton sighed, "My father would not have let the gods have such a tether in his territory. He would have already found who was responsible for interfering in Atlantis, and sent a message that could not be ignored."

He was lying down on his back atop the sculpted wave, staring up into the glowing cave ceiling, contemplating how his father would have done things better. It was then that I knew gods weren't all that different from mortals. Even Triton had self-doubt... and regrets.

Potentially seeing his dad again was stirring up a lot of resentment, and anxiety for Triton. What was Poseidon coming back to, but Atlantis, and the sea on the verge of war with the gods?

"Didn't you do that?" I contemplated out loud. Didn't Triton send a message, and find who was most likely responsible for the chaos happening in Atlantis? He summoned a meeting with Hera and spoke with one of the Fates of Zeus. It had to be one of them, right?

"Didn't you do what you said Poseidon would do? You confronted the king and queen of Olympus, and you sent a message to all the spies that you were stronger than ever, and marrying–" I stopped myself there, I couldn't bring myself to admit I was a goddess, but it was definitely a power play to tell all of Atlantis that he had a goddess, and the sea was powerful, he wasn't alone. But wasn't he?

"A goddess," he finished for me.

"What will you do next?" He had to have a plan, always thinking ahead of his rivals.

"I'm not marrying you because it helps strengthen the sea," he clarified before answering, "but I can't deny that you're right, showing you off to the spies is a good move. You were sent here because you were dangerous to whatever their plans are, and they thought I would be the one to dispose of that threat. You're alive, and you wear the crown of the sea on your head.

"The spies will send their messages. What happens next tells us a lot about what we're up against."

There was that 'we' again, and the more he said it, the more I got used to hearing it. It reminded me of my sister. It was always 'we' with her. Us against the world, though at the time it was more us against time to crunch for studying, or who could eat the most apple pie while watching the latest thriller.

I doubted any of those movies would have helped me find a way out of this predicament. The only thing I could think of was that whoever set me up knew I wouldn't let someone drown even when the odds were against me. Someone who knew me, but that would have been nearly impossible.

What's already happened could also tell us a lot about who 'we', I tried that pronoun on for size, it still felt weird, were up against.

"How do they know me?" I said out loud.

Triton hesitated, but answered anyway, "They don't, not really. They know who you were, in another life perhaps."

"No," he misunderstood, "they know me, the me now, or someone that does. Where I would be, when I would be there, and convinced your daughter to be there.

"I thought the people with the missing memories were from her, but they weren't, were they…"

They were from Triton, returning stolen mortals from the smugglers. Which means Coraline wasn't where she normally would be, and she used the fake memories of the returned victims to add a few mortals to her own entourage thinking they would be lumped in as a few humans that didn't survive drowning, the ones the other returned mortals weren't able to save, lost to sea.

Just another statistic.

I still didn't have enough information.

"You said you went to Apollo University," Triton followed my lead, looking for avenues where one of the gods found me.

"I do." I didn't like how he changed it to past tense. My studies weren't over. When this was done, if I survived, I'd go back.

"You were good at your studies." It wasn't a question. I was dedicated to doing well, but I always held back from being top of the class. I stayed in the middle, blended in like my mom, and my sister, wanted.

Theo, she was here.

She was a gladiator.

She told me to stay away from the sea, it couldn't be her.

I nodded at his assessment of my studies.

"But not too good," he guessed at my reluctance to continue down his clue path, "Apollo loves Poseidon. I don't believe he would have done this, even if he did know who you were.

"Artemis, however, is the best hunter there is, and she's loyal to Athena, and Hera, but she still would have had to notice you, or…"

"Or?"

He sat up at attention, staring in front of him when he said, "Viper-ess..." like he had an epiphany. But then I recalled what Sylvie called my sister. My sister.

He knew.

"How did I not see it?" He muttered to himself. "You have sisters," he thought through his musings.

"Sister," I amended.

"Sisters," he corrected right back, "the gorgons, my love, they were thought to have been killed off by heroes' feats centuries ago. If you still have one, and she's not merely a mortal that your mother placed you with..."

I was piecing the puzzle together, trying to keep up with his trail. "How would they know?"

"Poets back then only knew one side of the gorgon sister's story. The side of their hideous faces, hair made of snakes, and gnarled claws. That was the side they saw, because no mortal came to them without an objective of killing them. Each sister was beautiful, as you would imagine any sea siren to be, but they weren't sirens, they were goddess-es of Echidna, the she-viper. As powerful as a Titan, but made from the union of Gaia and Tartarus, instead of that of Uranus. Making her the mother of dark gods and goddesses—the Titans, her siblings, considered monsters.

"They were afraid of them..." he mused while descending from the statue, "as they are now afraid of you. That's it."

He figured something out, and it was all happening in his head.

"What is?"

"Olympianmachy. The rise of the dark gods, Apollo's prophecy. Zeus wants Poseidon to return to help defend the Olympian's from the rise of Tartarus's children to be the new reigning gods."

"Is that why we were labeled as monsters?"

This whole time, all those gods and goddesses of Tartarus were targeted as feats to be defeated by heroes to prevent this prophecy. A new order to the gods.

"So none of Tartarus' line would ascend to take over Mount Olympus. Yes, I believe so. They think you're the one to deliver this new order."

"Why? I want nothing to do with them," I exclaimed my exhaustion. Triton approached me, a sympathetic smile on his face.

"Because you are the terror of Tartarus, the sea creature that can not breathe under the water, yet flies above it. The lost dark goddess risen again and destined to defend a new era of gods. You are more than the Conqueror of the Coral Sea. You are the Queen that will balance the power between the realms.

"And they wished I'd take care of their problem for them. They would rather you die before you can threaten their rule."

"That's ridiculous," I folded my arms over my chest, and refused to accept this idea of some plot where I was some all-powerful goddess that would overthrow a monarchy of gods, "I have no reason to overthrow anything I didn't know existed, and if I'm so powerful then why was I almost killed multiple times?"

"The thunderbolt..."

"The thunderbolt?"

"The one I believe was used to kill Poseidon, but instead melted all of the fates of gods together. I find it hard to believe Zeus threw the thunderbolt to prevent Hera from cutting the threads. He doesn't miss his targets."

"You think he actually succeeded in severing a thread but didn't anticipate the heat from his thunderbolt would melt the threads back together?" I was finally catching up to what he was thinking.

"Linking many of the gods' fates together irreversibly. Including yours. I believe you were a side effect of his attack that he didn't want. Your fate was cut, and somehow, it found its way back to the melted mess of the gods' fates, but you haven't reached your immortality yet. It's farther down your timeline. Right now, you're vulnerable. And if you are vulnerable... so are others. So is Zeus."

So is Poseidon, I thought to myself.

Mo's words came back to me then. I was meant to defend him, without me... he was fated to die.

I knew what I had to do now, and somehow without realizing it, I was already planning for this very thing. I had to find Poseidon, and Mavron was going to help me do it.

For some reason, I couldn't bring myself to tell Triton. He was on the same page, wasn't he? He wanted to save the sea, and Atlantis from the gods that were afraid of their own death. He would want to help save his father, wouldn't he? Then why did a big lump form in my throat every time I tried to tell him what I planned on doing?

Why, too, did Mo try so hard to make sure I was the only one that heard my fate with Poseidon?

I couldn't do it, couldn't tell him.

So I said nothing.

Then the whole cave shook. A stalactite glowing with sapphire veins shattered behind me, and a few others throughout the underground museum of Triton's works. My wings burst from my back in fear, and without thinking, I lunged to cover Triton with my body. We fell to the ground with my wings sprouting on instinct to cover us, a shield of golden feathers.

My hands on either side of his face, his trident pressed against my back. The sound of breaking rock crumbling above us. A few scraps of rubble dusted on my neck, a weakness within my wingspan.

The rumbling stopped, and my chest heaved on top of his. Still reeling from the earthquake, under the sea.

What caused this?

"I should be the one protecting you." He smiled up at me, our noses touching.

"There's always next time," I joked, not actually wanting a next time to happen, but still trying to understand why I did it once again. Why did I keep throwing myself into danger? First, with Coraline, then Dion, and now with a god that was more than capable of defending himself.

"It would be my honor." Triton's nose nuzzled up, and my lips parted. Snapping my mouth shut, I knew if I stayed here like this, we were seconds away from being in the same position we were in earlier. I pushed up and dusted my thighs. Feathers drifted around us, and I plucked one from the ground, seeing speckles of red on it.

I didn't feel injured.

I patted myself down, searching myself just in case. Nothing.

Triton was already standing, his trident in his other hand, the other behind his back.

"This isn't mine..." I lifted the tainted feather. Then stared at him; he was acting rather suspicious.

He lifted a brow and then tapped the feather with the tip of his trident. It disintegrated to dust in my grasp.

Standing, I rushed at him to grab his hand from behind his back. He stood motionless, his spine stiff, as I examined the gash atop his hand where a rock had sliced it.

He gently pulled the hand back. "It's nothing," he insisted.

My eyes wide, I watched him in disbelief.

"You're vulnerable..."

His jaw tightened, and he looked away from me, ashamed. His hand was behind my back, underneath my wing, but outside of its protection, along with the trident.

My spine prickled, and I wiped away a few stray rock pieces caught in my hair. My weakness, he stopped one of the stalactites from landing on my neck between the folds of my wings.

"You saved me," I mumbled in shock.

"We saved each other," he corrected warmly.

I scanned the cave, assessing the damage, and my eyes landed on the head of Poseidon, his stone head had rolled—a crack down his face releasing one of his sapphire eyes.

"Atlantis is being attacked," Triton reached for me.

"Why now?"

"Because you live."

Chapter 15

Power Trap

L arge tentacles shadowed over the city of Atlantis, darkening the streets in waves as they moved to protect the land in the sea above us.

"I'll call Pegasus to get us back to the palace. We'll be safer there," Triton assured me, but was stopped by Ray.

"She won't come," Ray stumbled as the ground shook once more from the fight outside, "There are reports that she's helping whoever is attacking the Krag."

"She wouldn't," Triton denied before reassessing, "unless..."

Only Ray seemed to understand what he wasn't saying. "Yes," she agreed, "she was gifted to a demi-god to assist with a feat. One that involves Atlantis, or if we're lucky, just the Krag."

"Where's Dion?" Triton demanded, since that's who he asked her to find before we ditched her for the cenote, and he was his First Sentinel and if ever there was a moment to need your adviser and first guard, it was now.

Ray averted her eyes in shame. If he wasn't with us, it meant she failed in finding him or... I wouldn't think of it.

"He said if he had to go to the end of the world for you, he would, and that's what he was going to do, my king. He wouldn't say anything more."

"Fuck," Triton swore, and my eyes widened, not ever hearing him sound so distraught before, "it wasn't his burden to take... not alone."

"Where did he go?" I asked, worried, still remembering the hurt in his blue eyes when he saw me enter the Arena with a crown on my head and a very public engagement to his king.

Was this my fault?

Did he go on a suicide mission because of me?

"He went in search of Hera's last golden apple."

"How is a golden apple going to help us?"

It was Ray that answered first, "Haven't you heard of the god's ambrosia that grants immortality?"

"Ambrosia is merely a generic term for divine taste," Triton explained. "It was used to describe anything that tasted of the gods, but it was all made from the golden apple orchards. Nectar was the intoxicating taste of golden apple juice, and it was used for many purposes; one among them was immortality. That's what Dion is after now. He thinks we can use the apple to tip the scales in our favor and stop the Olympians from finding Poseidon and committing genocide of the rest of the Tartarus line of dark gods."

"By himself?" I exclaimed, incredulously. He was still injured from earlier. How could he go hunt a powerful relic alone?

"He's my First Sentinel for a reason," Triton sounded proud, "but, even a demi-god would run into trouble stealing the last known golden apple without favors from the gods themselves to balance the obstacles he might face."

"There are rumors..." Ray began. Triton and myself waited for her to continue. "I overheard Dion talking to one of the gladiators before he left. The guardian of the apple orchard has been petrified for centuries, and the nymphs of Atlas became trees themselves, waiting so long since the last harvest.

"With no apples to protect, and the guardians inert... if there was a last apple in the orchard then now would be the time while Hera and Zeus are distracted."

Triton shook his head. "Hera would never leave the orchard unprotected, even if the previous guards are benign, it's likely a trap."

Ray looked skeptical. "A trap?" She bit her lip and narrowed her brow, thinking the same thing I was. For who? For us? We didn't even know we would be going after the apple until now.

"You said he was talking with one of the gladiators?" Triton followed his instincts. And maybe this gladiator could help us find Dion before he left on his suicide mission.

"The redhead," she offered, and I had to stop myself from panicking. There was only one redhead I saw, and it was my sister, Theo.

"There aren't many that even know where to go to find the orchard. Knowing where it is, and finding it are two different things."

I sighed in relief. "Then there's nothing to worry about."

"Dion knows where it is." Triton squashed that hope.

"How?" I wanted him to be safe, and even if the apple could help, why did he have to do it on his own? And just as important, why was my sister involved?

"I told him." He didn't seem remorseful about it. "Hera knows we'll go after her orchard... even if the rumors that a single apple still exists are nothing but a lie. And with another rumor that there are no guards... the risk would be worth it."

"But you said it yourself... it's a trap."

"Maybe so, but it isn't any more dangerous than the status quo, is it?" Ray added, motioning to the shadows of the fight overhead between some demi-god and the Krag, guardian of Atlantis.

"We'll have to ask for a favor, then." Triton moved us through the alleyways. The structures were rather resilient considering the tremors throughout the island, but I guessed that would be expected with a lost city that was magically sunk to the bottom of the sea.

"There isn't much time," Ray advised. She quickly worked her way closer to the shore of the island.

"What about the Krag?" We couldn't leave the guardian to defend Atlantis by itself. I knew what happened to monsters in Greek mythology—all of them fell to the feats of the gods. Wasn't that the Krag's fate if we didn't help?

Shouldn't Triton use his trident to defend the city?

Wave it around or something?

"He's survived many who have tried to defeat him. This will be no different," Triton assured, but seeing my distress he struggled with agreeing to do something to help the giant octopus that would delay his efforts to catch up with Dion. "It is in you to defend," he understood, "but Atlantis is protected by more than the Krag. Look at the buildings as they shake—not even time will destroy them. Any who wish to conquer Atlantis must do so from within, and it will be done within the arena."

"What about the people who live here?"

"I have the trident," he reminded me, "if the demi-god makes it past the Krag I will know, and I will force them to prove themselves in the Arena. Upon winning they will, by law, be granted one triumph within my power to grant."

My mouth puckered. He didn't even think twice about the giant guardian of Atlantis. Either he was so certain the Krag wouldn't fail, despite all of the ballads that were sung of previous heroes, triumphs gained against monsters, or he didn't care.

That stung more than I thought it would.

I didn't really know him, did I?

"Or you could help the Krag now, and not have to leave in the middle of trying to help Dion." Did I have to explain everything? It was so obvious to me, that splitting now, would only lose both objectives. Time was important, I knew that, but we could arrive just in time, and still not be in time for anything if Triton had to suddenly disappear to protect Atlantis.

His jaw tensed up, and he grabbed my hand, ready to yank me into the water. Without looking over his shoulder, he ordered Ray, "Get back to the palace. We'll meet you there. It's safer if we don't draw attention by going together."

"See you there," Ray hesitated at the border of the air bubble, debating whether she should actually leave us, but then dived in.

Triton winced before revealing, "I can't do both."

"I don't understand." I drew attention to his trident and then searched his eyes for the answers. All I saw there was hardened resolve.

"Not without the apple," he clarified. "I can't fully control the trident, not for extended periods. If I help the Krag, then I may not be able to help Dion, at least... not right away."

"Maybe you don't have to."

"You don't understand. If I get the apple in time, then I can help Dion and protect my subjects. Not just today, but all the days after. I would no longer be weakened after using the trident. I'd be whole."

"You said it yourself... what if there is no apple? What then? You went into a trap and left your people defenseless."

"It's a risk I must take," he said in defiance, while straightening his back. His jaw was hard, and he was set in his path. He would leave to get the apple, even if it risked an actual trap that prevented him from coming back to Atlantis should the Krag fail.

"You'll go on your own then." I yanked my hand from his and took a step back.

"So be it. It's better you stay here where the gladiators can protect you." He backed away into the water, and with a point of the trident, a swirl of water rushed at me. Picking me up off the ground, it consumed me and when the white foam dissipated, I was back at the Arena, within the gladiator's staging area.

"My queen," Sylvie bowed in greeting.

With a glare, not intended for the old man, but unshakable, I immediately asked him, "Where is the Viperess?"

Chapter 16

Demi-Poison

"She said you'd want to see her," Sylvie replied pleasantly, with a smile as if I didn't just bark at him, "With the commotion outside the city, all the gladiators are coming from all parts of Atlantis, even those who have retired are preparing themselves. This is the safest place for you to be. The Arena will fill with all of Atlantis soon. Even the sentinels will come."

"Has this happened before?"

He chuckled. "The Krag has never failed before, but as the wise Poseidon used to say, 'Even the gods can fail, it's only a matter of when.'"

"How inspiring..."

He gave me a wrinkly smile. "It was after he had lost Athens," he remembered fondly as if he were there when Athens was deciding which god to worship, for all I knew... maybe he was, he looked old enough, "The bards liked to make their stories more thrilling at the time, and embellished how upset he was at losing the competition to his niece, but my mother was a bard, and history was her passion. She knew the stories as they were told, but she also sung her own accounts."

I hardly thought now was the best time to talk about history and stories when there was a fight still raging above the skies of Atlantis, in the sea surrounding us. But we were at least heading in the direction of where my sister supposedly was, and the more he talked the more my anger subsided. His voice was pleasant to listen to.

"You think the Krag will fail?" I had my suspicions as well. You hardly heard a myth reported of a hero failing after being given help from the gods. Hercules comes to mind. He basically bulldozed through a dozen feats, even with other gods against him. If this demi-god is anything like Hercules, then the best we can hope for is the Krag doesn't die when he's taken down.

"Everything fails, eventually. It's only a matter of when. Even Poseidon knew that when he lost, that's why we have the Arena to begin with. It used to be a temple, before the stands were made around the pillars. Specifically, a temple worshiping the sea, and Poseidon. It's designed so that the more people who gather, the stronger the temple becomes.

"When Atlantis is in danger, all residents gather in the Arena. Poseidon realized the reason he failed was he lost sight of what his people needed. A way to support themselves when he isn't around. It was because of Athens that many of his greatest achievements were created. One of which is this temple. When," he specifically emphasized the word, "the Krag fails, the temple will force whoever seeks to harm Atlantis to participate in the Arena. The Gladiators will battle against them preventing regular subjects of the sea from having to truly experience wars as they have been in the past."

"Why don't the gladiators help the Krag before it gets to that point?"

He shook his finger at the ceiling like he was having an epiphany before saying, "Ah, you see outside of the temple an army could be waiting, and our small city could be crushed by sheer numbers alone, before it was submerged into the sea. Poseidon made sure that victory over Atlantis would be made only by the strongest of warriors. Any warrior can be outnumbered, and overwhelmed, even the best. But if Atlantis has the best gladiators, then no army would win against us when they were stripped of their immortality. The Arena makes the enemy mortal, defeatable. This was his way of evening the scales in our favor, and it is the sea's favor that grows stronger here.

"Here we are," he stopped at a dressing room, and gave my hand a squeeze, "Because of you, every gladiator in the city will fight should it come to that. Having a queen in the Arena will give the temple even more power, and the gladiators will be unstoppable."

"They would risk their lives for me?"

The kind old man shook his head. "They would happily give their lives for the future of Atlantis. As Poseidon would say, 'If you aren't willing to lay down your life, then you aren't living a life worth having.'"

"Does he say anything less dark?" I mumbled.

"The sea may seem dark, but really it is your eyes that are blinded to its treasures. One day, the sea's brightest jewel will risk everything for Atlantis's future, but only if Atlantis is willing to risk everything first. Poseidon was always a thoughtful god, but he's lost quite a bit, as have his children."

"So, you'll risk everything, then."

"If you risk nothing, then that is what you shall have..."

"You're like a fortune cookie."

"Quit teasing the old man." From the door frame, my sister leaned in, watching us, and my lungs tightened at her voice.

It was only a few days ago that I would have given anything just to hear that voice, and for a while, I thought I had. In the dungeons, I'd hear her talking to me, like we were hanging out in our apartment. My eyes watered, and I waited to make sure I wasn't imagining what I was seeing.

She broke the silence between us, her own voice wavered, "I thought I told you to stay away from the sea," she chided while rushing to wrap her arms around me.

Squeezing her to me, I closed my eyes and absorbed everything she offered me. The comfort, the short reprieve from reality, and a small bit of normalcy.

"You could have explained things better," I choked out, forgetting about Sylvie, "like how I'd probably be kidnapped, and nearly murdered, imprisoned, and—"

"And engaged to a god of the sea?" she finished for me.

Pulling back, I balked at her teasing response. "What aren't you saying?"

"You wouldn't have believed me, and mom knew the risks of removing your memories. You wouldn't wake up; we didn't have much of a choice," Theo begged for forgiveness.

That wasn't what I was expecting her to say, and it was a blow to my reality. Removing my memories? What did she mean by that?

"What memories?" I backed away from her on instinct, feeling betrayed.

Theo groaned. "You didn't know..." she realized I was talking about something else she was keeping from me, thinking she would tell me about Dion and his plan to get the golden apple, and instead she revealed a past I didn't know I had. Mo had told me I had a past life, but it was somehow different to know that those memories were purposefully stolen from me. By my own family.

"Aless," she soothed, "You weren't waking up, and mom always planned on giving your memories back."

"When?" I accused. When I finally realized I didn't grow old? Or would they both find a way to take my immortality from me as well?

I could feel my skin ripple over my clenched knuckles as my claws formed.

"When you found someone else to love," she admitted with shame, turning her green eyes away so she didn't have to face me.

A lump grew in my throat.

"Theo..." the gravity of her statement hit me. Someone else to love... I was in love before.

Was that why Triton never gave up on me? Were we always in love before—until fate intervened?

My family would keep that from me...

I felt sick.

She quickly tried to explain more. "I understand what you're going through, believe me I do, but his fate is dangerous. You had the chance for a fresh start, and we didn't want to take that from you."

"We..." It was one thing for my mom to make this kind of decision, but Theo agreed to it.

"You took that choice from me." I shook my head, and took another step away, lifting my hand to stop her approach, "Even if I didn't believe you, even if the conversation would have been difficult, you should have offered me the choice."

"When?" she used my own question against me. "When you thought you were five? Would ten have been better? Should it have been a graduation surprise after high school? Or when you were finally a doctor? Don't be ridiculous, there is no right time, and if you weren't taken into the sea, then we could have told you when you came home for holiday. This would have been a funny joke, all until your naturally curious self decided you did want to know the truth. Then what? You would be here, in the sea, facing what we all were trying to avoid."

"You don't get to do that. You don't get to make that choice!"

Sylvie finally said something to distract us from our argument, "My queen," he steadied himself with the wall, "I've received word that the Krag is running out of time to finish the fight."

"Out of time?" That didn't sound like he was winning, but it also didn't sound like he was losing either.

"He means the Krag can't keep his form for much longer," Theo informed, while grabbing my arm and dragging me down the hall, "Thanks for everything old man, we need to relocate," when I pulled back from her, she added, "now."

"I'm not going anywhere until you tell me what happens when the Krag runs out of time."

The Krag didn't deserve to be abandoned to deal with the demi-god on his own.

Theo internally debated if she had time to deal with explaining anything to me, I knew that look, before she resigned, "Most 'monsters', as the Olympians would call them, are merely gods that were born from the wrong union."

"What does that have to do with the Krag running out of time?" I had gathered as much about the god's so-called monsters.

"I was getting to that. Impatient as ever."

"We're on a time crunch," I pressured.

"I know. I know. The dark gods have never been worshiped like the Olympians have in the past. Their myths usually end in tragedy, since the Olympian gods have always orchestrated their deaths, or their imprisonment, to do their bidding. It takes a lot of power and energy to maintain their godly forms, but most of the time, they look mortal...

"We look mortal," she pleaded for me to understand. "Outside of Tartarus or Olympus, we are barely connected to our essence, and it takes time to build up our power. When the Krag is tapped out, he'll return to mortal form. He'll still be powerful, but he might not be a match for the demi-god if they've lasted this long."

"He'll be vulnerable," I assessed, and I knew what I had to do.

"There's no changing your mind, is there..." Theo could tell I was determined.

"We have to help the Krag."

"Aless..."

"You're a gladiator, and you've been hiding whatever power you have, haven't you? You're a dark god."

"Well, yes... but–"

"What can you do?"

"I can poison people... my venom overheats the host until they shrivel into meat raisins," she deadpanned.

I cleared my throat. "I see."

"It's also the only known substance to melt petrification as long as you can cool off the person and keep them hydrated. My venom burns up just like the host, so stoned victims are the only ones who have survived it."

I saw my sister through new eyes. She wasn't just the person who helped take care of me anymore. She was a goddess that knew enough about killing people to know the only ones that survived her poison were those already smote by another god into petrification. How did she even find that out?

This was someone else I didn't even recognize as my sister.

"Right..." I was speechless at how casually she spoke about death. Death by her own touch. I tried not to think about it, instead focusing on the immediate need to help the Krag. Was I willing to poison a demi-god to save Atlantis? I shook my head.

There had to be another way.

"We just need to grab the Krag before the demi-god can harm him," I told her.

"They're riding Pegasus," she doubted the success of my plan. I could hear it in her voice, "we aren't fast enough."

"Maybe we don't have to be."

"You want to swim out there and have a chat with them?" She groaned. "You're impossible. We aren't dealing with a mortal, Aless. They came here for a purpose, and there is someone's life at stake should they fail.

"The gods wouldn't have sent him on a feat without high risk, high reward. They aren't simply here because a god told them to be. Someone they care about is in danger, and somehow this feat will give them something that will save them."

"Even more reason to talk with them," I doubled down, and yet part of me wasn't so sure anymore, "We might be able to help each other."

"Do you believe that?"

Part of me felt like I'd been in this situation before, or something similar. A sense of confidence came over me, and I nodded.

"I do."

"Okay." Theo came in for a hug, and squeezed me tight before releasing me with a new found determination. "The Arena dome is still up. We can exit straight up from there. It'll be the fastest way. And, Aless..."

"Yah."

"That crown should let you breathe under the water, but if it doesn't,we have a limited time before the lack of oxygen knocks us out. I'll grab the Krag and come back for you. Stay alive, or mom will literally kill me."

I didn't think she was joking about that.

"Literally...?"

She didn't smile when she replied, "She isn't winning any mother of the year awards before you."

"You're talking about the same woman that couldn't stand the sight of a scraped knee, and almost decided to lock me in my room instead of let me go to the playground..."

"She was always different with you." She lifted her arms up to help ease me into the water like I was still five. "We both are." I thought about the people she must have killed before and ignored her offered arms to step into the pool of water that led to the Arena myself.

My wings burst from my shoulders and without turning to see if she was following, I said, "I'm different too."

As the water lapped at the golden feathers, they seemed to melt together, forming a membrane. Did they always do that?

"You always were," she whispered, though with the crown I could still hear her like an echo through the shell before she spoke up, "You know, you remind mom of herself before the rise of the Olympians. Not that the Titans were really that much better," she amended while wading in the water, once we dove under we'd come out inside the arena, "but," she continued, "at least they didn't go out of their way to kill the other titans, or even the Olympians until the Titanomachy. That's what we're up against out there. It isn't just another demi-god wanting to prove themselves to the gods to join Olympus. They were set up by the gods they serve, and failure isn't an option for them.

Whatever they were asked to do, it is in service to end any possibility of the dark gods rising. Whether that's our death, or our freedom."

"If they aren't with us, they are against us. That's what you're saying, isn't it?"

"I'm saying talking might not be the answer."

"And fighting them is?"

"That's not–"

"I don't know the right answer, but it can't be turning into the kind of people that get rid of someone because they are a threat."

"What about Atlantis? What about the Krag?" I knew what she was saying. Should I be weighing the demi-god's life against the ones they threaten? How far will I be willing to go to try to save both? Is that even possible?

We were about the find out.

"What if that's what they want? We should find out who's fighting the Krag first and then get the Krag to safety." It was weird calling the giant octopus the Krag, since it made him sound like a monster. A monster that was protecting Atlantis, and that I recently discovered was a dark god, not so dissimilar to myself. He really should be called something else.

"Fine, I'll subdue the demi-god from behind, and you try to talk. But as soon as I run out of air, bets are off."

"How long?"

"Hard to say. Even water snakes need air, eventually. Not all of us were given royal sea crowns as an engagement gift." She teased, and I glared back at her.

"I'm not engaged."

"Does he know that?"

Ignoring her, I dove into the water, and my wings pushed through, propelling me forward. She was right. Since having the crown on, I hadn't felt like the sea was trying to choke me to death. Theo swam up beside me as we ascended up through the water dome. A large serpent tail replaced her legs, letting her glide through with ease. Her red hair moved on its own, countering the force of moving forward. Upon closer inspection it was integrated with red snakes.

I wanted to ask her more about it but knew she couldn't speak under the water the same way I could. At least, I didn't want to test the theory, or waste any air.

Tentacles spread out above us, casting shadows around us, and once we got closer, I realized avoiding the Krag's many arms was also part of the rescue mission. His body was larger than the arena dome, and from it his arms whipped through the water, creating forceful waves against our swim towards him. He was using his own body to protect the city, his arms reaching out as far as the island was long.

Then I saw the figure glinting between the tentacles, riding the bright white horse with wings. Like me, the wings changed from feathers to a membrane in the water, but like my sister Pegasus's body turned more seahorse than land horse with more of coral-like curved bottom.

I couldn't quite make out the rider, as they held a shield, and by the time I was done admiring Pegasus, they both blurred from an incoming attack from the Krag.

Before the tentacle could reach its target, they were gone, but more disturbingly... so was the tentacle. It seemed to shrivel up and snap back into the main body of the giant octopus.

Shit.

He was running out of time, and I had spent so much time talking, and understanding what was going on, that he might not be able to distract the demi-god enough for me to talk with them and find a way to let the Krag escape.

Paying too much attention to where the demi-god went, and still of the mindset that the Krag was on my side, I wasn't paying attention. A giant suction cup smacked into me and whisked me towards the main body. A large chasm was opening up, and it must have been the octopus's mouth. He was going to eat me!

"I'm here to help you!" I struggled against my wings being caught in one of his suckers that was larger than me.

The tentacle curled up on itself and transferred me from one sucker to another before my stomach leapt up into my throat at the whiplash of being slung along with the large tentacle. Nearly passing out from being tossed back and forth in the water as the sucker moved with me firmly stuck in its hold, the movement finally stopped enough for me to feel queasy all over again.

When I opened my eyes, I was face to face with the Krag's large eye.

"I want to," I stopped to almost hurl, but held back, "I want to try to talk to the demi-god. Stop the attack," I said, hoping he could understand me.

The pressure on my wings eased, and the tentacle rotated up like I was a display piece. Or I was in his hand... if he had one. One of his other tentacles opened up, and Theo slithered away with her arms crossed, unhappy with being detained. I could only assume that the Krag understood and was going to help us, since he didn't decide to eat us. Or crush us.

Another arm rolled out in front of me, curling up and blocking a hit from the demi-god. My wings wrapped around protectively on instinct, and they ached with the effort. As I turned towards where the attack came from, a large hole windowed a perfect frame displaying the demi-god atop Pegasus.

No longer distracted by how Pegasus was working against us, I could see the demi-god clearly through the sizzling muscle of the giant octopus tentacle. The Krag was weakening, and it showed. He wasn't able to stop the attack from reaching me, and steam bubbled up from the wound and from behind me. My wings... They stopped it. Whatever that flash of light was.

"That's Athena's shield," Theo shouted with a gurgle, and I panicked, wondering how much time that cut from her oxygen supply. I didn't know how it worked with water snakes, but I doubted they opened their mouths and stayed under the water much longer after. She sounded frantic, terrified even at the mention of the shield.

It didn't look all that threatening, though most things were deceptive that way. The stone shield was polished, but dented with use. The woman that held it was petite and had her hair shaved on the sides, revealing a raised scar. Her eyes glowed golden as she stared back at me, sizing me up the same way I was with her.

She obviously held her own against the Krag, and from the hole in one of his tentacles she had power; power enough to fry a giant muscle underneath the water.

Her elbow was bent behind her, and I noticed a golden hilt glinting before she pulled it at the ready, a long golden sword that seemed almost too big for her to carry. The buoyancy of the water must've helped, but even so, as she pulled it from behind both herself and the side of Pegasus's body, I was surprised I didn't notice it sooner. I must've, though at the time it was a shiny glint in the distance, blurring my senses.

Pegasus reared up; her wings flared before her neigh through the water reached my ears. "I have no choice." It was the only warning I was going to get. She was going to attack again, and I had no plan but to speak with someone who didn't seem interested in listening.

But Pegasus was...

"What does she want? Is there another way?" I shouted, hoping Pegasus could help. It was a long shot, but just because she was bound to help the demi-god, didn't mean she couldn't also help both of us?

It was worth a shot, though there wasn't much time, and I couldn't stay here unless I wanted the Krag to lose a limb.

Jumping up from the tentacle, my wings took over, and I darted away. Not that I could follow where Pegasus was going; she was much faster than I could track. I just had to hope that she heard me, and not even knowing where I was going would be enough to confuse a pursuer.

"She must defeat the Krag; there is no other way," Pegasus warned. She sounded defeated. She was helping destroy the only defense of her brother's city.

"Then that's what has to happen." I knew it was risky, but it was better than doing nothing. It had to be. I watched as the demi-god ignored me all together to throw her sword at another one of the Krag's limbs, severing one of them right off before it shriveled up and sucked back into his main body.

He couldn't take much more.

While one of the Krag's limbs disappeared, the demi-god swooped down his length looking to make a devastating blow to his core. The large, bulky tentacles were too slow to keep up with her movements now—she'd end him if I didn't do something.

Already I was swiftly making my way towards where she was heading without thinking about it. I was willing to place my own body in front of him, like he did for me. I was banking my life that my wings would defend me the same way they did last time. Her strike made it through his muscle, but not through my wings.

Swinging her sword, that same flash of light burst out that had blinded me from seeing the attack before. With this new vantage point, I saw something I missed before. Turning away from the light, I could see the Krag's body like it was under an x-ray. His entire exoskeleton lit up, throbbing at the back of his mantle were three hearts. One of which was hardly pumping at all, damaged from earlier in their fight.

A shadow approached one of the hearts, in the shape of wings and a rider... before that heart stopped along with the other.

He had one left.

When the light faded, so too did the vision of the Krag's organs. He floated still in the water, and I knew that turning back into his mortal form was the least of our worries. He would die before that happened with one more strike to his final heart.

That was her plan this whole time. Strategically targeting only his hearts.

Getting closer to where I saw the final heart, I needed to make sure she couldn't land the last blow.

Light flashed again, illuminating his body, and a pained cry vibrated through the creature.

Pinning the location of the heart, I launched myself, trying to protect a heart that was bigger than my whole body.

The other hearts were still functioning... but barely. Even the large sword was small in comparison to the creature's organs. I knew enough about anatomy to know you didn't have to obliterate the whole organ to make sure it couldn't do its job. Every valve, every section played a vital role, and the extra stress of the rest of the heart could cause the whole system to fail.

He may have been a dark god, but he was vulnerable, and he wouldn't be the first god to fall.

Another flash of light illuminated the final heart, and I knew the final blow would come soon. Then, as soon as I saw the heart in front of me, larger than a room, it disappeared.

Vanished.

My eyes too focused on where the heart had been, I didn't notice what had run into me, or me into it.

A limp body dangled in my arms.

Then, in the same instant, the pain seared my back. Arching back with the force of what hit me from behind. Then the pain was gone.

Shock took over. I knew it was only temporary.

Feathers exploded in a golden firework display around me and my mystery body that I clung to in frozen agony. My muscles tensed up, bearing down for what I would feel shortly.

My wings were gone, scattered around me, fizzling in a golden dust like they were burning under water.

Then we both sank as I screamed.

My claws dug into the flesh of my companion to ease the pain, but he couldn't seem to move or react to the new wounds. The weight of him dragged us down, but I couldn't let go. My claws still clung onto his back, digging in. His long, black hair wisped across his face as his head lulled back, and then I recognized him...

Mavron.

His arms twitched, one of them had a golf-ball sized hole through his forearm... the attack from earlier. The Krag.

The Krag was Mavron.

It was looking like neither of us was going to escape fate at this rate.

Groaning, Mavron stirred.

"We're both free now," he said, resigned.

"Don't give up on us yet," I gritted, barely above a whisper.

"I thought," he choked, "with the crown... you were ready..." he was fading, and I felt my own vision blur, but forced myself to stay conscious.

"Ready for what?"

"To protect..." he couldn't finish what he tried to say before going limp in my arms again.

"It's okay," I assured him. "I can fix this." At least I thought I could fix this. Maybe. It was a fifty-fifty shot really. I didn't know why my blood sometimes healed and sometimes poisoned. All I knew was that it did.

And if I was anything like my sister, then maybe it had to do with the location of where the blood came from. My sister's venom was at the back of her jaw and into her neck. As well as in the snakes within her hair.

Coraline bit my neck.

Maybe it had nothing to do with my blood at all?

With a renewed sense of confidence, I believed I could save him. Save us both.

But my whole body still couldn't move, and we were now drifting farther down, missing the city, disappearing into the darkness of a crevasse below.

The pressure of the water surrounding us squeezed, making us even heavier. Creatures I never imagined before began a light show more incredible than any firework display I had seen in my life.

Our presence... my presence stirred the beings of the deep to react, their bio-luminescence showing me a world I could hardly describe.

We caught on a rocky ledge covered in something similar to coral, but soft, and it sprayed a sticky dust up at us that covered our bodies in a kind of glowing spray paint of the sea.

"Aless..." Mavron groaned, bringing my attention to his current wakefulness.

"I'm still working on it." For some reason, I couldn't move my arms without searing pain down my shoulders and up my neck. Gritting my teeth, I tried to dislodge my claws from Mavron's back, making him growl and grunt, giving me new hope that he'd make it through this. If only I could give him my blood. Using the same finger I used when I was a kid to help a caterpillar that wouldn't move.

Letting his body ease away from me, I lifted my finger to his mouth, covered in his own blood that wouldn't wash away with the lack of current reaching us, but there wasn't much of a choice. I didn't have much more movement in me after this.

Whatever the demi-god did to me, it was bad, and I probably didn't even realize the full extent of the damage of what hit us.

"You need to bite down." I couldn't believe I was even suggesting this, but he was already half dead as it was, so even if I poisoned him, it was a mercy to go fast. And it couldn't hurt worse than what I was already feeling.

His eyes didn't even open, but his teeth pressed down slightly on the pad of my finger letting me know that he heard me before he used his canine tooth to only make a small prick that I couldn't even feel above the rest of my body's aches.

Without me saying anything more, he suckled, his tongue licking along my skin to capture my blood already knowing what he needed to do. After a few minutes, he spoke. "You're in worse shape than me, and I'm not sure your healing is helping enough to save either of us if we stay much longer."

"You...kay?" I mumbled, feeling myself become sleepy. Before I let myself take a nap, I had to know he was okay.

Mavron's face glowed with the sea paint looking otherworldly. He grabbed my hand gently between both of his hands and trailed the finger down his cheek to his chest, where two gashes were that I hadn't noticed since I was holding him to me as we descended into the darkness of the sea floor.

He stuck my finger to his wounds, and I watched as they closed up. Nothing festered. He wasn't convulsing. He was alive.

My mouth lifted in a small smile, knowing I could finally close my eyes.

The demi-god didn't succeed, but everyone who watched would believe he was dead. I had to tell him. Tell him he couldn't go back to Atlantis. That I made sure to break his oath with the king. He could leave. He could live. He could be free.

My eyes closed.

A pressure on my shoulder made me screech in pain. My lids flew open in alarm. Mavron had pushed his thumb into wherever my wound was. That's right... I remembered groggily; I was hurt too. I had forgotten—everything was numb.

He clamped his hand on my shoulder again, and I screamed before I could close my eyes again.

Mavron growled, "Stay awake. I'll get you out of here."

My fingers dug into his arms.

"No!" I had to tell him. He can't return. Other lives are at stake besides his own. "You can't go back. You need..." I had to spit it out. I was so tired, "stay dead."

Those dark black eyes softened in the glow of the sea paint.

"My Queen, that last blow from Chrysaor's sword was poisoned, and your blood hasn't stopped the infection."

"That's why they didn't follow..." He called me queen? His queen? I didn't marry Triton. I didn't, did I?

Atlantis's customs were ancient, but I didn't remember doing any-thing handfasting like.

"It's likely they believe both of us were infected–Shit," he swore, "stay with me."

I squirmed in his arms, and the coral beneath us puffed out more sea paint around us. The pain in my shoulder at him squeezing my wound was searing.

"Call Poseidon now," he said in a panic. "If we can't go back to Atlantis without dying then it's the only other way."

My teeth ground out. "I'm sure he's just swimming within earshot," I mocked.

"He's the god of the seas, and commonly forgotten a god of the land as well. You simply have to talk to him."

"Then you do it." I didn't mean it to sound rude, but I couldn't stay awake much longer. I was too tired, and if he wanted to have Poseidon help us, then he could do it himself. That's what he wanted to begin with , to be free of his oath to find him. He could do that. Poseidon wasn't reaching me in time for anything, if he even returned from whatever hole he dug for himself over the centuries.

I was going to take a nap and let the numbness ease the ache and sting of my back and shoulder.

"Stay awake or I'll have no choice but to keep causing you more pain."

I struggled to open my eyes again, but I didn't think I could take another squeeze. I'd probably just pass out from the pain. Before Atlantis, I'd have passed out long before now. Guess I could thank my stint in the dungeon for my new endurance. Mo would say things happen for a reason, I suspected.

Being a Fate and all.

"He wouldn't hear me," Mavron tried to explain, but before he could finish, the light show around us dimmed, all the life of the deep sea hushed, we were the only ones that glowed. His cheeks puffed out, and he spit into the water. Black ink surrounded us until we disappeared into the darkness.

Something was out there, bigger than us.

Scarier than whatever else lurked here to have the whole sea life quiet.

Then I heard him, the god of the sea itself. At least, that's who I imagined it to be in my delirium. "I don't have much time," a darkly husky voice vibrated through my enchanted crab shells.

"That makes two of us," I mocked with almost a laugh at the irony, but a deep part of me knew he wasn't pleased with that response. At least, in my imagination he could act concerned for my sake.

The water rippled over the dark features of Mavron, and it was bright blue eyes that stared out at me instead of his black ones. Poseidon was using Mavron almost like a lightning rod to focus his communication with me, or I was hallucinating. It didn't really matter which one at this point.

"I have no rule over the trident, little goddess. I have little power to give you, but what I have is yours to take. Will you have it?" He seemed near to begging me to accept, and a sudden clarity rushed through me. Was I actually talking with Poseidon, the sea god?

"Why?" Why would the god of the sea give me his power? Why would he be talking to me? It didn't make any sense. And with what Triton said to me about how he received his power, there was always a sacrifice to make. Something lost in order to gain. What did the god want from me? Was it the power of the golden crown of Amphitrite?

Just like the statue Triton made of Poseidon, his eyes were sad, distant as he replied, "The correct question is 'what'. What do I have to gain? And the answer is simple, little goddess. It's you."

My heart tugged in my ribcage at the way he talked. This was supposed to be the first time I ever spoke with Poseidon, but something about him was so familiar. I didn't want to let him go, but I knew he was right. There wasn't much time. And he needed his power to help Atlantis. To help Triton.

"Don't—" I stopped before I admitted to myself why it was so important to keep him with me. The dreaded thought stirred within me that the price paid to have his power was too high, and I wouldn't be the one to pay it.

I could feel my eyes swelling, and I was thankful for being surrounded by water and darkness to hide these unexplainable feelings.

Why did I feel like I was being torn apart and the pain wasn't even near where I was poisoned. It was so much deeper, in the pit of my gut, rising up and aching in my chest.

"You always were so soft hearted," Poseidon lifted a hand to cup my face, Mavron's hand covered in the ink and sea foam, "I know now, it is not a weakness to care. I'm braver now than I have ever been, and so are you."

"What are you going to do?" I narrowed my eyes at him.

Smiling his deep blue eyes twinkled back at me. "Now, you're asking the right questions. Deep down you already know what I must do, you just haven't accepted it."

"I'm supposed to protect you..." I began, feeling my panic grow.

"You have, more than you know."

"It's not enough. You need your power."

"You need it more."

Then his lips descended on me. Slow at first, with tenderness and warmth until I felt myself melt into him. Everything about his touch was electric. My whole system was shocked with a heat that burned behind my eyes until what I was left with was so raw.

All I saw was him, and his features sharpened, then all I saw was...

Dion.

But it wasn't Dion, it couldn't be. He wore the very same crown Triton wore, and the trident floated behind him almost like spikes sprung from his shoulders.

Dion released me, and his dark blue eyes watched with a chaotic mischief that was seductive and exciting. The call of the sea hung about him.

"I pray this will be the way you remember me always," he said with a soft smile, "because right now you look at me with wonder, as if without me you would be nothing..." Pausing he shook his head, "It is me who would be nothing without you."

I couldn't quite place it, but this wasn't happening right now. I knew that this had already happened. That this was already said before. And I remembered what I said back to him.

"You will live on without me, my love. You must. I've made up my mind," I told him, a flood of forgotten feelings coming over me. This had all happened before. Another time. Another life.

Dion backed away from me, annoyance on his face. Frustration. He groaned with frightening rage. Yet I smiled back at him, knowing that was his nature, and his rage wasn't intended for me.

"Why must you die for mortals you don't even know? This is how it has always been. You are being used! We are always being used. Countless dark gods were dead at the hands of quests and divine rites of passage. You will be nothing more than another tool for other's prosperity, I cannot allow—"

"It is my choice. I know Perseus is coming for me, Moirai is never wrong. I am fated to die tonight, and it's too late for you to stop it. Have faith that the plan will work." The words left my mouth, and they felt strange, like I was caught in a loop of the past.

"You're trusting Athena with your life…" Dion shook his head in disbelief, "the very god that cursed you. That cursed us!" I couldn't trust that he would listen to me, his rage would blind him. I took this choice from him.

I remembered now, at least this much. Athena helped spread the rumor that I was mortal, and she wasn't lying completely. All dark gods were vulnerable to death, even if we could live forever. Divine objects are capable of ending that life, but I had a gift.

I believed in that gift once, and it served me then.

"You've poisoned me." Dion clutched his throat, feeling himself grow solid, stiff as stone. He wouldn't stay that way for long, he wasn't meant to, he was a god, and it was but a drop.

But by the time he was free, I would be gone.

I kissed his firm lips, as the stone inched its way over his cheeks. I watched as his very eyes hardened to gems.

He was meant to live.

I gasped, feeling the heat of his power course through me, and my mind came back to the present.

Dion was in trouble…

And his image disappeared in the water, Mavron replacing him, shock on his face as he touched his lips, aware that he stood in for someone else's intimate moment.

I blushed, thinking of the way his lips moved against mine, but I was thankful it was much too dark to see clearly it was Mavron.

"Your shoulder… it's healed," he changed the subject.

Moving my joints around and feeling no pain, I confirmed his words.

"I guess you're right."

I knew who I was now. A little piece of my past returned.

I was Medusa, but I was also Aless.

Mostly Aless.

The few memories I had were like watching someone else's life, and whatever connection I had with it was distant. I knew I loved him. Loved Poseidon.

And somehow, that love overlapped onto Dion. He reminded me of him, and I knew in my gut something was wrong.

"You are more powerful now," Mavron could sense it.

"Poseidon gave me his power."

"He's more vulnerable than ever then…"

"I know," I said guiltily. I thought I stopped him in time for him to keep his power.

I also knew I was ready for it. Behind Mavron was a large predator fish that had spooked the rest of the life down in this crevasse. I could sense it now. Almost like the sea was speaking to me.

Waving my hand to shoo it away, the sea spoke for me, and the looming shadow quickly rushed farther into the deep. All of the luminescence of the darkest part, but also the brightest part of the sea lit up again, back to business as usual.

Before it was Mavron's ink that hid us from the danger of being eaten here, and now it was me, and the power of the sea. I was pretty sure having Poseidon's power was temporary, so I wasn't going to test how much time I had to protect him before it would return from where it came.

"Tell me where he is," I demanded of the sea, desperate to get to him in time.

"He gave you his power to save you, not for you to risk your life. He knew what he was doing when he gave you his power," Mavron tried to change my mind.

I grabbed his arm.

"We're both dead already," I joked, "might as well haunt a few folks while we're at it."

My wings burst forth from my shoulders, completely mended by my blood and Poseidon's power. We shot out from the crevasse faster than even Pegasus with the help of the sea, no one would see us coming.

There weren't many who knew the location of the golden orchard, but Poseidon knew, and by extension... the sea.

Chapter 17

Golden Apple

"You don't have to come with me," I gave Mavron his last chance to back out of helping. We were close now. I could feel it.

"I'm healed up from your blood, and letting you die isn't an option. Haven't you heard the prophecy? You're some kind of Queen of the Dark Gods, and every dark god left on this forsaken earth would have my head if you died."

"You already called me your queen," I teased.

"Yah, yah. I was in the heat of the moment. You just saved my life."

"Are you blushing? It's hard to tell under your—"

"Apollo was mistaken. You're much too green to inspire a rebellion or the Olympianmachy."

My grin faded. He was right.

"I don't really intend on surviving this to be anyone's queen," I admitted.

"Why go then? If you don't plan on winning, all you're doing is sacrificing more lives. You won't be doing anyone any favors."

Puffing my cheeks in frustration, I blew out bubbles in a huff.

"Triton will be there too. He's running into a trap."

"A trap we are willingly heading into ourselves?" He accurately assessed the situation.

"What if there is an apple left?" I had to hope there was, that all of this was real.

"Then one person lives if they get to it," he droned unenthusiastically about our lack of a plan.

I smiled sadly with an exaggerated shrug, and he finally got what I was getting at. Atlantis needs Poseidon or Triton, and that apple could help. Mavron tugged back to slow our swim.

"Don't you understand why he was attempting to get the apple to begin with? You think that was for himself?"

"He won't get it on his own... not without his power." Not with his power. Now, I didn't have to say what we were both thinking. If it weren't for me, then he might have been fine retrieving it alone.

Mavron shook his head, resigned.

"What aren't you saying?" He asked, and I could see he wasn't going to back down, already sensing where this was heading. The choice I had made.

"You got that from him, didn't you?" I asked, fondly remembering the way Dion thought about things, the way he knew the right questions to ask. "Never mind. Just know that fate was destined to repeat itself. I'm supposed to die. Might as well make use of what time I have left."

"Then you have me at your side. Two ghosts for one last battle."

My heart swelled with two different emotions—thankfulness and distress that I couldn't protect him again. What I was asking of him was a suicide mission, and we both knew it.

The orchard was at the next landmass. I knew it in the way the sea thrummed through me. We were here. Poseidon was close. Emerging from the water, the waves washed us up onto the shore. My wings flicked water from their leathery membranes until they transformed back into golden feathers with the last drops of water.

A hum in my head rustled my golden hair, and I knew my old friends were back. Now that I remembered them. One of my yellow snakes rubbed up against my cheek, licking a bit of moisture from my skin. I grinned. It was like a missing piece of me returned.

"Shhh, you're awake now." I palmed the snake in my hand and whispered, "I'm sorry." Not believing in the gods suppressed my abilities to call on them. They were very good at protecting me, sensing danger.

I turned my head at the sound of some of my snakes almost chuckling and saw Mavron with his eyes closed.

"It never worked like that," I couldn't help but find it humorous, "turning you into stone, that is, if it was, then no one would have known what I looked like. It's actually part of the poison... so don't get bit."

"Right," Mavron cleared his throat, and walked past me with gusto as if he wasn't concerned about it at all, and staring at his bare butt, I realized this whole time he was naked.

I blinked and quickly covered my eyes with one of my snakes.

I coughed.

I was the one embarrassed now.

"Um, are you going into the Orchard like that?"

"It didn't seem to bother you before," he teased, knowing he was off the hook for believing the rumors about people with snakes in their hair. Believe it or not, there used to be many dark gods with heads full of snakes. It wasn't all that un-ordinary of mom's children. Most of the myths just focused on my sisters and me, but there were lots of myths of lamia and nagas.

And none of them turned people to stone.

That was specific to my poison.

And now I remembered about Theo. Her poison could cure my snakes' poison.

My snakes' poison... Why was it important to specify?

I had another sister!

Younger than Theo, but older than me.

What was her name?

I couldn't remember.

"It's just up ahead," I warned Mavron.

"Do you have a plan?"

"Actually, I do... strange enough, I thought of this day a long time ago."

"Oh good, I thought I was committing suicide."

"Not quite," I said with a confidence I didn't know I possessed. It was still very much close to a suicide run, and the plan wasn't really fully formed. If you considered giving back these powers borrowed from Poseidon a plan.

Honestly, success weighed heavily on Poseidon's ability to tip the scales in our favor and get us the hell out of there. Which, in turn, was reliant on Triton giving him the trident.

That sounded reasonable in my head.

Why wouldn't Triton give his father the trident if it meant getting everyone out of the trap, and saving Atlantis?

I mean, the only thing protecting the city now was the people gathering to the Arena to strengthen the power there. Until the demi-god could win against all of the gladiators, however long that took. I knew Theo would try to stall as long as she could to protect Atlantis.

"Are you going to tell me what it is, or should I just be surprised when it happens?" Mavron pressed for more information, and I cringed.

"You don't have one, do you?" he accused.

"I do. It's just that suddenly I have doubts about what it would mean for Triton. I wasn't really thinking about him when I thought about a future where Poseidon was reunited with his trident."

"But now you are?"

I shoved his shoulder. "Get dressed or something." I changed the subject to avoid talking about it. I was conflicted, Triton was kind, and a bit pushy, but he seemed to genuinely care about his subjects, and even me. I touched my lips, and when I caught Mavron's black eyes again, he had sprouted a tentacle and wrapped it around himself, suction cup in so it stayed in place. Then another tentacle weaved, creating a makeshift toga. All of his tentacles were released from his back, except four, which I guessed were still being used as his arms and legs.

"How does that even work?" I kept imagining him transforming into the Krag, and all of his tentacles were all tangled up as he tried to defend himself. Then he would fumble and fall to the ground, which also didn't make sense because of swimming... buoyancy and stuff.

It didn't change the image in my mind though.

"Never mind," I didn't need to know, and we had more important things to do, and our time was limited.

Mavron shrugged, the ends of his tentacles sprawled out behind him like a creepy cape, or a sunburst in a land of invertebrates.

"If it comes down to it, I will knock you out and drag you back to Atlantis if it's the only option to save you."

"Aren't you loyal to Poseidon or Triton. What about them? Are you going to knock them out too?"

Unconcerned, he simply replied, "No."

"But you're loyal to me?"

His smile twisted, It was slightly unnerving, and I wondered if octopuses had sharp teeth like the merpeople, but his teeth looked normal. Now that I thought about it, I didn't see any teeth when he almost ate me either.

Loyalty probably had nothing to do with it.

"Let's just say, though the sea gods have spared me, my loyalty isn't with the Olympians."

"Right…" The dark gods, and I was one of them. Not just one of them, one prophesied by Apollo to lead them into a new hierarchy. One where the dark gods ruled. Bringing in the new generation of leaders. It didn't sound all that bad when I put it that way, not quite as scary sounding as the Olympianmachy, a fight between the Olympians and the Dark Gods.

Plus, why did we have to be called the dark gods, anyway? What was so dark about us?

Assessing Mavron didn't really help my case—black eyes, inky black hair, and skin. He was basically the epitome of dark, tall, and well, I wasn't going to inflate his ego anymore than that. He wasn't all that bad looking, but he did have a sinister quality to him.

And, my sisters and I… we all had a certain kind of poisonous quality about us. Guess we kind of were dark.

We were walking through barren trees covered in moss and rot. They resembled claws sprouting from the brown ground, waiting to grab you and take you to the Underworld.

Shit...

We were here. I'd been distracted, and we walked right in without any caution. This was the orchard; these were the apple trees.

They used to be, at one point.

Now, they were just dead.

I shivered.

The whole place creeped me out, and what's worse is that it was so quiet. At the very least we should have heard Dion, or Triton, somewhere, shouldn't we have?

Stopping, I grabbed for Mavron's arm, but ended up gripping a muscly tentacle instead. I would have thought it would have felt more slimy, or squishy, but it wasn't. It was firm, and almost like grabbing a smooth rock, except it pulsed... so, I naturally dropped it, but it served its purpose to stop Mavron from moving forward.

"Maybe they already got the apple?" Mavron joked, though both of us knew that wasn't the case.

"They're here." Instinct made my forearms ripple with armored golden feathers, and my claws grew out of my fingers. I was on edge.

Then I heard a rustle that made me dart behind one of the large husks of a rotten tree.

Following my lead, Mavron did the same. His tentacles pulled in close to himself, and the ones that didn't easily hid behind the twisted branches, becoming one with the tree.

"You were supposed to go with them," a deep voice reprimanded.

"They separated; I thought it prudent to join Triton. She'll be here eventually." It was Ray talking to someone.

Thank goodness, and before I thought it through, I jumped out.

"Where is Triton?"

She smiled, and Mavron slapped a tentacle to his face. Then I saw a slim man dressed in a suit next to her. Compared to her sentinel uniform and the normal attire I'd seen on Atlantis, the suit was strangely abnormal for the circumstances. And here I was dressed in the same golden dress Triton put me in for my first appearance to the Atlantians.

With a well-groomed beard, and wavy golden-brown hair he assessed me before responding.

My jaw dropped. I probably jumped the light a bit with assuming Ray would be helpful. She'd proved the opposite before.

"As you can see," he motioned to the surroundings with his chin, "the rumors about the last golden apple were just that... rumors." The suited man turned his back to me and proceeded to walk down the path between the trees. At one point, the trees were strategically placed, and probably were part of a beautiful garden long ago. Even the ground, if you scuffed it enough, you could see the stones used for a path, before they were overgrown with weeds and dirt.

Ray waved her hand excitedly to me for us to follow.

"Fate is funny sometimes, always bringing people together. We weren't the only ones curious about finding the last golden apple outside of Olympus."

"I guess," Mavron still wasn't convinced, and neither was I.

"Outside of Olympus," I repeated.

It was the suit that answered, "Yes, Hera moved her garden after the first time Atlas stole an apple for Hercules. She poisoned the orchard after she was able to spread the seeds behind her house. Now, if someone wants to take an apple without permission, they would have to go through Zeus.

"Between us, it's been said not even Zeus is allowed to enter the garden for fear he would use the apples for his side pieces."

Ray cleared her throat, uncomfortable with the conversation, which given her past conversations about 'fishing', I found odd.

"I thought the apples were a gift from Hera to Zeus for their wedding."

"Ah, so you know a bit about your history after all. But the truth is a bit more complex than that. Golden apples weren't created by any of the Olympians, it was created by Gaia, and she chose this island, at the edge of the world between sea, earth, mortals, death, and Olympus to give the gift of immortality to her children.

"The fruit of the gods was the reason why gods lived forever, so our own gifts could be given endlessly back into the land from which we all spawned."

It seemed like there would be consequences for destroying such a gift, even if she did move the garden to Olympus.

Mavron whispered, "Was this part of your plan?"

I shook my head, still debating if I should be following them or not. They were obviously part of the trap, or even if they weren't, they would probably lead us into the cross hairs.

"How did you know I would come?" My feet dug in, not willing to budge without an answer.

Ray huffed exasperated and pointed to her head then to me. "Everyone knows the crown lets you talk with whoever controls the trident."

The suit lifted a finger to object. "Love," he mocked the word like it was a silly notion that amused him, "Poseidon was a sap, and also a bit of a control freak. He made that crown to 'test' people. If they could hear him, then their love was true or some sad sop like that.

"It's ingenious, really. Who didn't want to wear a golden crown that would let them 'speak' with the sea? All while he made sure of their loyalty to him."

"She loves him?" Ray lifted a brow at me, disbelief evident.

"We'll soon find out," the suit said gleefully. I didn't like the way that sounded one bit.

I could hear lots of people with the crown, but from a distance... not once did I hear Triton's voice, not without seeing him.

I heard Poseidon. What did that mean?

Shaking the thought, I found myself growing more and more irritated with the familiar, friendly nature of this strange, suited man.

"Where is he?" I hissed, and even my scalp tingled with the need of my snakes. They wished to show themselves, but something in me warned not to.

Why was I protective about keeping my snakes hidden?

The confusion made even my threat towards this man fall flat.

"With the nymphs, of course. That's where we are headed, after all."

"What have you done with him?"

The man stopped and turned slowly to face me. All smiles he said, "Me? I've simply given him the same option I'll give you, to prove worthy of the last golden apple."

"You have the apple?" Mavron, ever the skeptic, wanted proof.

I couldn't blame him; it saved me the trouble of demanding proof myself.

He pointed to the oldest looking tree up ahead, the one tree larger, and not lined up quite like the others. The original golden apple tree. It must have been magnificent when it wasn't charred up and gray with death.

But I followed where his finger led and finally spotted it.

A single apple, small, almost hidden behind the black leaves... I should have noticed that before. It had leaves.

Very little, and nearly imperceptible with how black and decrepit the jangly branches were, but there all the same.

Even the apple was a bit rotten looking, but I wouldn't have called it an apple if someone else didn't call it that first. Certainly, a kind of fruit, but not what I would have imagined an apple looking like. The leaves hung over the fruit like a bloom, or husk. Only a peek of gold could be seen at the top, like the pollen of a flower.

Honestly, it appeared more like a poisonous flower than a fruit of the gods, and immortal life.

Lifting a brow I remarked, "You're joking..." I knew he wasn't, but even earlier he talked as if there wasn't an apple at all, and now he was revealing it to me. Why?

This was too easy.

Suspiciously easy, if all I had to do was grab it. Which, there had to be more to it.

"If that's the apple, then why haven't you grabbed it?" Did my suited man even know, or was he trying to get someone else to grab it for him, just in case?

Wait...

Was that what happened to Dion and Triton?

Why couldn't I hear either of them, even with the crown? Was it because we weren't in the sea?

They grabbed the apple, and they disappeared? Or were caught in a trap trying to get the apple?

The suit smiled, only fueling my unease.

"As I said before, you'll get the same treatment as the others, but maybe you'll satisfy the nymphs and retrieve your apple."

Not daring to approach the large apple tree, without first taking another glance around, I stayed where I was. There were a few trees that didn't match with an apple orchard, and also did not fit into the neat rows previously seen.

An elm, an oak, and a poplar.

And at the foot of the apple tree, underneath the branch that held the single fruit, was a large trunk, a natural platform.

How was it possible that any of these trees could be there, and especially the blackened stump so close to a tree that would have been guarded constantly?

"The trees are different here," I told Mavron, warning him, but also hoping maybe he would know more, having grown up in this world of gods.

"Those are not trees..." he said as one of the dead-looking trees whistled in the wind. A sweet song floating in the air drew me in.

The light in the sky dimmed, giving the orchard an eerie glow.

Ray took a step back, and the suit stayed where he was, waiting, watching.

"Do you wish to eat the fruit?" they sang, "Immortality you can choose, if you wish it to be true. Just one bite of divinities dew. Face the night, embrace your fright, and we'll give it to you."

"Do you hear them?" I wondered out loud.

"Sublimely beautiful, aren't they?" the suit said wistfully. "Well, shall we?"

"After you," I offered. If he thought I was dumb enough to be the first one to answer creepy tree nymphs call to face my fears, he was mistaken.

I didn't care about the damn apple. I just wanted to grab Triton and Dion. If they were here, then it stands to reason they probably took the nymph's challenge.

Ray gave me a 'go-get-er-girl' pat on the shoulder as encouragement, but even for a sentinel she was firm in not getting any closer than where she was.

"Did you just let Triton enter on his own?" I questioned her.

"He's a grown... I'd say, man, but is he really? Whatever, he wasn't interested in me following. I was to keep guard, and then this spicy delicacy showed up."

The spicy suit quirked a brow at Ray's description of himself. He still didn't offer an introduction, and I didn't care to ask him.

"You said you were expecting me..." I couldn't wrap my head around the inconsistencies.

"When he didn't come back right away, I figured you'd hear from him with your crown, and you couldn't help yourself but get into the weeds with him. It's your M.O. Tell you to stay away, try to keep you out of danger and you just reel yourself towards it, anyway.

"I bet he even told you he had it handled, and you—"

My face burned, remembering how I yelled at him, and he forcefully dragged me to the Arena, and stormed off to join Dion for the apple. Clenching my fist, he had chosen to come here instead of protecting his city, protecting Mavron.

The buzz of my snakes echoed in my ears, and I had to focus to make sure they didn't reveal themselves.

"He could have done this after protecting Atlantis," I fumed.

"Not likely," Ray leaned in, against any instinct she might have had that told her I was not to be messed with right now, she whispered, "He doesn't have full control over the trident."

My heart was hammering, worry overriding my anger. What did she know?

"How is that possible?"

"He's only a demi-god. Amphitrite was a powerful ocean nymph that rose to the status of god. He needs the golden apple to replenish his power so he can control the trident and take over as the god of the sea," Ray explained casually, like that was information everyone should know.

The suit couldn't help himself but to contribute to the conversation, "The sea will never be tamed. The more you try to control it, the more it fights against you. That is something Poseidon understood, and that is why he will never be dethroned. Even if he never wanted to be a king," he spoke fondly of Poseidon, and stared off at the tree like he was reliving a past life before seriously noting, "Now, that there is a queen, the sea will rise again."

"Another prophecy?"

The stranger's bright blue eyes sparkled. "Yes, the bastard will return whether or not he wants to." He straightened himself, and with a gleam about him, he marched forward towards the tree. I watched as he stepped up onto the willow trunk, and like a mirage about him, a full bloom willow tree encased him—what the trunk must have been in the past.

The suit smiled and released a deep-throated chuckle before magic swept through the inner circle of the orchard revealing an illusion over the reality of what the garden used to be.

His hand reached up to pluck the fruit, and before he could reach it... he screamed, and disappeared.

I gulped back my discomfort.

"That's encouraging..." I mumbled.

"Did your plan account for the nymphs?" Mavron prodded the holes in my initial idea of finding Triton, and giving the trident to Poseidon. I mean I was pretty sure Poseidon was here. Why else would the sea lead me to the garden?

"I'm pretty sure they're in the ground..." Ray offered, and I glared at her. Lifting her hands up in mock surrender, she quickly added, "The first time caught me off guard. I was paying attention this time. The light was coming from," she pointed to the willow trunk, which I wouldn't have known was a willow if it didn't fake bloom in front of us, "below him. There was still a shadow above him, and the light was dispersing around him. Plus," she turned on her sentinel all business mode, "Triton didn't step on the trunk to reach the apple."

"What did he do?" I demanded.

She nodded like she was relaying a report and continued, "He used his trident to send water to grab it. As soon as the water wrapped around the fruit, he froze before calling out your name."

I cringed, knowing I wasn't there because he forced me to stay. He never planned on bringing me with him.

"Then the light came, and created the mirage of the past garden..." I filled in the rest, then mused, "So, it only happens when you attempt to grab the fruit. Even if you do so from far away. How did Hercules do it?"

"He didn't," Mavron answered. "Atlas retrieved it for him. His daughters protect the tree. They used to be beautiful nymphs, but Hera didn't trust them not to eat the fruit themselves, and she didn't like the idea of them having more of the fruit than herself."

Ray laughed. "You would pick the story about how she cared how much the nymphs ate. She cared about Zeus seducing them and giving the fruit to his affairs."

"Hera turned them into trees," Mavron finished quickly.

"Then why is it that one of them is just a trunk?"

Ray shrugged. "Probably went fishing with Zeus before she decided to turn them into trees. You'd have to ask them to know for sure."

"You're not considering going wherever they took them, right?" Mavron was seriously considering knocking me out now, instead of later, to prevent falling into the trap.

"In the ground?" I asked Ray.

She nodded.

"As long as we don't reach for the apple, we should be fine to snoop around a bit."

"Sure..." he wasn't convinced, "but only if she joins us." I didn't blame him for being suspicious of Ray, but we didn't have much of a choice. I mean, sure there was a choice. We could leave, but without the trident, Atlantis was in danger.

"Fine, but I'm not touching the trees," she stormed past us, determined to prove her bravery, but also not dumb enough to tempt fate too much.

Mavron watched her closely.

"Where exactly did he stand last?" I ignored both of their glares at each other.

Ray pointed to a spot that was still wet. That made sense.

With my foot, I smeared the grime around, not sure what I was expecting to find.

Then I heard them sing again, "Into the light little bird, a true healer much stronger than myrrh. Dripping with life sea's lost goddess, you've stolen of Hades what was his to profess. Blood is your token, but entrance alone will not give what was taken. A choice must be made, a price will be paid.

"Sing for the goddess, darkness upon us, we welcome the queen of the night."

"We welcome the queen of the night."

"May the dark fly above the light," then their song repeated.

When I heard the last note again, the song turned to hums, and I remembered what Ray had said about a shadow above the light that took the suit.

Blood was my token.

I had wings...

Fly above the light, but where the shadow was...

"I got it!" I shouted before rushing to the trunk, my wings bursting from my back in my excitement. Fighting... I wasn't so great at, but I could handle a riddle!

"That's the first time they sang that song..." Ray added casually, not even a really strong effort to stop me, or give advice.

"Stop!" Mavron extended his tentacles to try to grab me, uncaring about his makeshift covering anymore. The light blossomed from the willow trunk as I approached.

Not every challenge was physical, and if I learned anything from Hercules, it was sometimes your wit could be just as strong as your might. I could do this.

What was all of my studying for, if I couldn't do this one thing? I'd bring back Triton and Dion.

"Protect Atlantis!" I called back at Mavron. If I didn't make it back out, he had to try again to make sure the demi-god didn't destroy Atlantis. I was hoping all the demi-god wanted was to kill Mavron, and thinking she succeeded, maybe she'd leave Atlantis alone, but I couldn't be sure, and he might be their last hope if I don't bring Triton back in time.

"F—," Mavron swore, and instead of heading away like I wanted him to, he latched on as a drop of my blood hit the trunk.

The tree bloomed, branches morphed into arms, then legs, and golden hair, not dissimilar to my own. Then it dimmed, turning a golden brown. And the orchard disappeared into a wasteland.

"Thank you," the nymph bristled with her new life. "It's been so long since I've stretched."

"Where is he?" I couldn't see Triton or Dion anywhere. It was a wasteland.

"You can call me, Gily," she said instead, folding her arms over her chest like I insulted her for not wanting to chitchat.

"Like for gills?" Mavron mocked her name.

She glared at him and pointed accusingly. "You cheated!" She huffed, and pulled at her hair, distressed, before adding, "It's pronounced GA-EL-Y, it's for Aegil, dumbass. I'm the dazzling light of the sisters of night." Then she blushed a fierce shade of red, hiding her face behind her hair.

She finally noticed the current state of my companion... naked. He didn't bring his seaweed with him this time, or even attempt to cover up with his tentacles. Those were swishing behind him like vipers ready to strike if he sensed any danger.

One was still wrapped around me.

I squirmed to free myself, and he released me reluctantly.

Seeing his opportunity, Mavron turned on his charm. Running his hand through his black hair, he flexed his arm with the action, and making a noise I could only describe as oddly carnal, like an animal mating call. I had to look away, but watching Gily, it was clear whatever you called what Mavron was doing, it was working.

He certainly wasn't ashamed of his body, and she was definitely faking her demureness earlier, because she was not attempting to avert her gaze away now.

They weren't doing anything, but I felt like I should be closing a door on them to give them privacy for fear that in moments I would see something I couldn't unsee. And seeing Mavron naked was enough for me.

Not that he wasn't attractive. I mean, I could appreciate his form, but I'd rather not.

I guess that didn't quite make sense, but it was what it was.

Mavron was perfectly not perfect for me.

I was about to gag, like watching a brother get all turned on by your best friend or something, not that Gily was a friend, or Mavron my brother. Ugh, it just needed to stop.

I groaned.

Mavron got the hint and got on with his flirting ruse.

"You didn't bring us here for nothing. Where are we meant to go, glowbug?"

I wrinkled my face at the pet name? If you could call 'glowbug' an endearment, I guess that's what he was doing, because she smiled.

Gods were weird.

"Zeus will be waiting for her at the river." She pointed west. "Mother can tell you the secrets that lie in the darkness, but you won't like them." She was talking to me in that last bit, and then she fluttered her eyes at Mavron. "So much delicious darkness deep in you. Now that you're here, I can not let you leave."

"What does Zeus want, glowbug, and I'll willingly stay for a while yet." The innuendo was obvious, and I cringed.

"He wishes for his brother to return. He has his son, his trident, his goddess, and his daughter. Poseidon will return, and with your blood, Zeus can finally break the spell over me. There is nothing that can stop his will."

"Zeus will not release you if it was his wife that changed you," Mavron chided her naivety.

"He made an oath to me," she growled in warning. He was treading on unstable territory.

"Fore the night falls on the light as darkness ascends, no more said the bird, and then there was three," Mavron recited.

"Trice does the river take, only two pay the price before day."

"Am I the bird in this story?"

"It's a poem, and what do you think?" He motioned to my wings. I was getting tired of being called a bird, like they were taunting me with how small I was.

"You're saying it wrong," Gily fumed at him, "it is *and then* the river replied thrice will I take from those that reach for the fruit. You're making it seem like the three is connected to me and my sisters."

"Isn't it?" He didn't know when to call it quits. She was definitely not going to want to sleep with him now, right?

"Enough!" I tried to stop their bickering, and as soon as I said it, both of them stared at me in shock.

Damn it.

"No more said the bird," Gily said in hushed tones.

"You better hope you're right about what the three means, or you're on the wrong side of the prophecy unfolding," Mavron sounded genuine in wanting her to be right, because if she wasn't it sounded suspiciously like either her or one of her sisters would not make it through to the end of the poem.

Clearing my throat, I changed the subject, "So, Triton..."

Gily nodded and seemed frazzled about her loyalties to Zeus or helping us. Then she conceded, "Zeus is watching him, but not even he will intervene with Nyx's judgment. She is the birth of chaos itself, and at the behest of Gaia helps guard the last of her golden fruit after Hera's choice to destroy the garden. Triton must choose the fate that will set him free, only he can do that."

"Nyx has him?"

"She didn't steal him, if that's what you're implying. He chose to enter the river himself. He won't get the apple otherwise."

"What happens if he chooses wrong?"

"His immortality will be stripped completely, and he will join Hades in the Underworld," she replied casually.

"He'll die!"

Gily didn't much care what his fate was; it was fear for her own fate that loosened her lips at all.

"What about Dion?"

Gily lifted a brow, confused by the name. "Who?"

"Poseidon?"

"He hasn't showed yet. He will when your life is in danger, and if not you, then his son, or his daughter. Just you guys and Triton have come so far."

"And the suit..." I was beginning to doubt this nymph's ability to know what was going on. The suit definitely was sucked up into her light, so either she was hiding something, or before I gave her my blood she wasn't quite all there. I couldn't decide what was more likely. They were both options.

"Oh, yah... *him*," she evaded. "He didn't choose to enter the river." Gily still acted shifty in her response, and I couldn't trust her entirely. Not that most myths really could trust a nymph, but Gily wasn't giving me the warm fuzzies.

Nymphs were known to be tricksters.

Then again, I shouldn't be judging when I was a dark god and thought to be a monster.

"If I'm to believe you—"

"You should," she interrupted.

"If I am," I pressed on. "Then according to the poem," seeing Mavron's approval at my word choice I smiled, "you're saying the river has only taken one out of the three from the prophecy. No one else entered the river yet?"

"Just Triton, so far," she affirmed.

"I would make two," I processed out loud, but according to her, Dion didn't come here. Ray said he came here, which is why Triton was so intent on rushing to get to the apple.

My eyes widened.

"Ray! Dion never came here..." I finally realized how I'd been tricked.

Gily shook her head. "Whoever that is? Is that the girl that's been pacing around the garden?"

"Are you stalling?" Mavron interrupted.

Gily lifted her shoulder to her cheek and blushed. "I'm hedging my bets on the prophecy. Can't be too careful, betraying Zeus could be the reason I never escape the willow."

"I'll handle the nymph, go get Triton," Mavron assured.

With a wink, Gily purred at Mavron. "I'm sure you will," she teased before sobering up enough to shoo me away, "off that way, you'll probably arrive in time to prevent Triton from forgetting the ethos of the sea."

"What about the third?" I asked. If Triton was one, and I was two... then who was the third?

"What about Poseidon's daughter?"

"You'll have to ask Zeus about that."

Was Pegasus the third?

I had to hurry.

"You got this?" I asked Mavron.

"Poseidon trusted me with his city."

I nodded; he had this. Whatever this was he was handling with Gily. It wasn't quite like guarding Atlantis.

I knew I hadn't known Mavron for very long, and really, I didn't know much about him, but it was his name and a promise of escape that got me through a desperate time. There's something about sharing life and death situations with a person that bond you, and I may not know much about him, but I do know he has my back. That's all I could really ask for, given the circumstances.

Debating sending him off with a hug was a short thought, and he saw the internal struggle with leaving him here, so he gave me a swat on the butt with his tentacle, and with a squeak, I rushed off.

"I'm going, I'm going," I assured him there was no need to add any more pressure with another swat. But as my wings took me west towards the river, I smiled at the ridiculousness of how much I cared about this stranger.

He better be alive when I got out of this mess.

Chapter 18

Betrayal

Poseidon's power hummed in my veins, and the closer I got to the river, I could feel the call of the water. But beyond even that, I felt something deeper stirring to the surface. A different kind of surge that did more than hum, it electrified.

Wings took me farther, faster, and an eagerness took over.

Thirst scorched my throat, and I had to get to the river. Faster, I thought. And faster I flew.

Until I was covered in water, and my wings were leathery like fins. The water was thick, slowing me down, and I struggled to keep going.

Moans surrounded me, and I blinked several times to come to my senses. Bodies, so many bodies. They all clawed and grabbed with desperation. Pulling me this way and that. The resistance that I thought was the water's current was actually bodies.

I struggled in their hold, and my wings caught—too stifled by the packed quarters.

My screams were lost in the chaos, and the more I fought against the hands and limbs dragging me under, the farther I slipped.

Darkness was below me, and it called to me the same way the river had called to Poseidon's power.

That static charge pressurized. I could sense its need to be freed.

I didn't know how, but my throat swelled, and my gums throbbed. I couldn't hold my snakes within me any longer. The golden beasts hissed and wrapped themselves around the faceless haunts that wished to take me deeper.

When we were surrounded in the darkness, so much different than the deepest part of the sea. There was no luminescence light show here, it was emptiness. And somehow, even the limbs that bruised me and yanked on my wings were a strange comfort.

To know that it wasn't nothingness here.

The comfort didn't last long, before knowing I wasn't alone was getting scarier. The haunts I could still see in my mind, but what if they weren't the only thing down here?

Something in me snapped.

That part of me I had forgotten years ago came out, and a film glazed over my eyes. The darkness wasn't so dark anymore.

I could see everything.

The tortured faces of people unidentifiable, like golems of mud, and clay.

I could hear their cries begging for release. They'd been here, in the dark for so long, they don't even know who they are anymore.

The pressure in my throat released like a cork, and I gasped. A strange liquid oozed like ink tainting the water. Spreading out around me.

Hands that were grabbing me drew back in alarm before hardening to stone. Soon, their screams silenced like an echo fading. Their vocal cords tightened until no vibration was left.

Flexing my wings, the forms behind me broke and shattered, floating in chunks until they sunk below.

I watched as everyone around me stared up, their hands frozen, reaching in vain. Their faces rippled as the last of their flesh turned to stone, but it wasn't terror in those gray rocks. They looked mortal, alive, more alive than they had when they moved moments before.

Floating there until every last one of them was too deep to see, I clutched at my heart.

What had I done?

And she had listened.

"You freed them," a melodic voice replied to a question I hadn't even said out loud. "Their souls have moved on to the Underworld, and their bodies will decorate my riverbed."

"What happened to them?" Torn between relief at not being dragged under and regret at how I had gone about it haunted me.

"The same thing that happens to all the souls that get lost here. They no longer remembered who they were, or why they lived. You can not possibly release them all, and really you shouldn't try."

"What are you saying?"

"They are still choosing to live, choosing their fate. To intervene when they are not completely lost is fruitless."

I could see what she meant now, as more bodies began to fill in the void I'd created. Not all of them are faceless, but the eyes I saw were hollow, lost in their own minds.

None of them grabbed for me. They weren't empty, yet.

Poisoning them to stone wouldn't be saving them, and I still questioned whether it was saving the others. Or if that was just a pleasant way of coping with my guilt.

"Where are you headed?" her voice was soothing, like a lullaby making my senses heavy. I struggled to keep my eyes open.

"I'm... I'm," I couldn't quite place my next thought, "I'm not sure."

"No worries, little bird. I'm sure it will come to you after you've rested. There is no hurry."

Right, I thought, I was tired. I wouldn't be good to anyone right now. My heart rate slowed, and the sound of the water lapping against me was calming.

The way she called me bird somehow triggered an annoyance in me, and I bristled just before my eyes closed.

Prying them open, I spotted a glint between the drifting mass of bodies. One bumped into me, and my mind jolted a bit at the contact.

Was that the trident?

My body ached with the movement of swimming through the molasses-like water. Cringing at the creepy act of easing limp forms around me to get closer to the glow I saw earlier.

A pulse rippled through the water, and bodies swayed away from the glint, creating a small clearing around the trident, and the man that held it—gripped in one hand.

Triton.

His eyes were closed, his face serene, as if sleeping. A hazy glow surrounded him. He really was a god. He was beautiful.

Finally, I reached him and cupped his cheek in my hand.

"Who are you?" I stared at this specimen of a man, and felt compelled to hold him to me. I gathered him up in my arms, pressing myself to his firm torso.

He stirred, if only for a moment.

A soft murmur bubbled from his lips.

"Aless..."

Smiling into his chest, I closed my eyes.

It felt nice here.

"Wake up," Dion called out to me.

I groaned, nuzzling into the warmth of a... a chest? Blinking away my sleep, a yawn bubbled from my mouth. Under the water, I was under water.

Shifting, I looked up into another sleeping face, his white hair long, and wafting behind him in waves.

How did he speak to me if he was sleeping?

I poked his cheek, and he twitched, but did not wake.

"You're not Dion..." I whispered softly to the sleeping man. Who was Dion? I knew the name, and I knew this wasn't him, but I couldn't bring myself to let go either.

Something told me if I did, I wouldn't find my way back again.

But why did I want to?

"Did you rest well, dark goddess?" A familiar, warm voice asked. Her presence was everything, yet nowhere.

"Yes," I replied. I felt rested and comfortable. The voice made me think of my mother. I grinned. My mother would be happy that I was safe. This voice was happy I was here.

Yes, I was supposed to be here.

"It's time for you to make a choice. Do you wish to stay here?" She asked, and it gave me pause. Why would she ask that? Of course I wanted to stay, this was happiness.

Here, with her, and...

I couldn't say his name.

It stopped me from telling her immediately that I would stay here, and I worried that I might offend her with my silence.

I had to tell her why, so she wouldn't be angry.

"Who is he?"

"No one important," she soothed my worry. She wasn't offended. I sighed in relief. "If you wish to keep him, you may. If you wish to let him—"

"No," I interrupted, unable to stomach the idea of letting go. Getting a hold of myself I amended, "I'm sorry. No, I don't wish to let go of him."

"That's fine," she said calmly, and she could tell I was biting my lip to prevent further upsetting her, if I had already. I hoped I hadn't. "Is there anything else?"

My cheeks puffed, not sure if I should say, but I asked anyway, "Is Dion here?"

I felt like she was smiling at me as a mom would a child, and with amusement she asked her own question of me, "Who is he to you?"

"I'm not sure," I pondered seriously.

"Maybe you need more rest, little goddess of the night."

"Maybe," I shook my head, "I don't think so." Clearing the cobwebs of my thoughts I held the man to me closer.

I remembered Dion told me to wake up. I must have needed to do something before I slept again. My lips pursed, trying to think.

"He never came here, my love. Does this upset you?" she confessed. She sounded sad for me.

My love. The words rang in my ears, echoing.

But it wasn't her voice.

"He didn't..." this did make me sad, but not for the reason I thought I would. He shouldn't be here.

He was in danger.

I had to help him.

"He needs me," I told her.

"You can go to him if you wish, but you must leave the other behind."

My wings curled protectively around the sleeping man. His white hair swept over his peaceful features like a caress. I brushed it from his eyes and behind his ear. A crown sat upon his head. He must be some kind of royalty. His armor was cool to the touch but seemed to mold to him like scales of a fish.

I pressed my ear to his exposed side of his chest, listening to his heartbeat. My eyes caught sight of a large fork that seemed to pulse. I remembered it.

The trident.

"He needs that. I need to bring that to Dion."

"If he wishes to give it to you, then you may take it," she offered. "Shall I wake him?"

"I don't want to leave him," I struggled with what I should do.

"I understand. Do you wish to keep both of them safe?"

I nodded fervently. The idea of both of them being safe made me happy.

"You must convince him to leave without the fruit he seeks, or he must give you the trident he keeps."

Seemed simple enough, I thought.

"And then he will be safe?"

"If that's what he chooses," she affirmed.

"Wake up," I gave him a squeeze.

"I must warn you, my love," her voice still soft and nurturing, "he's been shown his options in fate, and the choice is still his to take."

Before I could ask her what she meant, the man stirred from his sleep.

"It's time to choose King Triton, but first the goddess has a request," the mother of the river informed him as his eyes opened, bright blue like a summer lake in the sunshine.

He felt me in his arms, and he pressed his cheek into the top of my hair. A few golden snakes rose up to greet him, nuzzling their heads into his white, flowing hair, startling him.

Snakes, they were mine.

I knew that—they've always been a part of me.

"Aless...?"

"I need the trident," and as soon as I said the word ,his face fell, and his muscles tensed. A coldness entered his features, and I tried to explain, "I need you both to be safe."

Like I had stuffed my fist into my mouth, he distanced himself from me even more with my explanation. Triton's eyes glowed, and I flinched away from him.

"No one has ever betrayed me so blatantly before," he turned away from me, and the sadness there made my chest clench, as a tightness rose up my throat. I reached out to stop him, he was getting too far away from me, and I knew if he got too much farther I'd lose him.

"You must give up the apple," I tried once more to save him from being lost to the river, and it seemed like I couldn't say anything right to this ethereal man. His jaw set hard against the request and a power pulsed from him in anger.

"You've wounded me enough, goddess of darkness and deceit! You will not be the death of my people. Dion was right to warn me of tangling my fate with yours. We will discuss this after I've acquired the divine fruit. I will do the same to you as Zeus has done to Hera. You will not betray me again, wife!" With a wave of the trident the water whirled, and I watched him bolt through the water away from me.

Wife?

I tried to swim through the open path his power left behind, but it wasn't long before the bodies of the lost floated back, filling in the space, and I no longer could see him.

How had I angered him so much when all I wished to do was keep him safe, protect him? What have I done?

My knees curled up into my chest, golden wings encircled me in a cocoon.

"Do you still wish to save him?" The river goddess asked trying to comfort me with her melodic voice.

"What have I done?" I didn't understand, but I didn't have to. The disgust in his eyes was enough.

"Nothing, you have done nothing," she assured before asking again. "Knowing he will seek to force an oath from you, do you still wish to keep him safe?"

"He won't give up the apple, or the trident like you asked..." how was I supposed to keep them safe now? Dion needed the trident, and as long as the trident is lost here he won't have it, and as long as Triton stays here he won't be safe either. I knew that much, even if I didn't know exactly why it wasn't safe for him here.

"You ask for two fates to be altered, and one refuses to pay the price, while the other is not here to do so," she seemed to be pondering out loud, and then hesitated before continuing, "Do you wish to stay Queen of the Sea?"

"I can't be the queen of the sea," I protested, but then I recalled how Triton had called me his wife. Was he my husband? How could I forget something so important? He said I betrayed him... I pulled my knees in tighter to my chest.

"You do not wish to be queen?" She hummed a soothing melody, and I didn't have to answer for her to know the answer before she continued, of course I didn't, "It is those that have power thrust upon them that lead with care than those that seek it out and lead with force.

"For you I will give the king Gaia's fruit, and the path back to his kingdom, but the price would be left for you to carry."

Already racked with guilt over how Triton looked at me like I had stabbed him in the back, I had to do something. I knew he couldn't leave without my help, and Dion needed the trident, even if it wasn't from me. Would Triton even give Dion the trident? I had to make sure.

"Would Dion still be safe?"

I could almost see the smile in the river's voice as she responded, "Is there such a thing as safe?" she didn't mean it in a cruel way, I knew, but it hurt even still to hear her admit whatever I did here may not be enough.

"The choice is not only yours to make. Even fates change—fluid in their creation. Until it is past, only Chronos would dare to reweave what is made. But some actions are predictable, certain threads too set in their habits, in their ideals, and rarely moved to change that patterns form. You can disrupt those patterns... create a new thread of fate to grasp. But it is not your job to choose that path... it is ultimately theirs. All you can do is offer it, make it irresistible."

"I can do that?"

"I can teach you," she offered, and I knew then that I would have to stay. Would there be enough time? Urgency ran through me and threatened to keep me balled up in the fetal position forever for fear of failure.

"Time..." I echoed absently.

"I will help." She took that burden, and relief eased the tension in my shoulders.

Unfurling from my winged cocoon, I searched for the serenity in the river. The one that offered me hope.

A ribbon of fate, like the ones I saw surrounding Mo, appeared before me. Mo, I remembered her. One ribbon stood out, gleaming, sparkling, in the water's light, waiting for me to grab it. The most obvious of choices, the easiest to reach.

The most irresistible, like the river goddess said.

But a small, frayed string barely caught my eye. Only the smallest movement as it unraveled took my notice. Black, charred, and decaying with every second, I almost couldn't see it in the darkness, but for the brightness of the ribbon being offered to me. I might not have even seen it.

I pushed the ribbon closer to the thread, dissolving, making it farther from my grasp as I examined it. Reaching, stretching my arm and my fingertips as far as I could to grab the dying black thread, it was just out of reach.

With a push through the heavy water, my hand fisted the string, too fragile to stay together with my touch.

The ribbon glowing around me, wrapped itself, thick and strong, around my body, making it more difficult to move.

I only had one more chance to reach the thread before it disappeared into the dark waters, and everything in me wanted to grab it. My sister's words slammed into me at that moment when I was struggling, stretching, pushing myself. That moment before she confessed knowing about the magic of my blood. Before I knew that she was aware of gods and legends, I guess she always knew.

She used to say, 'Not even Zeus conquered the heavens by himself.'

Resigned that there was only so much I could control myself, I knew what I had to do. I took the ribbon, and I wrapped it around the thread. The ribbon weaved with the weak blackened fate, and like an ink it spread through the ribbon coloring it, and I let it consume me.

I was underneath the apple tree, above me was the golden fruit. With a closer look, I peeled back the black husk around it, and the inside resembled closer to a golden orange than an apple. Slivers of glowing golden juice sacks flowered out from the rotten looking husk, making it nearly impossible to transport without taking the husk with me.

Though before I did, I couldn't bring myself to rip it from the tree. Did I want this fruit? No, Triton had. And I thought Dion, but according to the nymph, and the river... he never showed.

I came for them, my memories slowly returning, but different this time.

Ray had lied to me.

Lied to Triton.

And then it hit me, her arrow to the one spot I couldn't defend, just behind my neck, where the feathers couldn't overlap enough to prevent just the right angle from entering. My hand around the husk of the fruit clamped down as pain radiated through my bones.

"You know, I honestly did hope you'd survive your judgment. I don't know how you did it, found a way to make even me feel like the bad guy for doing my duty," Ray didn't sound the least bit guilty about her actions, but I couldn't trust my ears when the only reason I could hear her was through a moment of stunned shock, where everything stilled.

"When history records your death, I'll go down as the hero that saved the last golden apple from the hands of Tartarus's monster to revive the Olympians and stop the Dark Gods from rising in Apollo's prophecy.

"Triton will be the next God of the Sea, and all he has to do is finish off his father and eat the divine fruit to do it. All thanks to you really, not that anyone will know that much of the story."

Crumpled on the stump of the willow tree, a single green shoot tickling my nose as I clutched the fruit in my grasp. Gily was revived, she would recover, she was still alive. I smiled to myself, remembering that she risked herself to tell the truth.

A chuckle escaped my trembling lips thinking about what she was doing with Mavron at the very moment. My blood dripped down my neck and down my chin to pool around the fresh sprout of the willow tree.

It wasn't her that would die, it was me.

Coughing, I wondered what I missed in the prophecy, the poem as Mavron would call it?

"You think I'm wrong?" Ray steamed over what she thought was me mocking her victory confession. But with the arrow sticking out of my neck, I couldn't speak with her to deny it, and even my chuckle was more of a bloody gurgle. The only reason I was still alive right now had everything to do with my blood, and as soon as it drained there would be nothing keeping me conscious.

Suddenly, I preferred the drowning in the water than this, because as soon as I passed out from that... I knew I would wake. Would I wake after this? Coraline proved even an immortal could end. Would this be mine?

"You think Triton actually cared for you? You think Dion came here to retrieve the golden apple? Triton sent him to go find your family, and he was more than happy to do something that would bring you a smile," she gagged. "I told you to leave Dion alone, but you still went out riding with him. Triton was convinced his father killed Dion and impersonated him, but not even a weakened god would be taken down by mere arrows."

My emotions were all over the place. I tried to speak, but all I made were choking sounds, and more blood drained from my mouth.

Dion, how did I forget him? He never came to get the apple... he was looking for my mom. He had to have found my sister... Ray said she saw them talking. I wanted to shake my head.

She was always lying to me.

"Medusa," Ray clucked her tongue, "I didn't realize it until now, but it makes sense why Triton thought you would be the one to bring his dad out of hiding." She laughed, reveling in the thought, "Marry the one love that took down a god. You're the reason Poseidon gave up everything. He didn't want eternity without you. Now, he won't have to. Both of you will die tonight, and he has you to thank for that. I'll be taking this fruit."

Ray shoved my ribcage with her boot, and then pressed her heel onto my wrist, prying the divine golden apple from my weak fingers. Fingers that were still clawed, my true form revealed. I was the monster of myths.

Snakes hissed up at her from my golden hair, and despite my weakness, they still tried to protect me.

One launched out, clinging on to her hand with its fangs. Ray swore, and yanked her arm so hard that the snake tore out from my scalp, making my vision blur. No screams, only blood suffocating me, and draining into my lungs.

"B—" she cursed. "You can meet Poseidon in Tartarus where your kind belong." To add insult to death, she sneered, "Goddess Nyx told Triton you're the reason she let him leave, and because of that... you're the reason Poseidon will die. And if you think I'll die from your attempt to poison me, you're wrong, because Triton doesn't need the whole apple to grab fate by the tits. I was promised divinity myself. I will be a god!"

The snakes, shaking from losing one of their own, still hissed at her. Ray scoffed at their display.

"It wasn't anything personal, Hera didn't know who you were, though if she did, you'd probably be worse off. My mom always said reach for the stars, and with this," she held the fruit in her stiff gloved hand, "I'll be part of the heavens.

"History always repeats itself Medusa. You die by beheading... again, an arrow through the throat is close enough, and a son succeeds their father while preventing Poseidon from helping you overthrow Hera and Zeus."

The order she listed the rulers of the heavens was telling, and Triton was right to not trust Hera, or Zeus, for that matter.

My eyes widened, and she smiled, giving me a shrug.

"Triton wanted me to infiltrate, and I took advantage of both sides. Better to have both gods want the same thing of me and get rewarded by all of them." She saw the hurt in my glassy eyes, as my body curled up on itself. "You'll find peace soon," she sympathized. "The arrow was laced with the deadliest poison known to man and god alike. A gift from Athena herself."

Ray flexed her fingers and only three fingers uncurled. She brought her hand up to her chest protectively, disgust clear on her features.

With an unsteady grip, she lifted the fruit up to her mouth and took a bite. Her whole body glowed brightly from within, a blessing of Gaia herself. Of life.

"It's like nothing I could have imagined," she cried out with joy, "so much power." She flexed her fingers, and gripped them tight. Plunging her fist into the ground, it rumbled and cracked as she laughed.

The elation quickly faded as she watched her hand crumble, and her glove dropped to the ground in the dust.

"How is that possible? I'm a goddess!" It was the hand my snake bit, and she glared at me accusingly. "You! No wonder the gods wanted you dead and didn't have the guts to do it themselves." She stormed towards me, and a nymph covered me with her own body. Gily...

She arched with a scream, collapsing onto my broken body with the force of Ray's boot. Not even a single wing could move to protect her, or myself. The quake from the impact split Gily's skin, and the stump beneath us cracked and splintered. The little sprout of life wilted, and trampled.

I watched her in wonder, asking her why?

With a sad smile, Gily replied, "I'd do anything for Zeus, but I'd also die to stop Hera from cutting another down."

I'm already dead, I wanted to tell her through my clogged throat. Blood pooled from my lips. She was sacrificing herself for nothing. My chest ached with something deeper than the pain of death and broken muscles.

"It doesn't matter. You can both die there in each other's arms for all I care. Hera will grant me a new hand after you're delivered to Hades."

"Hera doesn't care about your hand, or your life," Gily choked out, gasping for breath. With a whisper she wanted only me to hear, she continued, "When life and death hang by a thread, one must pay the toll to change their fate."

I didn't know what she was trying to tell me, but it was obvious she was reciting another part of the poem, the prophecy.

"Don't take too long to say 'hi' to Hades, I'll need my sword hand to help Triton finish the job when Poseidon comes to find his city in ruins, and his true love in Tartarus. I'll give you a proper send off."

With her new-found power from the gods, Ray stomped the ground, and had the land roll my body, along with Gily, back into the sea. The land and roots tumbled us out and flung us into the water's depths. There was no holding my breath, with lungs full of blood.

And Gily was not a water nymph.

"You'll live," a voice boomed in my head, "if I have to drag you from the depths of death itself, you will not leave me again."

Poseidon?

Chapter 19

Witness

S inking into the water, blood flowing from me even faster now, the salt stung in my wounds. I watched as my wings hardened to stone from the tips inward. Fingers followed, and then the heaviness took my toes.

Broken as Gily was, she struggled to lift us both back to the surface. But the more blood I lost, the heavier I became. The more my body turned to stone.

A dark man with pitch black hair floated beside us, watching us descend before he spoke. "You've evaded me for centuries, stolen countless lives from my kingdom, but still, I cannot take you. Not yet," he mused.

With a flick of his wrist, the blood from my lungs choked out of me, and I could speak.

"What do you want from me?"

His twilight eyes sparkled with intrigue.

"Come willingly to me," he offered, and the way his skin glowed like the night sky, and the universe was beyond his irises, I gasped.

"You will end here, Medusa—"

"Aless," I corrected him, and he grinned, amused.

"Aless," he humored me, "you will sink deep into the earth, where only Poseidon could find you under the sea, but you won't be dead, and you won't be alive. Only a pretty piece of art, lost forever. Not even my brother will come for you, because as we speak, he fights his own son for control of the trident, and the seas."

He disappeared, and then reappeared closer to me, overseeing my current decay.

"There isn't much time left. Come with me willingly, and I will let you save my brother before I take you across the river."

He saw the internal struggle about willingly going with him to what I assumed was Tartarus, like Ray wanted. She was wrong this entire time. My death wouldn't send me to Tartarus. I could fall to the bottom of the sea, and stay there unconscious for the rest of, well, my non-life. She would never see her damned hand again, and maybe, just maybe, that was enough to know Ray didn't win. Not fully.

Hades could see the resolution in my face, the determination to go down with one last defiance and he chuckled like he could read my thoughts.

"You would waste yourself at the edge of this realm just to prove a point? What point would you be making, dark goddess? What grander point would there be than to come back to life for long enough to save another? The very life Hera wishes to end so that she can take something important away from Zeus. You were always fated to die. We just never anticipated a goddess would be born with both life and death in her. So much that you can neither live nor die completely.

"A tragedy really, but there is so much more you can do in death. What is living, really? Do you wish to end in mystery, or have the chance to form a revolution, and be a true goddess of the night—of your grandfather Tartarus?

"You can fade into the sea, or you can inspire the rest of the dark gods to rise with your final act beyond death to save the true ruler of the sea, who will make sure no other dark god suffers the fate of monsters?"

"And all it costs is eternal service to you?" I guessed where this was heading. Hades wanted my soul.

"A small price to pay to outsmart fate, don't you think? Tick Tock, little bird. Even I can't bring you back without an agreement."

"You can help him?"

"You can," Hades corrected, "with my help." He held out his crown for me to grab.

Gily squeezed me tighter, her arms becoming wooden vines. A tightness crept up my neck, hardening my skin. I couldn't move my arms to reach for it even if I wanted to.

"A simple nod, or a blink of the eye, will do," he said with charm.

Theo used to say the way the gods tricked so many was an open-ended agreement. Or vague oaths, that leave room for interpretation. They've fallen victim to their own understanding of what they said yes to. I could be agreeing to an afterlife of torture in Tartarus, instead of the blissful absence of nothing that awaited me at the bottom of the sea.

But I couldn't stop hearing his voice telling me to live, to fight, to come back to him. To Poseidon.

My flesh, turning to stone, was creeping up my throat. I wouldn't have much time to talk soon.

To negotiate.

To act like them.

Like a god.

"I'll help you," I croaked, my voice box closing up on me. "A favor for a favor, as they say."

He grinned, happy that I would go with him. It was up to Nyx now how a favor would be interpreted, but it was better than a blanket contract of my whole existence. It was the best I could do to muddle the deal.

"You think I'll let you go with a simple trick of the words?" My heart sank, practically falling out beneath me. He tsked. "I've been making deals since before you existed. I'll let this one slide for now, since we're running out of time, and your voice is a bit tied up at the moment, but I'll have your oath by the end of this, Aless."

He snapped his fingers, and my spirit pulled itself from my body. My soul.

I watched as Gily turned into a willow tree, her trunk twined around my stone body as we sunk beneath the darkness.

We, I touched myself, verifying I could still feel. And I could. I didn't feel any different from normal, except there was no pain.

I felt alive...

But I was also dead... wasn't I?

Hades offered me his hand, and without a choice, my claws betrayed me and grabbed it... willingly.

I've made a deal with the devil himself.

"Shall we?" With another snap of his fingers, we reappeared in the Arena of Atlantis.

The whole process was disorientating. I stumbled. I guess being dead didn't change feeling vertigo when my equilibrium was warped.

"Now, go say your goodbyes, and give the fruit to my brother. Inspire the gods and all that business. I'll fetch you when you're done.

You have," he paused considering and then nodded to himself, "a few hours should be enough time. Don't try to hide from me. I'm sure my brother will try to convince you to run away with him, but like me, you are bound to the Underworld now, and you will not be able to stay away for long."

He handed me his crown, and I grabbed it absently, still gawking at him.

"It's the helm of invisibility—use it wisely."

Glancing down at the crown for only a moment was enough time for Hades to disappear. Guess he didn't need the helm to do that act. Leaving with no explanation of how I was supposed to save Poseidon, Hades was gone. I mean, he did say to give him the fruit, the golden apple that I didn't have in my possession anymore.

It was almost like he didn't really care if I succeeded or not.

Some favor indeed.

"My queen?" Sylvie questioned cautiously before his voice strengthened, "My queen! Triton has been waiting for you."

That didn't make any sense. He had Ray wait to murder me. Why would he be waiting for me?

"Where is he?"

"In the Arena," he sounded like I should have already known that. "Dion was able to defeat the demi-god from taking over Atlantis... but during the fight, well, it's better you see for yourself."

I glared at him, not wanting to be tossed into the unknown again with no information.

The old man didn't cower, but sighed with sympathy before nodding his assent, "Dion, as victor of the Arena, Protector of Atlantis, demanded the trident be given to him."

I sighed in relief, and Sylvie lifted a brow.

"Triton is required by oath to grant the victor of the Arena anything they ask," I tried to confirm.

"That may be so, but the trident is the one thing that can't just be given, even if Triton willingly wished to give it."

"I don't understand?"

"They must fight each other. And in the Arena, all immortality is stripped. One of them will die, the victor will claim the trident. Dion has asked that the queen be present for the feat. That you be present."

"Me?" I wasn't a queen. "I'm not—"

Sylvie silenced me with a gentle squeeze of his hand. He could see my hair, the one indicator of who I truly was. I wasn't just Alessandra anymore; I was Medusa.

"You wear the crown, you need not marry either of them to claim the right to the sea. I'm an old man, my queen. I've told you before I've sung many songs of history. Your history, your fate."

"My fate?"

His old eyes gleamed, his mother was a bard, and before he was the Grand Master of the Arena, he too was a bard.

"My mother was there when Apollo warned Poseidon. Of course, Apollo liked to give his prophesies in layers, so the story was incomplete."

Lacing my hand through Sylvie's arm, he guided me up from beneath the Arena, towards the stands where spectators watched. The closer we got the louder the noise of people filled the air.

Sylvie cleared his throat.

"It's been a long time. Forgive me, my queen."

Then he sang, "Angels, they say, are the gods of the heavens, but none are as fair as the heir to the sea.

"Jealous are they that don't dare to compare to the bird that holds both life and death's key.

"Blood for blood does the prophecy offer, but it will be hers that befalls the final judgment of Olympian's altar.

"It is she; it is she who rules the heart of the water, and all those oppose will find themselves lost in the chaos of uncertainty.

"Queen of the sea, terror of the guilty, protector of the dark, she will be. Gone are the days of old Olympus, when it is she that sees victory."

Speechless, Sylvie's voice was beautiful, and echoed in my mind as he released me to the royal viewing box.

Before he left me, I quickly asked, "The Viperess... Did she—"

He gave me one last reassuring squeeze.

"She was not part of the Arena battles."

Where was my sister?

Did that mean she was alive? Or did that mean she never made it back after the fight with the demi-god? I changed my mind. I needed to find the fruit and give it to Theo.

My ears heated, sensing I was now being watched. All of Atlantis could see me in the royal viewing box.

But it was his eyes that mattered.

They were the first I landed on, and I smiled knowing he was alive still, before I remembered why I was there. To witness their bloodshed.

Dion.

Triton's voice interrupted our brief contact. "*Wife*, I see you've decided to join us." The way he said wife was strained, and I glared at him, remembering how we left things in the river.

Giving him a feigned smile, I prodded, "I'm sorry to disappoint you. Ray wasn't quite the finisher you hoped for."

There was a moment of confusion on his face, before his mask of anger returned, and a sense of doubt came over me.

Didn't he want me dead?

"We'll talk after I settle this matter," Triton gritted, and rotated the trident like a javelin prepared to fight Dion.

Something felt off, and things weren't adding up exactly as I pictured. Would he finish the job that Ray left to sink to the bottom of the sea?

He wouldn't get the chance. The Underworld had already laid claim.

But that moment of hesitation, and possibly concern, made me question things. Question instinct versus my head... versus my heart.

I was torn between two feelings—betrayal and trust.

For both of them.

Dion was his First Sentinel, and yet there they both were ready to fight each other to the death. Only one of them was supposed to survive this duel for the trident, for control over the sea.

"Why?" I shook my head at both of them. If the demi-god was defeated while I was gone, and Atlantis was safe, then why did they have to fight each other?

Chapter 20

Poseidon

It was only after the first clash of metal on metal did I realize Dion had stopped staring at me, and Triton had called me his wife? Proposed to, maybe. Wife, how was that possible?

Triton spun his trident around like it was a second arm, and it moved so fluidly, spinning in circles, creating a current in front of him. The sound I heard was the trident clashing with Dion's spear, if you could even call it that. I didn't have a name for what he was holding. It was two poles joined together with sharp hooks on both ends, and a two-pronged sword jutting from one side.

White bubbles splashed around Dion's body as he lunged and hooked his spear onto the trident to stop its spin before the whirlpool was too strong to swim against. I had to remind myself to breathe as they both collided with one another.

First Sentinel vs King of Atlantis.

Both vulnerable to death inside of the Arena.

But something was off with Dion. He seemed defeated before things even got brutal, and I knew anything claiming a fight to the death would get agonizingly unbearable. Sure, he was holding his own, but every 'attack' he placed was merely to stall or disengage Triton. Exhaustion was written on his beautiful face. I watched him, and felt my heart tug, wanting to put an end to this disaster of a day.

He must have felt the ache in me, because it was then our eyes met, and he simply stopped. Dion wasn't paying attention to the fight any longer, and for a brief moment, neither was I.

Suspended in time, he gave me a simple nod of acceptance. I didn't know what he was agreeing to, or what he thought I wanted from him, but I felt my tears brimming, not ready for what was to come.

I shook my head, unable to form words.

Then I screamed as I watched Triton plunge his trident into Dion's chest while his words echoed in my mind, "You'll live..." his haunted, beautiful voice faded.

The same words, the same voice.

I recognized it then.

Why end hiding it this whole time?

The look of shock on Triton's face said it all. Not even the king knew who he had slain until that moment. Dion grabbed the trident with one hand, suspended in the water, with a prong sticking out of his shoulder, and the other two in his chest at an angle. His whole left arm hung heavy and lifeless from the trident, severing the connection to his nerves.

"I didn't think you'd have the guts to show yourself," a woman's voice floated down from the heavens like a mist. Light beamed from the top of the Arena, and an ethereal glow faded to show the woman in Triton's rooms when I first arrived, Hera.

"What is the meaning of this?" Triton boomed, looking from Dion back to Hera, accusing them both.

"Isn't that obvious?" Hera chided, "Poseidon has decided to step down as God of the Sea. And become mortal. Congratulations are in order, Triton. You will be welcomed into Olympus as the heir to the throne."

Dion coughed up blood, creating a red murkiness in the water of the Arena.

"He is the only being exempt from the magic of this arena," Triton objected.

Hera tsked. "It's the trident that strips him of his power, and his willingness to die to ensure you live."

Triton yanked on the sea fork to release Dion. With his one free hand, Dion held on, preventing Triton from releasing him. Why would he do that? I could hear him grunt through the crown's connection to him, a pained, sickening sound filling my ears.

Then he did the unthinkable. Dion pulled himself farther onto the trident, his body butting up against the ends of the prongs, jutting out from his back.

Choking from his punctured lungs, he rasped to Triton, "Keep her safe."

The snakes in my hair hissed, a sad cry echoing around me, since he was too far away, and I clutched the railing of my viewing podium with death's grip. I had come back for nothing, gave up blissful emptiness for pain and suffering. To watch the suffering etched on both of their beautiful faces.

"You would give your life for her?" a voice resonated through the crowded stands, angry, bitter.

"He's made his decision love, let's not make things more difficult for them," Hera dismissed, resentment in her pet name for our new guest, "It's a win-win, Triton ascends to rule the sea, and you no longer must worry about a fated prophecy of an uprising. Let's leave them to deal with the fallout of their decisions, shall we?"

"I'll decide when I'm finished with you brother," Zeus bellowed, "Mark my words, if you die here today in mortal flesh I will rend you from the Underworld, and make sure you serve your time beside our father until you beg to spend the rest of your existence back in the pit of his stomach!"

And with that pleasant note, Hera floated through the water to stroke Triton's frozen face.

"As promised, you will rule, and have the Queen of the Seas at your side." Remorseless, Hera smiled at Dion. "I never wanted your suffering to be taken on by another. You've done well here today. Both your son and the queen will live. I may just forgive you one day." She leaned in brushing Dion's hair from his face, and then gently kissed his forehead.

Realization hit hard with Hera's words. Poseidon's sacrifice was for us, for Triton and me? But he was doing it in vain. I was already lost, and Triton had the golden apple... Hera lifted up into a blinding light, disappearing in a hazy flash the same as she had come.

Dion's hand on the trident went limp, unable to hold on any longer.

A weak smile touched those soft lips. "You both have my blessing," he whispered.

The bluest-blue of his eyes dulled, and his body collapsed one final time.

I hadn't noticed before, but the Arena was eerily quiet waiting to see what their King, the God of the Sea, would do next with his father, the beloved First Sentinel of Atlantis, and previous ruler, Poseidon.

Slowly, Triton eased his father from the trident, and caught him in his arm. He was careful and gentle as he guided Dion's head onto his shoulder. He may not have been fond of his father, but he knew what was sacrificed for him, and he respected it. The crowd hummed with hushed whispers:

"For our kingdom."

"May he rise again."

"Zeus have mercy. Let him live."

"We believe in you."

"Pray to the Queen. Let him live."

Cascading through the over-stuffed rows of Atlantians, their eyes traveled up to me. Begging me to give them their rightful ruler back. Have mercy on the God of the Sea and Land. Have mercy on Poseidon. My body warmed with their worship, amplified by the arena's magic. I felt their power, their belief, their hope crash into me. Burning me up from the inside out.

I watched as Triton too looked up to me, not at all irritated by the betrayal of his people begging for his father's return instead of accepting him as the next ruler of the seas. He accepted it, and turned away from me, guilt written all over his features. With reverence he swam with his father in his arms to the exit underneath the stadium. Pushing off from the balcony railing, I rushed to meet him in the gladiator's quarters. The fastest way was through the Arena, and I wasn't thinking about anything else but reaching Poseidon's side. Leaping from the balcony, my wings unfurling before I dove into the watery bubble darting down towards where Triton disappeared.

The prayers kept coming in waves, imbuing me with their unified desire to save Poseidon. They may have had hate in their hearts for abandoning them, but had he really? Did all of them realize Poseidon never really left them, but became one of them, became their protector, a Sentinel of Atlantis? He didn't want the recognition of a god. He simply became part of their society, serving his own son for years.

This was all my fault, for being here in Atlantis, for inserting myself into Mavron's fight when Poseidon was here all along. He'd given me his power, his strength, and then his life. What else did he have to give? I'm sure he'd give that, too.

When I surfaced, Triton, Sylvie, and my sister Theo hovered over his body. In Triton's hand was the golden apple.

I held my breath.

He didn't eat it himself?

With his hand fisted above Poseidon's mouth, he squeezed the fruit. Juices dripped between his slack open lips before Triton forced the jaw shut and lifted his chin to make sure he swallowed. It was the nectar of the gods. It could heal anything.

Couldn't it?

We all waited eagerly for the life in his blue eyes to change from their current dull gray.

And waited.

But no reaction from Poseidon.

Impatiently, Triton ripped open his father's shirt to smear the blood away from his wounds.

They were healed, but our Poseidon hadn't returned to his body.

Shoulder's slumped in defeat, all except Triton, who pounded his fists into the lifeless husk of his father.

"You asshole! You don't get the easy way out. Gods damn you for becoming my best friend, and making me love you," by the end his revelation about his feelings towards his father were so quiet you could barely make out his confession. This whole time he thought his father abandoned him, and instead he was right by his side, and no one else's, serving him in any way possible. Allowing him to rule in his own right and befriending him like no one else ever could. Dion stayed by his side, for who knew how long. Was he someone else before Dion? Had he been around for centuries, or merely decades?

Did it matter, when Triton's heart was broken now that he was gone?

"Had I known, had you said something..." Triton buried his face in Dion's chest, hugging him tightly, unable to release him to the afterlife.

As if he knew we were thinking about his realm, Hades returned leaning against the wall like a fly on the wall biding his time to announce himself.

"You've done exactly what I needed of you King of Atlantis, son of Poseidon, newest member of Olympus," he congratulated with a slow clap that ruffled my feathers raising my ires.

"What do you want, Uncle?" Triton glared without honoring Hades with his actual attention, not willing to look at him directly.

"You've proven yourself worthy of entering Olympus by giving up the fruit. I would not have allowed you to enter even with your invitation if you hadn't. I knew you would though," he prefaced, "That's the kind of god you've become over time. Not the same selfishness in you as ages before. I can admire that, and even count on it to save my brother."

The only thing I clung to was that last part. Poseidon is saved.

"He's alive..." I let out a breath of relief, then in equal parts my annoyance grew. Hades knew I wasn't needed at all to save Poseidon, it was all taken care of by Triton. But he made a deal with me, tugging on my heart strings to join him in shoving it to the gods by saving Poseidon myself. He tricked me...

But so did I, I thought. Our deal was for a favor, nothing more.

Hades watched me as the emotions played out across my face, and right on queue he continued, "Your time is up, my little terror. You must come with me."

I kept my feet planted where I was.

"I'm not going anywhere with you," I hissed. Even my snakes chimed in, but it sounded more melodic than scary in my opinion. Like the power of Atlantis coursing into me was altering my state of being.

They didn't have to channel their belief into me and make me strong. It wasn't me they should have been praying to.

It was Triton.

He had saved Poseidon.

Not me.

"I thought you might say that," Hades said nonchalantly, uncaring about my defiance. "It's a good thing I have leverage to make you comply."

"I don't understand?" I said, confused, while Triton growled at his uncle.

"You will leave here at once! She is my queen and is to stay here by my side!"

My sister quickly jumped up between Hades and me defensively, and Triton tapped the trident on the ground in warning. The magic of the trident summoned the water from behind me and lifted Poseidon up in a gentle water cocoon before squaring his shoulders off to fight for me.

"Ah nephew, you have much to learn still. She is not your queen. She has always been referred to as The Queen of the Seas. Not once did Hera ever say otherwise, though she might have implied," Hades chuckled, "she's a wily one from time to time. The last gathering of the gods, she drank so much elixir she bedded Zeus's prize to spite him. It was deliciously entertaining."

"No one wants to hear about your jovial gatherings of Olympus," Triton boomed, the full authority of his position behind his voice.

"Yes well," Hades cleared his throat, "as much as The Queen of the Sea may have developed unpredicted emotional attachment to you, it won't last. She is my brother's fated mate, and she can't be separated from him, even if she denies her bond to him for all of eternity, keeping her heart chilly and cold. She will follow him, she will stay by his side, and share that connection with him. Always."

That statement alone bit deep into Triton, and I could see his resolve to protect me crumble. The betrayal that he felt from earlier was still strong in his heart.

"Triton..." I wanted to explain myself, but I didn't know what to say.

I ached for him.

But I couldn't deny I equally ached for Dion, or as he was... Poseidon.

"Now, it's time we stop delaying the inevitable. Medusa, I have Poseidon in Tartarus, and he will never return to his people unless you come with me."

"She's not going anywhere with you!" Theo's nails extended, ready to swipe at him. Her red snakes swayed about her head, preparing to strike if necessary. She didn't stand a chance against the god of death himself. I placed a hand on her shoulder, and she knew I had made my decision.

Atlantis needed their god, and all of their hopes and dreams of his return were filling me up near to bursting. I couldn't let them down. And I had made a promise to give Hades a favor. That was the only thing he had over me. I wasn't naive enough to think following him

right now evened the debt of pulling me from death at the bottom of
the edge of the mortal realm, but I knew whatever Hades had planned
for me it wouldn't be forever.

"Mom will be devastated..." Theo tried to plead with me one last
time amending, "I will be devastated."

I pulled Theo into a hug and whispered in her ear, "It's only as long
as a favor."

My sister sucked in a breath, biting her lip. She squeezed me hard.
"It isn't all the food that's dangerous... just the pomegranate. You'll be
immune to any secret traces, being Tartarus's daughter..." She let that
sink in, that she knew all along we didn't have the same father. "But if
you willingly accept..."

I got the idea.

I'd never leave the land of the dead.

But what kind of fool would I be to willingly accept being stuck in
the Underworld?

"You don't have to go," Triton interrupted my thoughts. "You
are the Goddess of the Sea, The Queen, and accepted by the people
of Atlantis. They will lend you their strength, and together we are
powerful enough to protect the mortals, and our people from interference from the gods," he paused clutching at his chest, "and you've
stolen something from me, my wife," he sounded broken, "I will never
be whole without you now that I've tasted a small morsel of your
kindness, your passion..."

I touched my lips, recalling our kiss.

My heart beat rapidly in my chest at the memory.

Mo's words came back to haunt me:

He knows the truth. The truth... that protecting him, protecting
the sea, joining the Olympians will begin your curse anew. Too beau-

tiful, too powerful, and much too virtuous little goddess. Death comes for both of you.

If I protect Poseidon, I'll be cursed to die.

I hesitated taking Hades's hand.

As if he was reading my mind, Hades assured, "In my realm you are protected from true death. No curse will reach you there, and the sea needs my brother, for Triton never wanted such a burden himself."

My hand touched his skin, and he clamped down softly, as if not wanting to scare me away. He pet one of my snakes under the jaw, amused by them. Even my snakes betrayed me, easily manipulated by Hades's charm.

"Your half-brother is excited to see you again," he casually added. "Cerberus has been pacing non-stop since I told him I was to fetch you."

I gulped. Was he talking about the three-headed, giant dog that guarded the Underworld?

My brother?

Before I could think on it more, Hades pulled me in close and we disappeared to the Underworld.

Chapter 21

Underworld

Arriving in the Underworld was a lot easier than I thought it would be, but I supposed I had my escort to thank for that. This was his land, and he didn't need to jump through hoops to rejoin it. My hands tingled like my body was adapting to its new existence here.

"Cerberus will be upset that I didn't take you through the entrance to greet him, but you have plenty of time to say hi later, I wanted you to greet another guest first," Hades waved over to the man resting his head on his forearm against the wall of books in what could only be described as a magnificent library.

The man looked up, and my mouth hung open.

What was he doing here?

"You've gone too far, brother." Poseidon glared at Hades.

"Call it insurance," he replied offhandedly.

"I did this for her! For my son! They are in love..." the way he broke on the word love, had my muscles clench.

"Are they though?" Hades didn't seem convinced. "Would she have come if she were? You were fine, your son gave you the fruit, and they both could have had a wonderful life together while you hung out with me in Hell for a few millennia." He sauntered over to a sitting area and flung himself into the black leather seat, throwing his feet up onto an end table.

A new bit of hope entered those once dull gray eyes, a vivid blue re-entering those orbs like lightning, just as quickly gone. Unable to allow himself to keep hold of his hope, Poseidon pinched the bridge of his nose, trying to understand.

"So, you're letting us both go?" Now, it was Poseidon that wasn't convinced.

Hades laughed. "And let Zeus hurl you attached to a lightning bolt into the lowest regions of Tartarus to join our father; that sounds like a wonderful idea."

Poseidon grimaced. Not wanting to be spurned by Zeus, and trapped with his own father, he acted as if he'd been there before, and it wasn't an experience he wanted to relive.

In all seriousness Hades added, "You're welcome to leave whenever you choose brother, that is the deal I made with the little goddess. But both of you are not to leave this realm together. She will stay with me in the Underworld."

"That is unacceptable!" Poseidon roared, slamming the side of his fist into the bookshelves, making them quake. A few books fell to the floor with a thud. I stared at him, unable to reconcile I still saw him as Dion, and no matter the circumstances he always remained so calm. To see him like this, distraught and angry, was different, and so unlike him.

But I didn't really know him at all, I thought. He wasn't really Dion, and the short time that I spent with him wasn't enough to truly know who he was, was it?

"Medusa, you owe me a favor, and I've named it little goddess," I waited to find out my fate. "You will protect the dark gods for me. You see, I'm quite fond of the 'monsters' Zeus likes to send demi-gods out to defeat to prove their worth to him, to earn his favor."

My heart stopped.

I'd be bound to the Underworld forever if I didn't find a loophole in the favor he asked of me. Because I knew...

There will always be monsters.

And Zeus will not stop hunting them on my account.

The only way to secure my freedom from this favor was exactly what the gods feared.

I would be forced to storm Olympus if that's what it took.

The dark gods will rise.

***

Thank you for reading *Taking Medusa*, please take a moment to help support this series by rating/reviewing in all the places reviews/ratings are found, so this story can reach more readers like you!

You can continue reading Medusa's story with book two, Breaking Fate!https://books.steviemarie.com/breakingfate

Author Note

T hank you for being part of my author journey and taking a chance on reading a new, self-published author such as myself! When I was younger, and told people I wanted to be an author for a living, the response I got was, "Yes, but what are you going to do for money?" or "That's a nice hobby or dream." The impostor syndrome struggle was real, and for the longest time I took those comments to heart and wrote my stories in secret, and never actually finished a single one. Now, as a mom, I couldn't, in good conscience, tell my daughter to pursue her heart's desire if I didn't do it myself. So, I've dedicated myself to being a full-time indie author, and with the love and support of readers like you, I've been turning my "babymoon project" into a "job" that I love!

As they say, if you're doing something you love, you'll never "work" a day in your life.

A special thank you to the super fans that joined my street team and helped catch typos and spread the word about my stories.

If you enjoyed Taking Medusa, I'd really appreciate spreading that joy with sharing your thoughts on all the places review/ratings are found. Every star helps those algorithms to reach more readers.

Read the rest of Medusa's story and the dark gods, with book two Breaking Fate: https://books.steviemarie.com/breakingfate

If you're aching for some more romance and fantasy, perhaps a bit of sci-fi you can grab a free novella My Abett when you join my weekly Thursday newsletter: https://dl.bookfunnel.com/pzx6j7x29n You get access to lots of fun content, indie highlights, and exclusive bonus scenes. Stay tuned!

Steviemarie.com

~ Stevie
https://linktr.ee/authorsteviemarie

Breaking Fate

Death will take me, in its flames, I will rise.

In a world of gods and monsters, prophecy and fate sway hearts and minds until a monster rises to rule them all, and darkness rises on Olympus.

"A Medusa who is worthy of admiration." - Amazon Reviewer

The continuation of the award-winning *Taking Medusa, Dark Gods Rising Series.*

Caught in a deal with the King of the Underworld, Medusa must learn to embrace her power and conquer the darkness in her own mind to protect the dark gods and free herself from the ties that bind her. Reconciling the truth of the past and accepting control over her future, she discovers the strings of fate aren't so easily unraveled. Hades and Poseidon play games with her life, but with the help of new and old allies she pushes to reclaim her destiny for herself. She just didn't expect her heart to play such a vital role in deciding what fate she fights for while the very lives of the deathless gods hang in the balance.

Dive into this slow-burn fantasy adventure with a romance that defies prophecy in this page-turning continuation of Medusa's untold story.

Using current known Greek myths as we know them and retelling them from Medusa's perspective. After all, history is written by the victors, and the bards got the story all wrong. Poets were influenced by the reigning Olympians, and Medusa still lives and she's fighting through fate to become whole so she can save the very gods that wish to destroy her to keep the one who's stolen her heart.

A paranormal myth and legends adventure romance, plot with spice, that will have you flipping pages well past your bedtime to know what happens next as the dark gods rise up and prove being a hero is a matter of perspective and plot twists that will have you squirming for more.

Continue the Dark Gods Rising Series with Breaking Fate: https ://books.steviemarie.com/breakingfate

Chapter One: Bounty

No sooner had I entered the Underworld was I put to work. And I found out the true cost of grabbing Hades's crown of invisibility on that fateful day of Poseidon's fall. I remembered it as clear as if it was yesterday. As soon as he told me what kind of favor he required for "saving" me from being a decoration of the ocean's floor at the edge of the world. He had tricked me into thinking I was needed to help save Atlantis, and it was already set in motion without me. I was just there for the show.

Typical.

I should have known better. And I might have, if my family was a bit more clear on the gods being more than myth and legends.

"Medusa, you owe me a favor, and I've named it, Little Terror," Hades had said to me, "You see, I'm quite fond of the 'monsters' Zeus likes to send his mortal children to defeat in an effort to prove their worth to him... to earn his favor. You will protect the dark gods for me. I have no power to help anyone without a deal."

"It's Aless," I corrected him. No matter who I might have been in the past, that wasn't me anymore. Little bits of my memories were returning here and there, but it was more like seeing someone else's life, a kind of disconnection from knowing and feeling them. I was still me, whatever that meant now.

Hades grinned with amusement but didn't acknowledge that he would call me anything different. With a flick of his finger, the crown of invisibility that was hanging from my elbow snapped against my bicep. I didn't dare put the thing on when he gave it to me but kept it all the same, just in case I might have needed it. But that was when I thought I was needed at all to help save Atlantis. To help save Dion... I was just a witness to what would have happened, regardless. My eyes had darted to Poseidon, standing there in Hades's throne room, as if he would have the answers to what his brother had planned for me. My face contorted in shock as the crown of invisibility shrunk around my arm and embedded itself into my bicep like a tattooed collar. When the dark smog emanating from it faded, I glanced up to see Poseidon was gone.

Or more accurately, I was gone. Invisible. We were gone from each other's perception.

"What did you do?" I could still hear Poseidon growl through the golden crab shells secured behind my ears. They were magically connected with him, regardless of what Hades did, at least for the briefest of moments before realizing those were the last words I'd hear from him without Hades's permission.

"Fate is such a tricky mistress," Hades began with a cool demeanor. He wasn't talking to me, I realized soon enough. "I had a fated mate myself, brother. I followed my path and yet I was spurned for doing so. You avoid your own, and what? I'm supposed to congratulate you and hand her over without you proving to me your fate deserves to be happier than mine?" His haunted laugh still echoed in my mind as he finished with ignoring his brother that I could no longer see nor hear, then faced me to say, "I control who sees you, Little Goddess. Do a good job in your new role as protector and I will grant you time to do with as you choose. Do you choose to see your fated mate? Or perhaps you choose to see *someone else*?"

It was clear what he meant. Would I choose to see Poseidon, or Triton, instead? Or my sister?

"Are you the only one who can see me?" I asked first, ignoring his interest in my love life.

"Of course not," he balked. "It would grow tiresome. You'd become a pest that would never leave me alone. No, you have access to all the Underworld, and of course any dark god you wish to extend your protection to. As for other gods... that's a case-by-case basis. If they know what they're looking for then I can't say my protection will hold. But in the Underworld, the crown's power is absolute. It is where you will be safest when the time comes that Olympus discovers what you are up to."

"And what *am* I up to?" I wanted him to clarify my new role as an Underworld servant.

"My brother," he said plainly before he lifted a brow and clarified, "the one you aren't fated to, is overly obsessed with results. To the point that if there is even a miniscule chance that Apollo's prophecy can be interpreted a different way, he will see to squashing it. Anyone with Tartarus blood will be hunted, and as soon as you start to protect them, they'll begin to gather, growing in number. Well, I don't need to spell it out for you, do I?"

"He'll think I'm building an army for war," I finished for him, my voice trailing off in thought.

"I knew you were clever," he mocked and then yawned like he was bored with our conversation. What was needed to be said was already said according to him. "You can chat with Cerberus about the details. He's been briefed and will help you acclimate to your new job. I don't care what you call yourself, but I think he's under the impression that you'll be called the Fate Breaker Legion. Do tell him that a legion requires at least three thousand, and there are currently only the two of you. Follow the river to the cave. Cerberus will meet you there." He lifted his feet up onto his throne of obsidian rock embedded with skulls and bones and then waved his hand once more. Even he disappeared from my view, and I didn't know whether it was simply him using the Helm of Invisibility to control who I saw, like he did with Poseidon, or he was actually gone. I guess it didn't matter, and I turned to leave the room and find my way out of this damned castle.

Keep reading Breaking Fate: https://books.steviemarie.com/breakingfate

About the Author

S.M. McCoy is a mom of two tiny humans in training, narrates audiobooks for fantasy/sci-fi indie authors, and when she isn't writing (which is MOST of the time) you can find her consuming copi-ous amounts of coffee, promoting indie authors, reading alien smut, fantasy, sci-fi and romance books, chowing down on Indian butter chicken, and when she actually hangs out with people in person, in real life, outside of the internet, (gasps) she's playing board or card games. All around nerd, lover of the strange, and all things fantastical. Grab your first free alien monster fated mates romance Her Alien Exchange for free when you join the Romance Newsletter: https://sendfox.com/lp/m2gyw5

Books by S.M. McCoy:

Taking Medusa: https://books.steviemarie.com/takingmedusa
Breaking Fate: https://books.steviemarie.com/breakingfate

Want More?

For more information about upcoming books in the Dark Gods Universe (or any other books by S.M. McCoy) like me on Facebook or subscribe to my newsletter.

Check out more books by S.M. McCoy and follow on Bookbub: https://www.bookbub.com/profile/s-m-mccoy

Thanks for reading! You are a book hero!

All the squishies,

Stevie

xoxo

https://linktr.ee/authorsteviemarie

Join my newsletter, grab a free book.

Do you like Alien Romances?

Check out Books by my pen name Sky Robert:

https://www.bookbub.com/profile/sky-robert

Grab a free book Her Alien Exchange here: https://books.stevie marie.com/heralienexchange